Praise for *Searching for Amy* by Becky Jones

'I devoured this book from start to finish.
The story was compelling, the characters vivid
- I loved Amy - and the moral is very much
a modern one. Everyone should read it'.

Alice Smellie, author and journalist

'Raw, resilient, and ultimately triumphant—
Searching for Amy reminds us that sometimes
finding yourself means facing what you fear most.
A compelling and beautifully written debut.'

Helen Francis, Literary consultant

'A clear new voice, and a strong protagonist
whom I found very convincing. I was swept
along on Amy's journey from the word go. Her
most private moment is made public and once
it's out there, it's impossible to reel back.'

M J Camilleri, author

'A gripping story that tackles difficult
issues with compassion and truth.'

Kate McDermott, author

'A compelling and powerful examination of one of
the most pressing issues for young people today'.

Tanith Carey, author

'You can't escape your past until you find yourself. *Searching for Amy* thoughtfully explores contemporary themes. A triumph.'

Nicky Downes, author

'As we follow the twists and turns of Amy's story, what emerges is not just an engaging tale but a great read too. By turns heartbreaking and heartwarming, *Searching for Amy* is essential reading for teenagers and their parents.'

Alan Fraser, author

SEARCHING FOR AMY

BECKY JONES

ELM BOOKS

PART ONE
THEN AND NOW

1

THEN

When Harry asked me to the party, it took less than thirty seconds to say yes. I've spent every waking moment since regretting it. I thought leaving home would mean leaving it behind. But it wasn't that easy. In all this time, I've never told the whole story out loud. I guess it's time I did.

It all began on a Thursday. Like every lunchtime, I was sitting on the radiator with my Pepsi Max, listening to Maria and Rosie, my best friends from forever. They were a great double-act, born storytellers. If you believed what they said, every lesson was full of drama and incident. Especially Religious Studies. Who knew A-level R.S. could be so entertaining? This time it was a scandalous debate about sex before marriage that they were finding particularly hilarious. I laughed along, but for once I wasn't really listening. I was distracted by the boys at the other end of the room. In recent weeks, I'd found myself ever more distracted by them. Well, one of them. They weren't doing anything that interesting, just flicking through someone's phone. When they found the track they were looking for, they started jumping around, crashing into each other, their energy infecting the whole room and making me smile. He saw me and grinned back as he bounced. Harry. I quickly looked away.

Maria and Rosie were still mid-story. Maria was putting on a convincing Scottish accent for comic effect and tossing her blonde hair around. She looked like a girl who got up at the crack of dawn to straighten her hair and do her make up, but I knew she'd pretty much woken up like that.

Rosie definitely didn't look like she got up early to groom herself - scraped back ponytail, make-up only when forced to. She moaned like hell about her lack of boobs and bum, but her boyish athleticism suited her. The official version was that her sun-kissed skin was the result of an outdoor lifestyle, but we knew she was no stranger to the odd bottle of Skinny Tan. And me? I sometimes felt like their shadow; the brunette contrast to all the blonde, with curves that Mum tried to tell me were an asset and messy hair that you could flatteringly describe as wavy. Charlie's Angels, Rosie's Dad used to call us, as if we were some kind of film stars. Maybe that's how we looked to the rest of the world, but it didn't feel like that on the inside.

'I don't mind this song when I'm pissed on a dance floor, but it's not really the right music for conversation at break, is it?' said Rosie, rubbing her temples.

'Been using your brain this morning, have we?'

Out of the blue, Harry was there at the edge of our group. How the hell had he crossed the room so fast without me noticing? My heart rate shot up and I tried to look cool and collected, if there is any way you can do that whilst sitting on a radiator. I tried to remember if I'd put on my mascara that morning.

'More than you, for sure!' Rosie ruffled his hair, trying to annoy him. I felt a little stab of jealousy. I wished I was the one ruffling his hair. Although it was different for her, she was his cousin.

'So, what are you three up to this weekend?' he asked, ducking away from Rosie's hand and flopping his hair back. 'Oli's mum and dad are away and he's having a party on Saturday night. Wanna come?'

Rosie raised an eyebrow. 'Oli wants me to come to his party?'

Harry flicked his eyes skywards. 'Ancient history, cuz. Course he does.'

She gave a wry smile. 'Alright. What do you think, girls?'

'Could do,' Maria said, sounding bored. Maria, as usual, was pulling off cool and collected a million times better than I was. In our little group of three, she was always warm and funny, but she could put her resting bitch face on at any time. It made people think she was full of herself. It also seemed to make her ridiculously popular - she got invited to every social event going. I sometimes felt I was lucky to be her tag-along. Not that she would ever have seen it like that.

'How about you, Amy?' he said, turning to me.

I froze. Having him look straight at me and say my name made me feel like he'd turned his headlights on and fixed me in the glare.

'Saturday? I... um, I don't finish work until eight.'

'Doesn't start until nine so you'll be fine.'

And there it was, my first chance to change the course of history. I had a valid reason not to go to the party. The work excuse. But he dismissed it easily, swotting it away like an annoying fly, and I just let him.

'That's sorted then.' He nodded and I caught the smallest hint of a smile as he turned to walk away. I dared to hope it was for me.

'Rosie, I can pick you up if you want,' he called over his shoulder.

'Looks like we're partying on Saturday then, girls,' Maria said when he was out of earshot. 'Good thing I'm getting my nails done later.'

2
NOW

The first time I walked into Jon's café was the first time I fully realised that university made me anxious. *Common Grounds* it said across the window, in a funky modern font. Good name, I thought as I pushed open the door.

It was Saturday and the whole place was humming; older women laughing and chatting loudly around a pot of tea, young families with toddlers spraying crumbs and juice all over themselves and the floor. I felt instantly comfortable, like I never did on campus. I seemed to spend my time trying to hide from all the clever-clever people my age, armed with their fake smiles and too many questions. It was nice to be surrounded by ordinary people - as in, not students. I joined the queue and watched as the guy behind the counter expertly handled one order after another, frothing and steaming and banging out coffee grounds, rubbing down the machine in between customers with real care.

'So, how are you today? And what would you like?' Laughter lines around his eyes and a flash of grey at the front of his hair made him seem older than he looked from the back, and he asked the questions as if he really cared about my answers. Long time since anyone did that.

'I'd like a flat white, please. Do you have any non-dairy?'

He raised his eyebrows.

'Of course. In fact, I have a new oat milk that I think you'll like.'

He made it sound reasonable that he might know what I'd like. I watched the performance as he moved between the coffee machine and the milk, all his actions speedy but precise, slowing down abruptly to smoothly feather milk across the dark espresso. I almost felt the need to clap when he put my coffee down on the counter with a flourish.

'That's what you call a flat white,' he said, admiring his own handiwork. 'It's a special barista oat milk that gives that froth...' He looked up. 'Sorry, you're probably far less interested in that than I am.'

I laughed, then stopped when I realised he was waiting for me to say something.

'No! Not at all. It's interesting.' The effort of speaking to someone new made my face hot, but when I looked up, his eyes were twinkling at me.

'Nice of you to humour me. I know I'm a coffee geek. Card or cash?'

I took my coffee to a scrubbed wooden table at the back. Something about the delicious smells and friendly noise felt like home. Home as it used to be. And it was so cool - red brick walls, polished copper pipes, stripped back tables and floorboards, a great playlist at just the right volume. And the flat white was amazing. The caffeine hit, and I started to relax.

'Well thanks! You can come again.' the barista said, smiling, when I took my empty cup back to the counter. 'I definitely will.' He nodded, then as an afterthought. 'I'm Jon, by the way.' I smiled awkwardly and walked away without telling him my name.

I managed to find very regular excuses to keep my word. For morning coffee when I wasn't in class, it was an easy choice between one of Jon's flat whites or something out of a machine on campus. When lectures finished early, I'd head there with a book. More often than not, I'd stay until Jon told me it was time to go home. And on Saturday afternoons, when the weekend yawned ahead of me without plans or structure, I'd kill time by sitting at the counter in the window on my laptop. It had rapidly become the place I most wanted to be, so when I saw a poster on the door saying *Saturday staff wanted,* it felt like a sign meant just for me.

Of course, I got the job. And a purple *Grounds Crew* apron to go with it. I was a bit nervous at first, but I found it was different there than on campus. There, I was the waitress, the Saturday- and sometimes Other-Day-girl, no difficult questions to be answered, no need to try to be anything else. And Jon was great at training me - he didn't just stick me in the kitchen washing up. Although some days, that might have been a good idea.

Like that Saturday, two weeks or so after I started. I'd done a sweep of the tables and was balancing a load of cups and a small plate with the remains of a flapjack that looked like it had been trodden on. Squeezing past the queue at the counter I saw, second in line, a guy I'd noticed the week before. Noticed. Who was I trying to kid? This guy was so gorgeous I couldn't even speak to him when I gave him his coffee. I did a quick calculation and worked out that I could time my walk to the kitchen so Jon would get to Gorgeous Guy before I got back. I didn't think he'd seen me; not that he would have remembered if he had. But I hadn't forgotten. I'd had the image of his hypnotic green eyes in my head all week. Jon was serving Gladys - that was always a long one. If I stacked all the pots into the dishwasher instead of dumping them on the sink, I thought I might get away with not having to speak to Gorgeous Guy at all. I couldn't trust myself not to say something dumb.

I tried to give myself a talking to while I dropped the furry flapjack into the food bin and slid the fork and teaspoons into the cutlery basket. The fact he was back was nothing to do with me. He was probably just some regular who came in every week for Jon's coffee. I hadn't been there nearly long enough to know who was a regular. Although I thought I should probably ask Jon about that one. Whether he came in at the same time every week, for example. And whether that might be a good time for me to take my break.

I waited ten more seconds by the sink, wiping down the already clean surface, then headed cautiously back to the counter, only to bump into Jon coming the other way with a food ticket.

'There you are! Thought you'd got lost. Gladys wants a toastie, can you do drinks for a bit?'

'Sure', I said, stepping aside. Shit, I thought as Jon cleared my line of vision. He's still there. He's next. I took a deep breath, rubbed my hands on my apron and said, 'Morning, what can I get you?' hoping really hard that I wouldn't have to say too much more.

Gorgeous Guy smiled and said he'd like a latte please, with oat milk. I managed something like a nod to acknowledge his order without saying anything or properly looking at his face. But oat milk. I hadn't clocked that last week. I added 'possibly vegan' to the list of things I liked about him. Which, to be honest, was quite a lot from just two coffee orders.

Jon had left his usual mess and there wasn't a clean frothing jug for non-dairy. I cursed him; this was taking forever. Behind my back, there was a queue forming, and I felt Gorgeous Guy's eyes watching my hands as I fiddled around opening a new carton, rinsing a jug. I could hear Gladys laughing with another of the old cronies. Bloody woman, wanting a toastie at eleven in the morning. This could all have been avoided.

I poured the oaty froth onto the double shot, fixed a smile and turned to face him. He was frowning at his phone. I hadn't taken that long, had I? Whose eyes were boring into my back then? A quick glance at the queue showed a few possible contenders, none of them looking that pleased. Hurriedly I cleared my throat.

'Here you go, oat latte. Can I get you anything else?'

He looked up quickly, the frown instantly melting. He smiled. Oh wow. I tried not to look into his eyes. It was like fighting the feeling you get at the top of a skyscraper when you want to throw yourself off. Stop it, I told myself. You know how it ends. A catastrophic crash onto a pavement.

I pulled myself back to the job in hand and realised he was looking at me, expectantly. Oh god, he'd said something and I had no idea what. My brain had been on its flight of fancy and now I was standing there looking at him stupidly when all he'd done was answer my question.

'Do you have any today?' he continued. 'I had one last week, it was delicious.'

Last week, what did he have last week? Date flapjack! Got it. Vegan. I grabbed one from the back of the glass shelf and put it on a plate, handed it to him and offered the card reader without daring to say anything else. God only knew what I might come out with if I tried any small talk. He paid, took his coffee and cake, and just as I was about to start breathing normally again, he said, 'Thank you… Amy, isn't it?'

I looked straight at him, startled. My mouth went dry.

'I, uh, I heard your boss say your name. When you were in the kitchen.'

I nodded dumbly. That made sense.

'Well, thank you, Amy. Nice to see you. Again,' he said as he walked away.

Trying to ignore how my hands were shaking, I dealt with the rest of the queue as quickly as I could, serving teas and Americanos and several date flapjacks - he seemed to have set a trend. By the time Jon got back from delivering the toastie, I'd restored order to the coffee station and managed to only look in the direction of table four once. Well twice. But the second time it was only because the back of his head with its soft dark curls fell into my eyeline as I wiped down the frother. Yeah right.

'Jon, are you back here now? Shall I go and see what kind of mess you've left in the kitchen?'

Jon laughed at the running joke and I retreated quickly to safety.

Even Jon couldn't cause too much carnage with a toastie, so there wasn't much to do. I cling-filmed a bowl of grated cheese and threw some food tickets into the recycling, then sat on the side, swinging my legs and gazing out of the window. It was ridiculous. It was months since it happened. Why was it so hard to talk to some random guy? There had to come a time when I was ready to deal with all this stuff. Maybe Mum was right and I should talk to someone about it. But no. She wasn't. I was doing fine as I was.

'Hey, there are plenty of chairs out there if you need a sit down?' Jon said, bringing a tray of cups in. I slid guiltily off the counter-top.

'I didn't get a five for hygiene by having my weekend staff sitting on the food prep areas, you know.'

'Sorry, Jon, I just...'

My neck prickled unpleasantly and I bit my lip as I looked at him. But he was smiling.

'It's okay, kiddo, I'm teasing. You okay? Need a break? Why don't you grab yourself whatever vegan concoction you feel like today and go have a sit down?'

I didn't really want to go have a sit down. Not out there. But the kitchen was spotless and I couldn't think of another excuse.

'You sure you can manage?'

'Yeah, I think I can probably cope,' he said. 'You got rid of the queue nicely, probably got a half-hour lull before lunch, take your break.'

He stacked the cups and plates into the dishwasher and without looking round, said, 'I think your good-looking friend has left already though.'

Shit! Had I made it that obvious? But at least he'd gone, so I exited the kitchen before Jon could make any more unwelcome observations and went to make myself a flat white.

3

THEN

Thursday afternoons were never that great – I had realistically low expectations of an English teacher who confessed that he didn't like Shakespeare. The yawning and eye-rolling hadn't quite ruined it for me, although I had to admit *Twelfth Night* wasn't my favourite either. But that day, I had other things to think about. I spent much of the lesson trying to work out what it meant that Harry had invited me to the party. Made a point of it. I was trying not to let myself think that he might actually like me. I'd never told anyone how I felt about him, because he was Rosie's cousin and it was too awkward. But there was no mistaking that he'd specifically asked me to go. Which meant what? I didn't really know.

Rosie and Maria were waiting for me at the gate when the bell went, and we dawdled along, doing our typical run-through of everything that might possibly happen at the party.

'I'm not sure Oli really would want me to come,' said Rosie. 'Do you think I should message him to check?'

I shot Maria a look. Boys loved Rosie and she was so at ease with them - she never blushed with embarrassment or seemed lost for words. Unlike me. So we were mystified that, from her vast array of possibilities, she was still interested in Oli who she'd had a brief thing with and who was, frankly, a complete wanker. Too many evenings had ended with one or both of us holed up in a loo with Rosie crying because he'd left with someone else. He was a waste of time and emotional energy. We just hadn't quite dared to spell it out for her yet.

'I wouldn't bother. You can talk to him there. Anyway, I feel like a bit of a dance,' said Maria, hurriedly changing the subject. 'I hope they've got some decent music. Can't stand it when the whole night turns into a battle of phones and you don't get more than twenty seconds of a decent song before someone sticks some poppy retro crap on.'

'Someone said Oli's older brother is DJ-ing. He's quite into music,' Rosie said. 'Although whether it's your idea of good dance music I wouldn't know.'

'DJ-ing? What, he's put a playlist together on his phone?'

They were laughing. While they went into a discussion of the best possible party playlist songs, I let my thoughts wander back to the Harry question. They carried on for a couple of blocks then Rosie interrupted my daydreaming.

'You're quiet, Ames, what's up?'

'Oh, nothing. Just, I'm not a massive party animal, plus I'll have to go home after work otherwise I'll turn up smelling like the inside of a pizza oven. Not sure it will be worth it by the time I get there.'

I didn't really want to tell them what I'd actually been thinking about. Did Harry want me to go to the party because he thought something might happen between us? I didn't want to let myself believe that. He was way too good-looking, too popular. And too close to home. But now I'd thought about it as a possibility, the idea it might not happen was too much. So I was thinking it was probably better to stay away, avoid the potential disappointment.

But no chance. Rosie and Maria jumped on me.

'Don't be stupid! No one will even get there until nine-thirty, you'll only miss the pres, and you're a lightweight anyway!'

'You have to come! Don't leave me to mop up the mess that is our dear friend Rosie at the end of the evening.'

Rosie dug Maria in the back and we all laughed.

'Oh okay.' I relented too easily, again. 'Promise me you won't have disappeared off with Oli again before I even get there.'

'Promise,' said Rosie. 'Harry's giving me a lift so we'll probably all just hang out together until you arrive.'

'Until I arrive?' Maybe she knew more than I did. I tried not to sound too interested.

'Well, then he might have other people he wants to hang out with.' She winked. 'He seemed pretty keen for you to come, can't imagine all that dancing around the common room was to impress me.'

So she'd noticed it too.

'Oh, ummm... I don't know about that. He's always pretty friendly but, you know, I didn't know if cousins were off limits...'

'No! Not at all. Go for it.' She and Maria swapped knowing glances. 'Knew you liked him.' She winked again.

'Stop bloody winking at me!' In spite of myself, I was laughing. As if I'd thought I could hide anything from those two. But I had the green light from his cousin. That, plus the memory of his smile when he thought I'd said yes; it was all the encouragement I needed.

'See you tomorrow, you bullies.'

I turned off towards my end of town, leaving them laughing and diving straight into what could have been an endless discussion of what they were going to wear. Rosie's suggestion that he'd been trying to impress me just added fuel to the fire of anticipation that was smouldering in my gut. Me and Harry. Harry and me. I grinned all the way home.

4
NOW

'Lifesaver,' Jon said as I walked in. It was a Tuesday morning, and I'd got a frantic text an hour before. 'This bloody counter is constantly flickering and ticking like an indicator. Got to go and get a new bulb or something.'

I wasn't massively bothered by it, but it seemed to put Jon in a foul mood, and I was delighted to help whenever he needed me. Time went so much faster at work.

'Good job I'm not epileptic,' he said, grabbing his keys and wallet. 'If I can't get the right bulb, I'm going to have to put up a strobe warning.'

I laughed as he raised a hand in farewell and left me to it.

The radio was on in the kitchen as I started some early lunch prep. Jon had obviously been in early – I was sure that man was an insomniac. There was a batch of fresh flapjack and two trays of brownies cooling on the side, and the kitchen smelt of cinnamon and chocolate. I hummed along to the radio, sorting everything out on the work surface so I'd be able to rustle up a salad garnish in seconds. The song stopped and the news jingle cut in – ten o'clock. Probably start to get busy soon. I wasn't really listening, the news was always the same old crap – I chopped some spring onions, started to wash the lettuce, then I heard the words social media and image abuse. All my senses jumped to attention. Some new statistics about the number of people who took their own lives after being abused on social media. The media companies needed to start taking action. There had been too many cases. I tried to keep my mind on the salad, but I couldn't focus. Come on, I told myself. This isn't about you. The bell on the door jangled. Gratefully I wiped my hands on my apron and walked out of earshot of the radio.

A trickle of tea and coffee orders kept me busy, but the flickering light was quite annoying. I was grateful when Jon reappeared with a large bag and a look of determination.

'Right, let me at it. I've got three different widgets in here that the guy promised would fix the issue.'

I stepped in as he started to destroy the cake display in an effort to get to the flickering bulb. 'Go and take your coat off,' I said. 'I'll empty the shelves.'

'Go on then.' He headed off to the staff room. 'You can make me a coffee too, I'm gasping.'

It was quite tricky to work with Jon in the way, swearing at the counter, the electrician who put it in and his own lack of wiring ability. But when he'd finished, it did look a lot better. I replaced the cakes and topped up some of the fresh brownies.

'You're good at displays.' Jon said, picking up his tools and giving the glass top a final polish. 'That looks very photogenic. Great food porn.'

I flinched at the word, but he carried on, seeming not to notice.

'That reminds me. Been meaning to talk to you about something. I keep forgetting. Think the strobe effect's been scrambling my brain.'

I laughed and shook my head.

'Any excuse. I think we'd call it age?'

'Cheek! I'm still the right side of forty-five. Just... Anyway, that's my point.'

'Sorry, what is?'

'Well, it's good to have you giving me ideas. I know I wasn't too keen at first, but sales of vegan bakes are up.'

My brain flipped briefly to the Gorgeous Guy. I hoped he wasn't only interested in the flapjack. Jon was still talking.

'Anyway, I have to say it. You were right and I was wrong. And I like that we have more young people coming in now. That's definitely since you started.'

I squirmed. I really hoped people weren't coming in to see me. Maybe he just meant the vegan stuff.

'So, I was thinking, is there a way we could be more 'down with the kids'?'

I shoved away the paranoid thoughts and laughed.

'Saying things like that really doesn't help you! But yeah, I think there are things we could do. A QR code for the menu, for example. iPads for ordering?'

He shook his head. 'Steady on, nothing that modern. Too much tech. I like having a blackboard for the menu and bits of paper I can lose for the food orders. No, I was meaning publicity. Could you help get the word out?'

I picked up a cloth and started to wipe down the already spotless counter. If he meant he wanted me to tell all my friends, he might end up a bit disappointed.

'What do you mean? Posters? I'll have a go but I'm not great at design.'

'Well, you can design a nice cake display! But no, I meant social media. I've never bothered, not my thing. I know the big chains all have apps and whatever showing off what they serve. We could do that. Post our own food porn.'

I wished he'd stop saying that. I put down the cloth and started to pull at my sleeves, praying for someone to come in.

'Umm. Well, it's not really my thing either. I mean, I don't do Instagram and stuff.'

Jon folded his arms and looked at me in mock disbelief.

'What? You're eighteen years old and you're not into social media?' I flinched and looked away, hoping he hadn't noticed. 'I was thinking maybe you could set us up on Instagram and Twitter? Get us an online presence or whatever you call it.'

I could feel him watching me, so I half-smiled but I still couldn't meet his eye. I needed to just say no, and close down the conversation. But Jon was undeterred.

'Thought maybe you'd like an extra level of responsibility? I'd pay you a bit more for it.'

It was like he was deliberately not reading the signs. He pointed enthusiastically at the counter.

'These cakes for example. And the new, unflickering counter. Could be a lovely post. Or is it a story? See, I need help!'

He made me laugh, and I gave in. I looked again at the display I'd chucked together. If I was going to photograph it, I'd need to put the vegan stuff towards the front.

'Oh, alright then. Fame to the vegan flapjack. Why not? I'm not sure it will bring that many more people in, but I'll give it a go. If that's what you want.'

Jon looked pleased and went out to clear some coffee cups from table three. I watched him humming to himself, content with his morning's achievements. Why did I just say yes to that? Oh well. Arty shots of a beautiful flat white and today's specials on the blackboard wouldn't get me into too much trouble, I guessed.

The door opened. Finally.

'I've got this,' I said as he went past me with the cups, narrowly missing tripping over the mess on the floor. 'Get rid of these bloody screwdrivers, will you?'

5
THEN

Most weeks I didn't stay in school all day on Fridays as I only had two proper lessons. That week, however, I hung around in the library, had lunch in the canteen and spent a whole free period in the common room pretending to myself that I was getting ahead with nineteenth century history. What I was, in fact, doing was looking for Harry, and I didn't see him once.

I was standing at my locker, wondering if now would be a good time for a sort out, when Rosie came wandering around the corner, her face breaking into a grin when she saw me.

'Oh good! You're still here. Thought you had Friday afternoons off? Maria's stuck in R.S. finishing an essay, want to come outside with me?'

I nodded and shoved the locker door shut.

'Far too sunny to even think about clearing out my locker,' I said as I followed her down the corridor.

'Ames, your locker is tidier than most and we still have three weeks at school. You can do it another day.' She looked at me sideways. 'You stayed in school this afternoon for that?'

'Not exactly. Hey, do you fancy a coke?' We were passing the vending machine, just at the right moment. I was suddenly embarrassed to admit I was hoping to see Harry.

We took our drinks to the grassy area outside the side door where no one ever seemed to go. Rosie stretched out in the sun, and I sat beside her, hugging my knees, and absent-mindedly picking daisies.

'So…' I started.

She half-opened one eye and looked up at me.

'You want to talk about Harry, don't you?'

I laughed. I was in that phase where Harry was all I wanted to talk about.

'Well, you know yesterday you said... I mean...'

'Come on! Spit it out. You gone all shy on me?'

I bit my lip sheepishly.

'I just wanted to know. You said you thought he was trying to impress me. Has he... has he said anything?'

Rosie sat up and took a swig of her coke.

'Yeah, he never shuts up about you.'

I turned to look at her to see if she was winding me up.

'Really?'

'Uh-huh. It's been ages. Since that day we went to Party in the Park. Remember?'

Of course I remembered. One day last summer, Mum was at work and Maria was off on holiday. I'd joined Rosie and her family at an outdoor music thing - picnics and local bands down by the river. Harry had never really talked to me much before then, I'd always thought he just saw me as Rosie's mate. He'd known me long enough; he'd always been at her birthday parties in the phase where your parents are in charge of the guest list. Then obviously there'd been several years where there was no way you'd invite a boy, even if it was your cousin.

'I remember. But are you sure? He's literally hardly spoken to me since.'

I thought of how we'd talked about music, found a few bands we both liked. I'd sent him the link to one of the local bands' Instagrams afterwards, but he never replied. I just thought he'd only been friendly that day because I happened to be there.

Rosie lay back down.

'Well, don't be mad. I didn't think you were into him. So I sort of warned him off you.'

'What? Why?'

'He's a bit of a tart. I was pissed off with him that summer; he'd been with loads of girls and I was getting the shit from it. I didn't want him just adding you to his list.'

I pushed my nail through the stalk of a daisy and threaded another one through.

'Oh. Right.'

She shifted onto her hip and turned towards me, leaning on an elbow.

'Are you mad? Don't be. Honestly, I thought he'd dick you around so I told him to stay away. But I think he actually really likes you. He's not short of offers, but he always asks me about you. So if you like him too, why not?' She smiled mischievously. 'Who am I to stand in the path of true love?'

'Bloody cheek!' I said and threw the half daisy chain at her. She rolled away from me.

'He thinks you're gorgeous. I told him you were too good for him but he's worn me down. Go for it.'

The little glow inside that had started the day before got very much warmer.

'Thanks for granting permission,' I said. 'Anyway, where is he today? Not going to lie, I've been trying to bump into him all day.'

'Stalker,' she said, brushing the daisies off her skirt and getting up. 'He's off. Got a bug, Mum said.'

I must have looked momentarily alarmed.

'Don't worry! I'm sure he'll be fine tomorrow. Missing school is a bit different from missing a party. Shit, it's nearly two. I've got drama. Talk later.'

She sped off. I picked up her half-drunk coke and my empty can and dropped them into a bin, then gathered up my things and headed for the gate. If Harry wasn't there, I might as well go home.

I let myself in to my house, dropped my bag onto the shiny hall floor and chucked my coat over the end of the banister. Mum had left a mop and bucket leaning against the kitchen door and there was a familiar smell of polish - she must have given the floor a clean before she went to work. It was a little house, but Mum would always say it was perfect for the two of us, making me feel that we were something special. There'd only ever been the two of us. When I was born, apparently we lived with Gran for a bit, but I was too young to remember. Somehow it had always been okay that I hadn't had a dad. Well, of course I had one. He just didn't want to know about me. Mum always joked that most people came out of uni with a useless degree and she was the lucky one who came out with a baby. Sometimes kids at school would ask why I didn't have a daddy, and teachers would always make too much of a fuss when it was Father's Day or Take your Dad to School day or something tactless. But most of the time, I didn't mind. You can't miss what you never had. Mum was enough.

I made our dinner – I'm not much of a cook, but I have a few things I can make, and my veggie pasta sauce is legendary. My phone was beeping away as I chopped pepper and aubergine – excited emojis on the party WhatsApp, and snaps from Rosie and Maria of possible outfits. And a message.

Hope you're coming tomorrow?

It was from Harry. My heart did a flip. I stared at the message for a second, then put the phone down and whizzed the vegetables round in the pan, trying to dampen down the unmistakable tingle of excitement. But there was no chance of that. It fizzed and bubbled, making me dizzy and breathless. But I left the phone a full five minutes before replying. Just four short words and no kiss.

Yes, see you there.

It was, of course, a massively busy shift at work on the Saturday night and I didn't get out until nearly quarter past eight. I was in a total panic thinking I was going to be late, but there was Mum, sitting in the carpark.

'Thought you might need a lift,' she said as I dived into the passenger seat and kissed her.

'Oh, thank you! It was so busy tonight; I've never cleared up so fast.'

'It's the very famous law of sod, my darling. Don't worry, still plenty of time to make yourself beautiful.'

I looked sideways at Mum. I hadn't even mentioned Harry to her, but in her usual all-knowing maternal way, she'd worked out there was someone I needed to impress.

I got into the shower with relief - it was always such a pleasure to get the smell of the kitchen off me after work. Probably the pizza oven needed a good old clean. When I got out, Mum was waiting on my bed nursing a gin and tonic, and there was another one on my dressing table.

'Thought we might start the party here if you're going to be a bit late.'

'Oh brilliant, I might need it.'

Casually I pulled my best jeans and a black top out of the wardrobe, as if I hadn't spent the last two days planning my outfit.

'So, who's the lucky guy?'

I could see her in the mirror, looking at me to see my reaction. I continued pulling on the jeans.

'How do you know there's a lucky guy? Couldn't I be going for a fun night out with my friends?'

She sipped her gin and gave a knowing smile.

'Well, you could. But you haven't sat down for more than five minutes at a time for the past two days, you're in need of Dutch courage, you're wearing your best black top, and you've just put perfume on for the third time, so I'm guessing it's not just a night with Rosie and Maria.'

I laughed. Why bother trying to hide things when she could see straight through me?

I always knew how lucky I was to have my mum. That's not a thing most teenagers would say, I know, even if it was true. And I probably didn't let her know it all the time. But we were a team. She got us through the ups and downs of life as a single parent family without any lasting damage. And that can't have been easy. She could always tell as soon as I was worrying about anything. When I was being picked on by the cute blonde class bully in year five, she got it out of me before we'd even pulled out of the school carpark. When I was twelve and starting to get boobs, she turned up with M&S cotton bras in two sizes and said, 'Try these. Then you can take that big jumper off and not worry about what's going on under your t-shirt.'

I told her about my first kiss, when I was so embarrassed that a boy wanted to put his hand up my shirt. She'd hold my hair while I was being sick, regardless of whether it was totally self-inflicted. She'd pick me up at all hours of the morning, even when I'd said I'd get a taxi. She'd make my favourite chocolate sponge pudding when she knew I had premenstrual sugar cravings. She knew me inside out and back to front and there was nothing we couldn't talk about. Before the party, that is.

I told her who the lucky guy was without any hesitation. 'It's Harry. Rosie's cousin.'

'Ah, the good-looking rugby player. I know the one.'

'Yeah, that's the one. He sort of invited us... me... I mean, it's not his party, it's at his friend's house. Oli.'

'Oli Nelson? I used to work with his mum. Do they still live on Romney Road?'

'Yeah, they do. Number seven.'

'Well, it's already nine o'clock. Get that hair dried and I'll drop you off.'

She left me to it as I tipped my head upside down and blasted my curls into submission. I wish she'd stayed there longer. I wish we'd talked and I'd said, actually Mum let's just hang out tonight, I don't want to go to a party. But of course, I didn't. I dried my hair, grabbed my phone and a lip gloss and called out 'Ready' as I left my bedroom. I was going to the party to see Harry and there was no stopping me.

6
NOW

Quiet lunchtimes were few and far between, but for whatever reason it was one-thirty and there was hardly anyone in. Jon looked at his watch and surveyed the scene - two customers already eating, and that was it.

'Doesn't really look like you needed the extra pair of hands today?' I said, catching him looking. I felt a flicker of guilt about the social media I hadn't set up yet. 'Wonder where everyone is?'

'Oh, it's nothing to worry about. You get days like these. Mondays are never that busy.'

'Do you want me to go?' I asked, reluctantly. 'No point having to pay me to stand around.'

'No, it's been good, I've done a load of batch cooking. And I need to go to the bank and a few other bits and pieces I never make time for. Will you be okay for an hour or so?'

I laughed, relieved. 'I think I'll cope. Unless there's a late rush of hungry vegans waiting round the corner until they see you leave.'

Something about the image obviously struck Jon and he laughed out loud.

'You could always keep them at bay with the egg and dairy free quiches I made earlier. They look totally inedible, probably be better used as defensive weapons.'

'They can't be that bad! I'll try one for my lunch and let you know.'

'Maybe wait until I get back just in case you keel over.' He laughed as he put on his jacket. I pulled a face that was supposed to look as if I was having an allergic reaction, hoping to make him laugh again.

But as he left, who should walk in but Gorgeous Guy. Of course he did. I quickly pulled my features back into what I hoped was a welcoming smile. Please god don't let him have seen the choking face. I tried to act normal. That always works.

'Hey! You're here! I didn't know you worked Mondays.'

He sounded genuine. He couldn't have seen the choking face. Phew. I wasn't sure of the correct answer, so I just said, 'Not always. What can I get you? We still have all the specials.' I waved vaguely at the board. Just him being there made me unable to think what acting normal was.

'Oh, not today thanks. I just wanted a coffee actually. Flat white. With oat milk please.'

I dared myself to meet his eyes, but I had to quickly look away.

'I hadn't forgotten the oat milk. I'm dairy-free too. Vegan.'

I foamed the milk and feathered it across the coffee, trying not to smile like an idiot. How cool, maybe we were both vegan. I half-thought about telling him how many oat milks we'd tried before we found the perfect froth, but I decided he might not be that interested. The flat white did look pretty, though, when I placed it down in front of him and handed him the card machine.

'So, how long have you been vegan?' he asked as he handed it back.

'Oh, only since I've been at uni. So not long.'

I finished the transaction and looked up at him as I handed over the receipt. He was listening so closely that I felt suddenly self-conscious. I looked away and reached for a cloth so I could occupy myself with wiping something.

'I'm not very virtuous about it though. When I go home, I'm pretty sure I'll cave in for a roast dinner,' I said. He burst out laughing. I jumped - I hadn't meant to be funny, it was just something to say really, the silence of him listening to me was a bit too intense.

'Oh thank god for that! I'm a pushover for a bacon sandwich. Or roast pork. I didn't want to let on that I am, at best, veganish. I thought you might judge me.'

'As if I would!' I said with conviction. If he only knew. Judging other people was not something I bothered wasting time on. I was far too preoccupied with wondering whether they were judging me. Surely it was the moment to take his coffee and sit down, but he took a sip and stayed at the counter. 'So where's home?'

'Oh, just my mum's,' I said, vaguely. Bollocks. Why did I mention home? I put the cloth down and started to rearrange some cups that were fine where they were.

'I guessed that bit! I meant which part of the country. I detect a slight northern accent?'

Bollocks. Damnit. He had been listening carefully.

'Yeah, you're right. I thought it had nearly gone, I don't go home that often so I'm losing it more and more.' I hesitated but he seemed to be waiting for an actual answer.

'I'm from the north-west. Tiny place, you wouldn't have heard of it.' I wished desperately for another customer to come in and give me a reason to stop the line of conversation without seeming rude. No one did.

'Try me.' He put his head on one side. Shit, I'd have to lie to him.

'Ummm, Whitbarrow,' I stammered. It was my standard answer. I wasn't even sure it was a real place, but it sounded like it might be. 'It's near... um... Rochdale.'

'Oh, no, you're right. Never heard of it.'

He was smiling. I relaxed a bit. Maybe he had literally been trying to carry on the conversation, not as a means of interrogation. But I was always careful.

The door went. Gladys. Thank God. I smiled at Gorgeous Guy and he gave a nod - thank you and goodbye rolled into one - and went to sit down, although he had practically finished his coffee already.

I took my time over Gladys, you had to. Today she talked me through her whole decision process about which of the cakes she'd allow herself, although she really shouldn't, but then a little bit of what you fancy does you good, apparently. I hovered the tongs over the flapjack, then the fruit scones, then back to the flapjack as the final choice was made.

'And an Americano. Cold milk, dear. You know me.'

I stole a look towards his table as I turned to make the coffee. He caught my eye, got up from his seat and gave a wave.

'Bye, bye, Amy from near Rochdale. See you soon.'

I breathed a sigh of relief as he left, and almost instantly wondered when I'd see him next. Gladys was telling me that the butcher didn't have any lamb cutlets again and bemoaning the weather. She handed me a twenty-pound note, and as I was getting the change, she lowered her voice and leant forwards over the counter.

'So. That nice young man who keeps turning up.' I froze, the till drawer open in front of me. I counted out the change slowly and turned back towards Gladys, my smile back in place.

'Which one? There are so many!' I laughed, falsely. Gladys gave me a knowing look.

'That one. That just left. I've noticed him here a lot. Never used to come in before a certain young waitress started.'

My hairs stood on end and my stomach felt hollow.

'When are you going to put him out of his misery and let him ask you out for a drink?' she said.

Blimey. That was direct.

'Ummm. I don't think... I mean, I'm not sure...' I floundered. Gladys nodded knowingly and picked up her coffee.

'Take it from me, nice young man like that won't stay interested for too long. Don't let him get away.'

She took the coffee and flapjack over to her usual table and struck up a conversation with one of the women already sitting there. I took some plates into the kitchen and mentally added Gladys and Gorgeous Guy to the list of the people I needed to avoid.

7
THEN

I'd like to say I remember every detail about that night, but I don't. Bits of it, yes. The bits I'd rather forget. They're stuck in my brain, triggered at any given moment by the smell of sweet vapes, the taste of warm coke, certain songs. I've relived those bits way too many times.

I was hit with a wall of sound and heat as I opened the front door onto a crowded hallway. The crowd continued through the whole ground floor – seemed like everyone in my year and everyone we'd ever spoken to from the year below had turned up. There were a few older boys I didn't know, I guessed Oli's brother and a few of his mates. It was carnage and not really that late – Mum probably dropped me off around nine-thirty, but the levels of drunkenness were way above the slight G and T buzz I was feeling. Sign of a good party. I was on the look-out for Harry from the minute I walked in, but first I needed to locate Maria and Rosie and the communal vodka.

I pushed through the hallway into the dining room, navigating a crowd of people flirting, snogging, slamming shots and yelling into each other's ears in an effort to have a conversation. Maria was on a makeshift dancefloor that looked as if it was usually the site of a dining table. She gave me a wobbly hug and shoved a bottle at me.

'Where's Rosie?' I managed to yell into her ear in between gulps.

She shrugged and mouthed, 'Oli?'.

'Already? So much for waiting for me.'

'Fuck 'em, let's dance.'

I shrugged and we carried on swigging from the bottle, flailing around, and in my case, scanning the sea of bodies for Harry.

Sometime into our random gyrations, the music shifted. Happy pop and dance tracks were replaced with something altogether darker and more grungy. We tried to keep going for a couple of songs, then Maria reached for me.

'This is shit, and I'm so hot! Shall we go outside for a bit?'

I nodded, grabbing her bag from the edge of the sticky dancefloor and following her to the back door. In the kitchen, there were glasses and bottles and half-drunk, murky-looking alcoholic concoctions on every surface. Maria went to pick up a cup of something that might have been punch but definitely should have been avoided. I steered her away from it and out through the door. Taking a clean mug from a shiny grey cupboard, I filled it with water and followed her out into the back garden.

I don't know why breathing in fresh air makes you feel even more drunk. We both reeled as it hit us and slumped down onto the nearest bench. I took a sip of the water and put the mug down on the grass. Even more people were hanging out in the garden. I didn't recognise a lot of them, although they all seemed pretty friendly. Hoping to nick a cigarette, Maria struck up a conversation with a bunch of smokers we'd never talked to before in our lives. We chatted away with them – I remember their listening faces, slightly glazed over, as I talked at them animatedly about God only knows what. Someone was passing round a joint – I said no thanks and passed it on, but whenever I smell weed it always takes me back there. From somewhere upstairs I heard sounds of laughter, then a window being suddenly closed. In the smoky vodka blur, it seems weird that I remember the window.

'Girls!' It was Rosie, in need of vodka. She pulled us into a hug and I passed her the coke bottle. She seemed much more sober than I felt and swigged it greedily.

'Where's Harry?' She voiced the question that had been in my head all night. 'Thought he'd be with you?'

I shrugged.

'Haven't seen him. I haven't seen Oli either, or any of them.'

She took another slug of vodka coke, screwed the lid back on and pulled me off the bench.

'No, me either. Come on, let's go find him.'

I let her drag me away, leaving Maria chatting with her new smoker friends.

Harry was surprisingly easy to find for someone who'd been invisible for the past two hours. Standing at the bottom of the stairs with Oli, beer in hand, chatting, laughing, looking like a nice boy having a good time at a mate's party. It didn't occur to me at the time to wonder where they'd been or what they'd been doing. As Rosie and I squeezed through a group of rugby lads, he spotted us and made us some space.

'Hey! Where have you been hiding?' He looked cool in a nice T-shirt and jeans and smelt of shampoo and body spray. For a second, I pictured him in his room at home, getting ready, choosing what to wear, just as I had done.

'Not hiding. Just dancing,' I replied, smiling. He leant in closer.

'What?'

'Dancing!' I yelled, laughing.

The four of us stood awkwardly. A group conversation was pointless; the music had got louder as people got more drunk, and none of us could hear a thing. Gradually Harry turned his back to the others, so that there were just the two of us. Rosie and Oli melted away. Well, I say that. For me they did. In fact, I think they probably stood there at the bottom of the stairs for quite a while. But all I could see was Harry from then on. Like we were the only focussed part of a very blurry picture, standing so close together, oblivious to the music, the bannisters pressing into my back, the sticky patch on the hall floor where someone had dropped a beer.

And then, it was that moment. We've all seen it in a million films. The two main characters have found each other, the ones you've known all along were destined to get together. Everything slows right down, they look at each other with a new intensity, and some weird current of energy passes between them. Then they kiss. Which sounds cringy and romantic, but it happens. Well, it happened to me. Once. His hands cupped my face and he pulled me into him and all the waiting and wondering and hoping were worth it. The rush of something that felt like pure excitement overwhelmed me. Nothing had ever felt that real before. My whole body was just nerve endings reacting to him. Maybe Rosie and Oli were still there, watching as the inevitable happened. Maybe they saw that it was me who, sometime into the eternity of that first kiss, grabbed his hand. Maybe they saw that it was me taking the lead, me who smiled as I guided him up the stairs. Sometimes when I think back to that night, I need to remind myself that a lot of it was my idea.

8
NOW

I went into work a bit early. Well, an hour early. If Jon asked, I'd say I'd figured he wouldn't mind an extra pair of hands. The truth was, I couldn't bear to be on my own any longer. I'd woken up stupidly early on a morning where sleeping in and rushing about to get ready would have been much better for me. I lay there, wishing I'd planned something more than just a normal day at work. Bustling through a Saturday shift with Jon would keep my mind occupied, but then what? Just an empty weekend stretching ahead. There were just three messages when I'd picked up my phone first thing. Mum, Maria, Auntie Joan. That was it. Maria's gif was cute, two girls chinking glasses and dancing. 'Will be us soon!' she promised. But Edinburgh felt such a long way away. Mum had sent love and put some money in my account, 'to spend on a nice meal with some friends'. Did Mum really think I might go out for dinner? I really should make a note of which 'friends' I'd mentioned by name, in case she asked. Other than that, a couple of junk emails with special offers. As I was pulling clean underwear from my drawer, the phone pinged again. I grabbed it, too hopefully. Anna, a girl from my course. Asking if she could borrow my copy of a set text, she'd left hers in the library. Disappointment flickered. Well, what did I expect? I hadn't told anyone it was my birthday.

There was already a Saturday morning buzz, and Jon looked grateful to see me, if a bit surprised. Turning up late and flustered was much more in character than strolling in an hour early. He raised a hand as I went to hang my jacket in what he lovingly referred to as 'the staff room'; it was actually a rather over-full, walk-in cupboard. Aproned and ready, I went into the kitchen to start on some salad prep, already feeling a bit better. There, on the spotless countertop was an envelope with my name on it, and a solitary cupcake with a candle sticking out of the chocolate frosting. For a second I had a lovely warm feeling, like seeing the pile of presents under the tree on Christmas morning, but then my brain caught up. Shit. Who knew it was my birthday and how?

'You going to open it then?' Jon made me jump.

'I...'

'Happy Birthday,' he said, scooping the envelope off the counter and handing it to me.

'Thank you.' I tried what I hoped was a warm smile and opened the card. '"To my favourite vegan, lettuce celebrate"' I read out loud, raising an eyebrow. Jon shrugged.

'It was better than "Avo great birthday".'

I laughed. It was. There were two twenty-pound notes inside.

'Wow! What's this for? Thank you!'

'Duh, it's your birthday!' Jon laughed. 'Birthday staff bonus. As one of only two staff, I don't think it's going to break the bank. I thought you might be able to use it for whatever crazy socialising you're planning this evening.'

I thought of the empty space on my calendar where my birthday plans should be. He must have picked up my hesitation.

'Have you got plans tonight? I can let you go early if you need to go and make yourself beautiful?'

As if. I shook my head.

'No, no, don't worry. I can stay until closing. Umm... nothing's starting until later. Thank you so much. I wasn't expecting this. In fact,' I carefully folded the twenty-pound notes back into the envelope, 'did I tell you it was my birthday?'

Jon looked at me sideways and put a finger to the side of his nose.

'I have my sources,' he said. Oh my god. What sources? I racked my brain, trying to think if there was anything that would give me away. A familiar prickle started down the back of my neck, but he was laughing.

'Don't worry, Miss Mysterious. You put your date of birth on your application form, remember? I took note.'

Phew. Of course! I'd been worrying for nothing. And what did it really matter if someone knew my date of birth?

'So I did. Well, thanks for taking note and remembering. I'll eat this later, looks amazing.'

Jon looked pleased and opened the dishwasher door, putting a stop to its merry beeping.

'What can I say? I'm the best boss you've got. But as you're here early, can you start on some salads? Rainy day today, I think we might be busy.'

I nodded and started to get lettuce, tomatoes and pea shoots out of the fridge. It was really sweet of him to do that. And I'd have something to tell Mum about my birthday that was actually true.

As predicted, it turned into a very busy lunchtime. We worked around each other like we'd both learnt the same choreographed dance, passing each other a jug or a pint of milk, keeping eye contact with the customer and listening to the next order. I'd learnt so much from him in the few weeks I'd been working there. It wasn't just about serving drinks, it was so much more than that. The café had an almost tangible welcoming feeling - I'd always noticed it when I was on the other side of the counter. And now I knew what it was. It was the way Jon was so good at remembering things about people. Like their birthdays, I thought, smiling about the cake and the bonus. And I was trying to do it too. Taking note and remembering what people ordered. Referring back to what they'd said last time they were in. Making sure I listened and got them what they wanted. Offering them new things they might like. Smiling. Apologising if required. Making them laugh. And that way, they'd probably come back.

The shift ranged from pretty busy to full-on packed. There was a steady queue, and at times it was standing room only, with people leaning on the counter and the shelf at the back. There were lots of regulars but loads of people just passing through too. Future regulars maybe, or perhaps they were just shoppers sheltering from the rain.

'Told you we'd be busy today!' Jon managed to say as I stood back to allow him past with a new bag of coffee beans. 'Must be your Instagram!'

I forced a laugh at the new running joke. I still hadn't got anything set up on social media and Jon was trying all sorts of less and less subtle ways to remind me. On days like this, I couldn't really see why he thought it was so important. But I'd said I'd do it and it really didn't look as if he was going to let it lie until I did.

The door went again, a girl and two boys. Students. One of the boys looked vaguely familiar. I wondered if I recognised him from my course. Made me feel uneasy to see them there, out of the campus context. Although, so what if it was someone from my course? Didn't mean he'd come in because of me. I busied myself with the cake order of the young family I was serving, but I tried to listen to their conversation. They were speaking too softly for me to hear, but one of them laughed, a low laugh that sounded like they were sharing a secret. I was sure they were looking at me. My hands started to sweat as I realised they were next in the queue.

'So, my young friends, what can I get you?' Out of nowhere, Jon appeared. Sometimes he really did seem to have a sixth sense. I squeezed past, leaving him behind the counter, and disappeared into the kitchen.

Sometime after lunch things calmed down a bit. When Jon came in with a load of dirty plates, I was staring into space, arms folded, standing next to the sink which was filled with soapy water.

'Hey, have we actually got some dishes that wash themselves now?' he said.

'Sorry, I was miles away.' I sprang into action, sticking some of the plates into the sink and looking around for a scourer. 'That was a busy one!'

'Wasn't it? Good job we were both here. I've even been wondering whether we should get someone else in. Although that would double my costs in terms of the annual staff bonus. And if the plates are washing themselves these days...'

I splashed some bubbles in his direction. 'Sounds like a plan,' I said.

'Yeah. I was wondering if you knew anyone?'

I was suddenly fully focussed on the milk jug I was scrubbing. 'Me? No, can't think of anyone.'

That was true at least.

'Did you know those three that were in before? Seemed about your age, I thought they looked as if they recognised you.'

'How do you look as if you recognise someone?' I asked, a little sharp. Jon picked up a tea towel and started to dry.

'I dunno, they seemed to be looking in your direction.'

I didn't need to look at him to know he was watching for a reaction. I pressed my lips together and carried on washing up.

'Well, I didn't recognise them. Anyway, wouldn't you want a school kid or someone for washing up? Based on the kitchens I've seen, I'm not sure any of the students I know would be any use at all.' My laugh was forced.

'Maybe I'll just stick an ad in the window, it worked last time.'

I looked up from the sink and relaxed to see he was smiling at me.

'You were just lucky I saw it.'

'Damn right. When you turned up, I was sitting there contemplating two teenagers who couldn't string a sentence together between them. Don't think I'll bother letting them know about the new vacancy.'

'They don't sound ideal.'

'I count my lucky stars every day that I appointed you and not one of the silent twins. Anyway, listen. Big decision. What soup shall I make for next week?'

Somehow he'd left me off whatever hook I thought I was on. 'That's a biggie. Let me have a think.'

I piled clean cups into my arms and went off to restack the counter before he could ask me any more difficult questions.

9
THEN

I'd slept with Harry. Sun streamed through the half-open curtains and, with it, the first thought of the morning after. I'm not a virgin anymore. The feeling spread through me like a smile as I ran my hands over my body to see if it felt any different. I felt fine – more than fine, I felt amazing. Well, maybe slightly hungover. I rolled out of bed and looked in the mirror. Did I look different? Would anyone be able to tell when they looked at me? Would Mum? A sketchy memory of the ride home drifted back, me sliding unsteadily into the passenger seat, Mum with an eyebrow raised, asking if I'd had fun. And then realising when I got back to my bedroom that my top was on inside out. So yeah, chances are Mum would know.

Rescuing my jeans off the floor, I dug around in the pockets, then checked through the pre-party debris on my dressing table. Where was my phone? I had a vague recollection of giving it to Maria when we were outside, but didn't remember if she gave it back. Oh well. I was sure she'd turn up with it sometime. Or maybe I'd left it in Mum's car. Anyway, it wasn't a bad thing not to have it. At least I didn't have to worry about whether to message Harry or wait for him to text me first.

I feel so grateful now for those phone-free hours before Maria showed up. I got back into bed for a while, reliving the night before. We found a guest room upstairs – Harry seemed to know his way around the house, from years of sleepovers and children's birthday parties, I guessed. He opened the door for me and I walked in, giggling. I thought of the way he turned on a lamp next to the bed, flooding the whole room with soft romantic lighting. I cringed a little bit when I remembered telling him it was my first time – he looked surprised, or taken aback, or maybe as if he was having second thoughts. But I wanted him to carry on. I've never thought you need to wait for 'the one'. But I did want it to be with someone special, and he felt special. It was all really natural; he told me what to do and I did it. He was gentle, but it did hurt a little bit, although I didn't mind at all. And he was so sweet, afterwards – finding my clothes for me, looking away almost embarrassed when I put my bra back on and got dressed. I played it all over in my mind, smiling to myself, thinking of what I'd tell Maria and Rosie and what I'd keep just for myself.

Mum interrupted my happy flashbacks by gently opening the bedroom door.

'Morning, Sleeping Beauty. Thought you might need these.' She plonked a cup of tea and two paracetamols down next to my bed.

'I don't feel too bad,' I said, slurping the tea.

'You don't feel too bad, or you feel good?'

'Good. Definitely good.'

Mum shuffled onto the edge of the bed, making me move over to let her in.

'So?' She looked straight at me. I burst out laughing.

'So what? You're so nosy. Mums aren't meant to hassle their teenage daughters for information. They're supposed to wait to be told.'

'Tell me then.'

I told her. She asked the appropriate Mum questions about whether we used a condom and whether I bled. Thank god she didn't ask for too many details about what it was like. Not that I'd know, I had nothing to compare it to. She hugged me and as she pulled away, I could see she looked teary.

'Mum? Be happy for me! I'm not the last virgin standing anymore!'

She did laugh, but she was thoughtful.

'I'm happy if you're happy, darling. But you're my baby and you're growing up. There's something there to be a little bit sad about too.'

But I didn't really get it and I wasn't sad at all. I was so pleased with myself I was almost purring. I was befuddled with hormones and a feeling of pride. I stood in front of the mirror as I got dressed, pretty sure I could see something different, and that other people would be able to see it too. And I was happy with the idea that people would know. For those few hours, I was really happy. Until Maria turned up with my phone.

10
NOW

'Hey, how are you getting on with recruitment?'

I felt obliged to ask. Jon had been interviewing on the Friday and although I felt a bit weird about it, clearing up wasn't my favourite bit of the job, so I was trying to look on the bright side. I was half-hoping he hadn't managed to get anyone, but knowing Jon, there'd be someone new starting today.

'Yeah, good!' he said, making my heart sink a little. 'Well, I don't know really. I did get a bit of interest but I only interviewed three. There was a girl who seemed okay, but I gave her a trial and she left loads of scraps in the sink, so...'

'You gave her a trial? What, like here's a load of mess I've made, can you clear it up?'

Jon looked round from the blackboard where he was scribbling the day's specials.

'Well, yeah. That's going to be the main part of the job, so seemed sensible.'

'I guess.' He'd misplaced an apostrophe on today's soup. Again. I'd correct it later when he wasn't looking.

'So, she didn't get it,' he said. 'Then I had two guys. One of them literally wouldn't have said boo to a goose. I know you don't need the charisma of a stand-up comedian to be a pot washer, but I kind of hoped we'd get someone you and I could get on with.'

I was pleased he'd considered me at least. I took my coat off and realised I'd left my apron at home. Damn it.

'Anyway, the third one I thought was good. Very personable. Looked me straight in the eye and answered my questions well. And I did ask some strange ones.' Jon chuckled to himself and I remembered what he'd asked me. If you had to eat only one cake for the rest of your life, what would you choose? It was a good question. I was still thinking about it.

'And did he get a trial too?' I asked.

'Certainly did. Spotless sink, everything dried and stacked and surfaces wiped. A star.'

'He sounds amazing.' Ridiculously I felt a prickle of something like jealousy. For god's sake, like I wanted to be the only person who was good at clearing up the kitchen.

'His name's Andrew. He starts today.'

Done deal. Oh well. Maybe he'd be nice. I really hoped so. Someone tried the door, which was still on the latch.

'Jon, it's nine. Shall I open up?'

'You do that, kiddo. Then go and find yourself an apron, you appear to have turned up incorrectly dressed.'

He was laughing and I rolled my eyes at him. He might be the most understanding and laid-back boss you'd ever find, but you couldn't get anything past him.

It was quiet for a Saturday. Typical. We could have managed easily without a new guy. It was only ever a problem when the morning was so busy that dirty pots were already stacked up by lunchtime. Oh well, better to ease him in gently on his first day. I was trying to be nice.

I didn't actually see Andrew arrive – there were a few people in and I was working my way through a list of complex drinks. You can always spot the one that's going to order an iced vanilla latte and change to caramel just as you pour the syrup. Jon said hi to someone I assumed was Andrew, and I saw the back of his head as he followed Jon into the kitchen. He was tall, solid-looking – I'd been expecting a school kid somehow, but he looked older.

When things settled down out front, I thought I'd better go and introduce myself. I walked into the kitchen with a few dirty plates. Andrew was at the sink, turned away from me. He was definitely not a school kid – he was probably six-foot, with broad shoulders and slightly sandy wavy hair, and was dressed in standard issue jeans and a cotton Polo shirt. He looked like a student, probably around my age. He moved his head and I caught a better look at his face in profile. Something about him gave me a chill. For some reason I couldn't get hold of, I felt sure I'd seen him before. The cheerful introduction I was about to offer dried up in my throat. Where did I know him from? As I was standing looking at him, he turned towards me and grinned, way too broadly, showing all his teeth.

'You must be Amy? Hi, I'm Andrew. The new guy. Pleased to meet you.'

He wiped his hand on his apron and reached for my free hand. The apron looked ridiculous on someone so big. He gripped my hand firmly and I desperately wanted him to let go.

'Hi!' I said, managing to sound bright and breezy. I hoped I'd got away without betraying myself, but as he released my hand, his brows creased into a little frown.

'Do we know each other?' he asked. 'I feel like I've seen you before. You look really familiar.'

I tried a laugh. Even someone who didn't know me would have realised how false it sounded.

'No, don't think so. I've just got one of those faces, I think. People often say that.' No one had ever said that.

'Are you a student here?' he said, undeterred.

I nodded, quickly grasping the straw. That was probably it. 'Uh-huh. I expect you've seen me on campus or something.'

I put the cake plates down in front of him, hoping to dismiss the conversation, or at least to distract him from the way he was staring.

'I believe these are your responsibility today.' I gave a smile, nearly as false as the laugh. He was still frowning.

'Oh, cheers.' He shook his head a little bit. 'Yeah, weird. I don't think it is from uni, but I definitely know you. Six degrees of separation, isn't it? Probably if we ask each other enough questions we'll work out we were both at the same Blossoms gig last summer or something.'

I tried to laugh it off, silently deciding never to give him enough time to ask me any questions at all.

'Well, I hate Blossoms so it's definitely not that!'

'They were great at that gig, you missed out.' He picked up the plates I'd left. 'Cheers for these, I'll get on with it.' He was still shaking his head slightly as he put the plates into the soapy water. 'I'll think of it though,' he said, fairly neutrally, but to my ears it sounded like a threat.

I left the kitchen, wracking my brain. There was something, and I wanted to be the one to think of it first. Just in case.

'You met Andrew then?' said Jon as I joined him behind the counter.

'Yeah, he seems nice.' It sounded like a bit of a lukewarm endorsement. Jon looked at me but didn't say anything. I gave him a smile. 'Yeah, very nice,' I lied. No point letting there be any suggestion of tension in the team. Last thing any of us needed.

I managed to let Jon do most of the table clearing and food orders; it was quite a busy lunchtime in the end. Towards two, as things were calming down a bit and I was just starting to think I could do with something to eat, the door went and there was Gorgeous Guy. I blushed. Really? I said to myself. Get a grip. I turned to him, my full-on waitress smile in place.

'Hello again.' Might as well get in there first.

'Hi,' he said. I thought maybe he looked pleased to see me. But it was hard to judge without being totally distracted by his eyes.

'So, am I too late for lunch?' he asked, smiling. I realised I was staring and snapped myself back into reality, waving at the blackboard.

'No, not really. We've still got most things on here, apart from the soup's changed. It's now roast butternut squash. Sorry, haven't had time to alter the blackboard.'

I rubbed at 'tomato and basil' with my finger, succeeding only in smudging it a bit and getting chalk dust up my nose. I sneezed. He laughed.

'Bless you. No worries at all about the blackboard. I absolutely prefer the sound of butternut soup anyway.'

I was being a bumbling idiot, yet again. I wrote the order on a little notepad.

'Anything with that? It comes with a hunk of bread...' I'd literally never used the phrase 'hunk of bread' before in my life. I cringed inwardly but he didn't seem to notice.

'Nothing else thanks. Maybe a coffee later.'

I passed him the card reader and decided I'd probably be in the kitchen when he needed his coffee; Jon could do it. Then I remembered Andrew. For god's sake, work was supposed to be my safe place. Gorgeous Guy was looking at me expectantly.

'Take a seat, I'll bring it over.'

'Thanks. I'll be there, in the corner.' He pointed to table four.

Course you will, I thought. That's where you always sit.

11

THEN

Mum had gone out, leaving me drifting around in a happy daze. I wasn't worried about the phone; I was pretty sure either Rosie or Maria would have it, and we had a well-worn ritual of getting together at mine the morning after the night before to piece it all back together. So I just waited for them to turn up, trying to stop grinning to myself. I had a shower, made toast, watched a bit of crap TV. My stomach was full of butterflies and my brain kept going over and over how we'd kissed, how he'd touched me. I wondered what he was thinking. I really wanted to see him again. I couldn't wait for my friends to arrive so I could talk and talk about Harry. Little did I know.

It was around midday when the doorbell went. Maria, on her own, wearing an inscrutable expression that wasn't her usual hungover face or her, "Oh my god, what did I do?" look. I couldn't read her at all.

'Hey, what's up?' I said, still cheerful, blissful in my ignorance. 'You look very serious. And where's Rosie?'

'Amy, can I come in? Rosie's... not coming.'

I stood to one side to let her in, my heart starting to beat a bit faster. This didn't feel like normal behaviour. Maria went into the kitchen and sat on one of the tall stools by the counter. She plonked my phone down on the worktop but, as I reached for it, she put her hand out to stop me.

'Look, before you check any messages or anything, I need to tell you something.'

'Shit, Maria, you're scaring me now. What the hell happened?' I had a sudden thought. 'Is Rosie okay?'

Maria nodded slowly, her hand still over my phone.

'Rosie's fine. Well, she's not hurt or anything if that's what you mean.'

I felt slightly relieved but Maria's face was stony.

'Amy, I don't know how to tell you this. Last night, with Harry...'

I grinned in spite of myself.

'Yeah, we did it. I'll tell you all about it if you...' She stopped me with a raised hand.

'You don't need to, Ames. I know. Everyone knows.'

She picked the phone up, pressed the screen and passed it to me. I was trying to understand what she'd just said, butterflies turning to something more twisty and sour inside me. On the screen, a video was playing. I turned the phone horizontal so the image filled the screen. Grainy and not that well-lit, a room with a bed just off centre of the frame. And two figures, a girl seated on the bed, her arms in the air, and a tall, athletic-looking blond-haired boy taking off her black top. Harry and me. On the bed in Oli's guest room. My breath caught in my throat. I looked desperately at Maria for explanation.

'What the...? Maria, what's going on? What the hell? Who did this? Who's seen it? Oh my god, delete it, we have to delete it, get it off here. Who's seen it? Tell me!'

Maria shook her head.

'I'm not sure who's seen it. It was a link, on the party chat. To this website. It says... three hundred and twenty-five views'

Blood rushed to my head, I felt hot, overwhelmingly dizzy. I didn't want to see any more but I couldn't tear my eyes away. The camera angle was such that we were almost in the background, an expanse of pink carpet filling up the foreground of the shot. You could see my top where he'd dropped it, and my jeans in a ball on the floor. Something was slightly obscuring the bottom left of the picture, but it didn't stop me from seeing what was going on as Harry undid my bra and threw it to the side. I watched, paralysed, as he moved me into position on top of him, my breasts clearly visible in the light from the bedside lamp, my hair falling across my face until he swept it away with his hand. The distance from the camera made the sound quite muffled, and there was some kind of musical backing track, but I could hear his voice, my moans, the creak of the floorboards. I started to shake.

Maria put her hand on my arm and gently took the phone off me.

'Babe. Don't watch any more,' she said. My head pounded.

'Is it all here?' I started to cry, frantic. 'The whole thing? Has Harry seen it?'

'Ames, I don't know! I just don't know.' Maria was starting to cry too. She reached out for me but I was beyond comfort. The images were still playing out on the phone, lying there on the kitchen worktop, the pumping pop backing track not quite masking the sounds of me and Harry having sex. I wanted to be sick.

'Who did this? Maria, who did it? What are we going to do?'

I sank to the kitchen floor. All joy had gone out of me. My body ached, my insides twisted, my head filled with images of the night before, now seen through the eyes of all those people who'd watched the video. I couldn't speak. I could barely breath in, the air seemed to stick in my throat as I fought silent sobs. Maria held me and rocked me like a baby. Gradually I crumpled further, making myself as small as I could, my cheek cold on the shiny floor, my tears tiny splash marks on the tiles. Maria got up, I could hear her speaking softly in the other room, then she came back into the kitchen and put the kettle on. Lowering herself to her knees, she stroked my hair.

'Amy. Come and sit on the sofa. Let me make you some tea. I just called your mum, she's coming home. Can you stand up? I think you're in shock, mate. But lying on the floor's not helping, let me get you into the lounge.'

Somehow, I stood. Maria more or less carried me to the sofa where I curled back up again. I wanted to die. I mean, I didn't want to actually kill myself and leave Mum grieving for her only child. But almost. I couldn't imagine how life could carry on. How could I ever leave the house? I tried to imagine walking through the main street, going to school, seeing my friends, my teachers. Anyone of them could have seen me naked. Watched me lose my innocence in a tacky pink guest room, drunk on vodka, pale-skinned, with underwear that didn't match, making noises like I was enjoying it. Oh god. They were the kind of images you can never unsee. And already more than three hundred people had seen them.

Maria's version of what had happened was incomplete. She'd felt sick after smoking too much, so she'd done what she often did and realised she needed to go home. Luckily for me, she'd picked up her bag and my phone. She remembered saying goodbye to Rosie, but not me – I was upstairs with Harry, she guessed. She said Rosie was a bit off and was in a heated discussion with Oli, but Maria was too drunk to care what was going on. She'd got a taxi and rolled into bed sometime around 1.30, she thought.

'So, this morning I felt like shit, and the phones were both beeping away. I went to turn them off so I could sleep some more, but...' She rubbed her hand across her forehead and leant heavily into it, as if trying to erase the memory.

'There were forty-seven notifications on my phone. I kind of realised something must be going on. So I looked at the party group, that was the one with the most messages.'

I was hanging off her every word, hoping somehow that this was going to turn out to be a mistake. Or even a joke. Pretty fucking horrible joke but I would have taken it.

'And yeah... well, that link. Most of it was comments so I scrolled back and realised they were all talking about that link. And so I clicked on it.'

I made a choking sound and shoved my fist into my mouth.

'Don't worry! I hardly watched any. Just enough to work out... to see what it was.' She shook her head.

'God, Ames, I couldn't believe it. And the messages were still coming in. So I started to contact people. I was telling them to stop sharing it, to take it down. I didn't know how to tell you; I was trying to make it right before I got here. But...'

'But?'

'There were too many, I just couldn't deal with it all. As soon as I sent a message, two more came, then others on other groups. I didn't know what to do. So I came round here.'

I nodded and held out my hand for the phone.

'Can I see?'

Maria held the phone closer to her chest.

'Do you want to? I think it's probably better if you...'

'Maria. Give me the phone. I want to see.'

I knew instantly why she didn't want me to look. Seeing myself naked on screen was one thing. The dimples of my buttocks, the flat stomach I'd always been quietly proud of, the breasts I'd privately thought were a good shape. Suddenly it all looked obscene. But the comments were something else. My friends, my so-called friends, saying all kinds of things they would never have said to my face. About my tits, my arse, the way I moved my body. There were voice messages impersonating me, "Oh Harry, yes, do that, yes, it's so good" with breathless giggling and grunts of ridiculing laughter. Taunting me for being a virgin, mocking me for the things I said. Slagging me off as a slut and a whore. How could I be all those things at once? I couldn't stop reading them although my chest hurt with the pain of trying to hold myself together.

'Mate. Stop. Please.'

Maria reached for the phone but I snatched it away and threw it across the room, hearing it smack against the cupboard, hoping it had shattered, wanting never to have to deal with the world again.

Tea sloshed around my empty stomach; my head pounded. Maria was going over and over how she'd tried to stop it, how she'd asked people to stop forwarding the link. Every few seconds her phone would beep and she'd start more frenzied messaging. Pouncing on every notification, telling people to stop, channeling an energy into her phone that I'd never seen before. But I couldn't move. My phone lay dead in the corner by the TV and I lay on the sofa, just as silent. My brain was in overdrive, calculating, recalculating. There must have been over a hundred people at the party, all of them capable of sending on the link to the video. God knows how many more group chats were alive with it. Maria had mentioned at least four. I curled further into myself, imagining the wildfire spreading, the link travelling through the ether as more and more people clicked on it. I wondered if I would ever leave my house again.

Maria gave a stifled gasp and looked up.

'What?'

'The views are over five hundred. We have to get this video down. I just don't know what to do!'

She looked really pale, her eyes despairing – I reached for her hand and she started to cry too.

'Oh god, Amy. You don't deserve this. How did this happen?'

She curled herself around me on the sofa, and that's where Mum found us, sobbing into the cushions, the phone buzzing every couple of seconds from the coffee table, sending out its evil messages without either of us picking it up.

12
NOW

It was a Tuesday afternoon, and I'd just had a lecture on some nineteenth-century poet my tutor was obsessed with. I was unimpressed, but I was a bit too tired to concentrate. I'd done a couple of busy shifts over the weekend, and then on Sunday night I'd finally managed to get the café social media set up. I didn't really know why Jon was so keen on it, and I definitely didn't know why I'd said yes. But the running joke about how I still hadn't done it had gone on too long. How hard could it be? So I'd started with X, that wasn't too difficult. But Instagram. I'd really struggled to go there again. Just looking at the icon on the App store made my heart race. But I'd done it, at some silly hour of the morning when I'd finally admitted to myself it was stopping me from sleeping. I'd realised if I set up a business account in the name of the café it didn't need anything on there that would allow anyone to find me. Assuming anyone wanted to. I used a photo I'd taken of the front window with the light falling across so you could read the logo really well. Account opened. It looked good. And Jon was pleased.

I drifted around the library for a bit looking for inspiration, but, not having found any, I gave up and headed out. Halfway down the stairs, someone called my name. I tried to carry on, pretending I hadn't heard, but heavy footsteps chased after me and he said it again, louder this time. Andrew.

'Hey! Fancy seeing you here. Almost didn't recognise you without the apron.'

Would there ever be a moment where Andrew would say something to me that didn't make me want to vomit?

'Hey!' I replied, trying to be non-committal. He matched my pace as we went down the stairs. 'Been trying to remember how I know you,' he said, oblivious to the fact I didn't want to talk. He started off on a load of tedious drivel, trying to find something that linked us. We got to the main door and I tried to read his body language so I could turn in the opposite direction, but he stopped and said, 'Where are you going? I'm free now, I was just going to grab a coffee…' He left it open but I could hear the invitation hanging in the air. I chose to ignore it.

'Well, enjoy!' I said, giving him a little wave and moving away. He stood there with a slight hangdog expression that did nothing to endear him to me.

'See you Saturday!' he called to my retreating back. Shit. Having him around really didn't make for happy workdays. I wished I could remember where it was that I'd seen him before, then maybe I could stop feeling so jumpy around him.

I didn't want to risk bumping into him again and I still hadn't found anywhere I felt comfortable sitting on my own, so I went back to my hall. At least it would be quiet there. I walked through the ground floor common room unnoticed – there were a bunch of people I vaguely recognised sprawled over the sofas, but they didn't pay me any attention. Safely in my room with the door closed, I chucked my bag down on the bed and pulled out my phone. I tried to FaceTime Maria but she didn't pick up – probably in a lecture or hanging out with some of her new friends, I thought, trying not to feel jealous. I sent Mum a little message telling her I was busy with work but I'd call her at the weekend. Jon had given me a new soft drink to try out – it looked a bit pink and a bit sweet, but in the absence of anything to do, I took a swig and started to flick through Instagram.

I checked out some of the opposition and noted that one of the big chains were promoting gingerbread latte. The café had six new followers and my first post, a lovely shot of a bowl of soup on one of the scrubbed wooden tabletops, had twenty-four likes. I felt quite pleased, even though I'd promised myself I wouldn't be one of those people who got their dopamine from likes. I made a mental note to tell Jon. Although I couldn't decide if he was more interested in the likes and the followers, or just the fact that I was actually doing something.

About to put the phone away, I spotted a message notification. Without thinking I clicked on it and an oh-so-familiar face appeared with a "Hi, how are you?" I closed the app as if it had stung me. My eyes lost the ability to focus and the world went unsteady for a few seconds. How could that have happened? How could anyone have reached me? Then a rage hit me. "Hi, how are you?" After all this time, that's the best you can do? Fuck you. I chucked the phone onto my desk, pulled on a coat and left my room, hoping air and space would let me shake off the feeling of being cornered.

I walked out onto the main road as daylight turned to dusk, losing myself in the sound of traffic, headlights staining the backs of my retinas as I marched alongside the commuters on their way home. But I couldn't stop thinking about it. I hated that the message was still there, festering away on my desk. I walked and walked, those four innocuous little words searing my brain, until I had missed dinner and had to buy a soggy wrap from the garage on the corner on the way back to campus.

As soon as I got to my room, I grabbed the phone, deleted the message and blocked the sender. But it was too late; I'd seen it and it wouldn't go away.

13
THEN

I still haven't ever really asked Mum how she felt that day. But however she felt, she read the situation the minute she walked in, and realised she needed to take over. Maria couldn't do any more – she'd done pretty well on a hangover and not much sleep, but she was wrung out. I was useless. I couldn't even speak, let alone make decisions or activate any kind of plan. Mum untangled us from our sobbing heap on the sofa and gave Maria the task of making us all tea. She sat next to me and silently stroked my hair for a few minutes, until Maria came back with the drinks.

'Thank you, Maria, just what we need,' she said. 'Now, can I have your phone?'

'No!' I instantly came to life. 'No, Mum, please. I don't want you to see…'

Mum gave me a very weak version of her usual smile.

'Darling, it's okay. I don't want to see either. I just want to know where the video is and who's watched it, so we can try and sort this out.'

I was ever so slightly relieved. The idea of Mum watching me doing those things with Harry was more than I could stand. I went back into my foetal position and watched as she got out her laptop and a notebook and pen.

Mum's working knowledge of social media went as far as fifty friends on Facebook and enthusiastic use of WhatsApp, so she really didn't know what she was dealing with. Credit to her though, she didn't let that stop her.

'Okay, Maria, I don't really need your phone, as long as you can help me. First of all, I want you to tell me all of the groups and apps you've seen with messages on about Amy.'

Maria nodded and applied herself to the task with a new-found energy, relieved that an adult was taking charge. She scrolled through WhatsApp – the video link had appeared in five different groups, she reported. And there were about a hundred and twenty people in those groups in total, she worked out, when pressed. Mum started to write a list of names – the girl I used to share lifts to ballet with, a boy from my Maths class I'd never spoken to, a friend from drama club who hadn't even been at the party. Names and more names, and numbers, and the WhatsApp group they belonged to. Mum wrote it all down, Maria flicking through and dealing with notifications as they came in. Then they went through Instagram. Then Messages. And Messenger. And the same with Snapchat.

'And the link? What is that?' I shrank into myself, Maria gave me a quick look and managed to not die of embarrassment at saying the name of a porn site to my mum. Mum frowned slightly but wrote it down.

I just watched. My mum and my friend, battling the world for me. Maria with her phone and Mum with her unshakeable belief that there isn't a problem too big to be tackled with a list. I loved them, and I envied their optimism that somehow they could stop what was happening. Because I already knew. That video was out there. Mum could contact whatever hideous website it was and get it taken down, that was the first thing she was going to do. She could call the school and get every single person on that list in front of the head. She was going to do that tomorrow. But the video had a life of its own by now. Downloaded, shared, circulated way beyond the reach of the head of Queen Katherine School. The damage was done.

Sometime mid-afternoon, Mum took Maria home and left me with instructions to have a bath. I still hadn't eaten anything, and two of the four cups of tea Maria had made sat grey, cold and untouched on the coffee table. Alone in the house, I stared at the wall for a while, trying to get the energy to stand up. Maybe Mum was right, maybe a bath would make me feel better. Anything was worth a try. Somehow I hauled myself off the sofa and went upstairs.

I turned on the taps and stood looking at my reflection until the mirror steamed up and I disappeared. I thought back just twenty-four hours - how happy I'd felt with my reflection, my shoulders in the black halter top, the flatness of my stomach, the tightness of the jeans on my curves. I thought of me in that bedroom with Harry undressing me, smiling with the sure knowledge I was about to have sex with him. It was like remembering a book I'd read, or a character someone else had told me about that I'd almost forgotten. That version of me no longer existed. I tore my clothes off and threw them on the floor. They were clothes I'd chosen in a different life-time, before I realised my body was a thing of shame.

I stuck an elbow in the water and the heat sent shivers up my arm and gave me goosebumps. Too hot. I turned the cold back on, waited a few seconds. But as I stood there, I caught a glimpse of my naked reflection, distorted by condensation on the shiny taps. It repulsed me. I wasn't clean. I needed to be clean. I couldn't wait. I turned off the cold water and lowered myself into the bath with a shudder. I grabbed a cloth and started scrubbing my skin in a frenzy, rubbing at it until it turned red. The water wasn't hot enough. I turned the tap on full, my nerves tingled, a new sensation, so hot it might have been cold, a physical pain that couldn't drown out the agony inside me. The steam got thicker and thicker in the room; I scrubbed and scrubbed at myself, my skin raw with the heat and the fury. I couldn't get clean, no matter how hard I tried.

Then suddenly Mum burst into the room, emerging through the fog. A brief expression of relief crossed her face as she saw my head above water, but then the heat, the colour of my skin, the sobbing.

'Amy!' she cried out in alarm. 'Amy, my god!' She turned off the hot tap, pulled the plug and somehow managed to haul me out of the water onto the bathroom floor. She wrapped me gently in a towel, careful not to chafe my scalded skin, enveloping me in her arms. We sat there, a twisted grown-up version of me and Mum from years before: me wrapped in a towel with a hood, baby curls springy and soft, smelling of Johnson's shampoo. Mum singing *Five Little Ducks* on a continuous loop until it was time for bed.

She rocked me on the bathmat as the steam left through the open door and the boiling hot water gurgled away. I leant into her, wishing for the days when a fluffy towel and five little ducks was enough to make it all okay.

'Amy,' she whispered into my hair. 'Oh my darling girl, I shouldn't have left you. What have you done to yourself?'

14
THEN

My school's policy on absence was pretty uncompromising – if you could get up, you should be at school. Monday morning dawned and Mum came in to wake me. She was always a believer in the power of a good night's sleep – sadly for her, I'd only slept for a few fitful hours, with dreams full of flickering screens and the sounds of phone notifications. She sat on my bed and stroked my hair. Neither of us mentioned the scenes of hysteria from the night before when she'd covered my red raw skin in lotion and tried to coax me to eat something while I sobbed and shook, unable to say a word.

'Amy. It's seven. How do you feel about school today?'

I shook my head and pulled the duvet over my face so she couldn't see me and couldn't stroke my hair anymore.

'Darling. I understand. I know you think you can't face people. But at some point you're going to have to go back. Maybe it's better to face it head on, get it over with. I'm sure once you get there and see your friends...'

I'm assuming the sentence was heading for something like 'it won't be as bad as you think', but I didn't let her finish. I threw the duvet back.

'Mum, I can't!' I screamed at her. 'I can't! You didn't see it. You didn't read the comments. How can I walk into school knowing every single person watched me losing my virginity? Everyone's seen me naked.'

Mum looked taken aback by the speed I got up to full volume, but credit to her, she didn't try to interrupt.

'You know those anxiety dreams when you walk into a room and you have no clothes on?' I said. 'That's actually happened to me! You say you know how I feel. You can't know. You can't possibly know! You don't have a clue about social media. I bet there's no one in this town under the age of thirty who hasn't seen it. And that will include some of my teachers. I don't know how I can ever go back.'

My tired lungs somehow found the energy to sob again. Mum tried to comfort me but there was nothing she could say. I cowered back under the duvet, rejecting her strokes and attempts to hold me. After a while, she went away. I could hear her on the phone, probably letting school know I was ill and wouldn't be in today. I pictured the knowing look of the school receptionist as she hung up the phone. Her son was in my year.

Mum went to work, reluctantly leaving me alone. I must have slept a bit because I woke up to that awful feeling when you know something terrible has happened but your conscious mind hasn't quite caught up. Two seconds of relative peace before the memory flooded back. I screwed my face up and pulled the pillow over my head, as if stopping the light getting in could make the thoughts disappear. It didn't work. I thought about staying where I was, curling up in a ball and hiding from the world. But I felt weak from lack of food and too much crying, so I forced myself out of bed, into my dressing gown and downstairs.

Mum had cleared up all the cups and plates from yesterday and plumped the sofa cushions, but my phone still lay in the corner of the room where I'd thrown it. Gingerly I walked towards it as if I was approaching a land mine. It hadn't smashed, but the battery was long dead, although it seemed to radiate an energy all of its own; as if the messages, the shares, the number of views, likes and comments it was hiding were giving it life. Suddenly I needed to see it all for myself. All my instincts of self-preservation were overwhelmed by morbid curiosity, and a desperate need to understand if things were really as bad as I thought. I dug a charger out from behind the TV and plugged my phone in.

It seemed to take ages before the screen woke up, the little white apple on the black teasing me with what it knew that I didn't. I had all my social media apps grouped together in one folder – there were two hundred and eighty-nine notifications. Taking a deep breath, I tapped WhatsApp. The party group was still the one that had the most notifications, but when I opened it, I could see that Maria had done her best. Lots of people had deleted their comments and the original link had been removed. Deep down, I allowed myself a very small feeling of relief. The same thing was true on the other chats – lots of deleted messages, making it hard for me to work out which of my so-called friends had been sharing the link and which had been commenting. But I could still see their names. Anna Rowe – This message is deleted. Rob Gardner – This message is deleted. Didn't really need to know what they'd said, it turned out – my mind could fill in the gaps with its own nightmare imaginings. And I could still see which of them had been thoughtless enough to put it all into groups that I belonged to. Too many to list.

I turned to Snapchat. The screen taunted me with all its colourful circles telling me which of my friends had posted new snap stories. I wondered whether to just delete it, but some masochistic streak made me start flicking through. You'd imagine there are controls on social media about sharing a sex video, and you'd be right. I wondered at the cruelty of the creative geniuses who had managed to get me into their stories without showing anything that would get them into real trouble. One image flicked to the next, some just zoomed in on the bed using graphics to make mention of what everyone had seen and didn't need to see again. *Oh, Amy, you're so hot,* declared one in jiggly orange text and decorated with a flame emoji. There was one of two images next to each other, labelled "Before and After" - a shot of the unmade bed alongside a really unflattering still of me nearly fully dressed afterwards. I recoiled at the hideousness of my body, no longer just mine to share. But I couldn't stop. It was like I wanted it to hurt. Like I needed to see just how shameful I was. Oli's story was a screenshot of me and Harry, frozen in time at the moment we entered the room, hand-in-hand. I was smiling at Harry; he was looking just over my shoulder. I shuddered and moved on. Flick, flick, flick, image after image, each one hitting me like a blow to the guts.

Suddenly I realised something. I went back to the various message apps – there was absolutely nothing from Harry. No how are you, no sharing of the shame. And more than that. All of the jokes were at the expense of my body, things I'd said, what I did. Nothing about him. There were just a couple of congratulatory, shitty laddish comments, the sort of thing that should be outdated in this day and age. Cogs whirring, I went back and found Oli's story. I zoomed in. Harry was looking straight at the camera, with an expression of slight concentration, someone looking over their shoulder to check they were in the right place. I thought of the way he put on the light, positioned us on the bed, moved away afterwards as I got dressed. Oh my god.

He'd known about it. Whoever had set up that camera, Harry knew it was there.

It was about two o'clock. I knew Maria would be in double RS until the end of the school day but I desperately needed to talk to her. This felt like a discovery – whoever put the camera there and shared the video, it was a plot. I had no idea why I was the victim, but it gave me hope. We might be able to get rid of it all somehow if we knew for sure where it started. It was, at most, a vague glimmer of hope, but it was the first time I'd felt anything other than utter desolation. I sent her a message.

Hey. Please come over after school, I need to find out how today was, plus I think I have an idea of who did this.

Mum had left her notebook on the side next to the TV. I picked it up – she and Maria had done a good job of trying to list everyone. It almost made me smile, her familiar handwriting transforming the list of names into something almost sweet and friendly. But it wasn't a list of who to invite to my birthday party, or the names of people to thank for their Christmas presents. It was a register of all the people in my life I could no longer trust. I scanned it; there were so many names. Amazing that people who never even spoke to me had been happy to share their comments. And totally sickening that people I used to consider my friends had been too. Dani, Alex, Martha, Oli, Izzy. And at the end, in Mum's curly blue scrawl, the name that had been hovering around in my subconscious for the last two days. Rosie. Written with a question mark next to it. Rosie? Yes, that was indeed a very good question. Where the fuck was she and why hadn't she been to see me?

By the time Maria arrived, I'd managed to shower and get dressed. I'd had some toast and a yoghurt and I was feeling a bit better - there was a definite sense of purpose to me on that Monday afternoon, a glimmer of the strength I was going to need to get through it.

I went to the door – Maria still looked exhausted, but in a worn-down way like she'd spent the day in battle. We hugged, a deep and heartfelt hug that lasted minutes as we teetered on the edge of all the shit that was still to come.

'I'm so happy to see you. Today's been looong. Cup of tea?' I tried a smile, thinking back to the unending stream of un-drunk tea from yesterday, but it was still too soon.

'Actually, yes please. Haven't had one today yet.'

We delayed the conversation by putting the kettle on, Maria getting the mugs, me rooting through the cupboard to see if there was any chocolate. We took the tea into the lounge and I saw Maria look at my phone and Mum's notebook open on the table.

'So,' I said, perching on the sofa. 'I need to know. What was school like? I'm going to have to come back, I know, but I wondered if I left it a few days...'

Maria looked at me grimly.

'Ames, I'm not going to lie to you. It was all anyone was talking about. I mean, down to a proper lecture on sharing sexual images. Mrs Jameson got the whole sixth form into the common room and gave us a proper bollocking.'

I felt sick. So the school had seen it. It was inevitable, I supposed. Maria carried on.

'I mean, I didn't think that was fair, getting us all in like we'd been part of it. I went to see her straight after, to tell her I'd been trying to get it taken down. That you didn't know, how upset you were...'

'And?'

She shook her head.

'Well, she did say I'd been a good friend. But she was kind of saying you can't pick and choose how you use social media. Like it's all evil and if we want to dance with the devil, that's what might happen.'

She paused. 'I did have the feeling she'd been looking through everyone's Instagrams.'

I cringed, thinking of all the posts she might have looked at – selfies of new clothes, posing with my friends, mirror selfies showing my body off in shorts, new jeans – God, I think I posted a bikini one last summer. Suddenly all of that seemed outrageous. Did I not realise that meant anyone could see it? Including my head of sixth form?

'What, so because we've all posted selfies and pictures of our milkshakes, we've got what was coming to us?'

She nodded.

'Yeah, pretty much.'

The feelings of hopelessness and shame overwhelmed me again and I crumpled.

'Mate, she might be different with you. You weren't there. I mean, there's no doubt who the victim is in this case, she probably just seized the moment to talk to everyone because you weren't there to hear it.'

'It's not just her though,' I said through my sobs. 'It's everyone. I feel violated by every single person who's watched it. You say I'm the victim but even so, it feels like it's my fault. I'm so ashamed. I wanted to sleep with Harry, you know that. So maybe I did ask for it.'

Maria rushed over to me on the sofa and took my shoulders in her hands.

'No! Don't you ever say that again. You did not ask for this. You didn't do anything wrong. You are a victim, they completely knew what they were doing...' She stopped.

'They?' I asked. She took a deep breath.

'Okay, look. I said I'm not going to lie to you. If we're going to fight this, you need to know everything. You ready?'

I steeled myself and nodded.

'I didn't know all of this yesterday. I knew nothing really, only what I'd seen on the WhatsApp group. I told you, I left the party not long after you went upstairs. I was pissed and you know what I'm like, I had that moment where I just had to leave. So I had my bag, money for a taxi, I just went. You know the drill.'

I did. Brief memories of me and Rosie hunting her down in a nightclub when she was already tucked up in her bed almost made me smile.

'You were obviously off somewhere, and I said goodbye to Rosie on the way out. I told you that too. She wasn't really listening to me, which again isn't that unusual.' Maria paused and took a mouthful of tea.

'So yesterday morning with all the messages and stuff, of course I immediately called her to see what we should do. I thought we could come over together, like we always do. Both of us be here when we told you. She didn't answer. I figured she was still asleep, so I left it a bit, but when I tried again, she still didn't answer.'

Rosie was always the one who was up earliest, and she was never far from her phone. Maria carried on talking but my thoughts were racing. This was weird behaviour.

'I wracked my hungover brain and thought about when I'd last seen her. She'd been talking to Oli. Well, more than talking, having a proper row it looked like. I mean, odd right? I know she can be an argumentative cow sometimes when she's had a drink, but more likely to be crying on me and you than arguing with Oli. So I thought it was odd. I tried to phone her again – no reply, so I went over there.'

Maria paused for breath and another drink of her tea.

'She was there. She let me in. I said, God what a shitshow – she'd obviously seen all the messages. I said come with me to see Amy... and she wouldn't.'

'What?' I started to cry again.

'Ah, Ames, don't cry. I'm so sorry. I tried. She just wouldn't. She said she felt too close to it because Harry's her cousin and she didn't want to get involved.'

I tried to imagine Rosie saying no to Maria. Saying no to coming to see me, her friend from forever.

Words tumbled out through the tears. 'So she doesn't want to see me? At all? Does she blame me for this? I don't understand. I don't know why being Harry's cousin means she can't come and talk to me. Ask me how I am. Jesus!'

Maria picked at the hem of her school skirt and didn't meet my eye.

'Maria?'

She let her breath out in a rush.

'Okay. The thing is Ames, there was a plan. The boys, they had this hilarious idea to set up a camera in the guest room to catch anyone who was in there. Then of course, they all got pissed and started daring each other. It was, well, like a bit of a competition...'

I looked at her in disbelief.

'A competition? What competition?'

'Well, who could get laid and get it all recorded. Without the girl knowing.'

I felt utterly sick to the core, sicker than I'd felt up until that point. The short-lived sense of purpose had evaporated and the shame that was already threatening to bury me suddenly increased tenfold.

'Harry knew the camera was there? Of course. That shot of him in Oli's post. He was looking right at it. He knew it was there. That's why he slept with me?'

All of the warm feelings, the memories of his gentle hands on me, him peeling off his t-shirt, holding me to him, the thrill I felt with him there, so close. There was nothing good left. I hated him.

'And wait a minute? Rosie is somehow siding with this, this sick monster, because he's her cousin? She's choosing him over me?'

Maria sighed.

'I don't know that for a fact. When I saw her yesterday, she didn't tell me all that. Just that she felt too close to it all. I found out today by all the bragging and the chat going round. Harry was strutting around like he thinks he's some kind of sex god. To be fair he did look a bit sheepish when he saw me.' I saw the smallest flash of self-satisfaction in her eyes. 'I gave him a load of shit.'

I pictured her fronting up to Harry, six foot tall, strong and good-looking and backed by his rugby team mates, and I could see just a small part of why she was looking so battle-scarred.

'Thank you.'

She smiled weakly.

'But, Rosie, what did she say about it all?'

'She wasn't in today either and she's not picking up my messages.'

'I need to talk to her'

'You can try.' Maria chucked me my phone. I shook my head.

'No. I'm not phoning. She'll ghost me too. I'm going round to her house.'

15

NOW

The unwanted message had rattled me, no doubt about it, but I couldn't tell Jon what had happened without way too much explaining. I finally got hold of Maria, thinking if anyone would get it, she would. She seemed pretty unconcerned.

'You know, it's that stage of uni where people start to get nostalgic about school. That's probably all it is.' She was using her best consoling voice, although her words were a bit muffled. I imagined her brushing her hair with a hair band held between her teeth.

'Yeah, well, nostalgia about school isn't something I suffer from really. I just can't work out how I could be linked with that account? I don't want any more personal messages. And I'm definitely not replying.'

'No, that's fair. Honestly, mate, I wouldn't worry about it. It's nothing. Sorry, I'm just on my way out. Are you okay now?'

'Yeah, yeah I'm fine. Was just a little panic about nothing. Have fun.'

'Will do! You should come and visit.'

I said I would, and she hung up. I tried to take some kind of comfort from what she'd said, although it didn't sound like she was taking it that seriously. But what bothered me most was how anyone could have linked me with the café, or the account. I hadn't even told Mum about it. I knew what she was like, she'd have got all over-excited about it and starting following, even though she was two hundred and fifty miles away. Posting uncool comments and saying how clever I was or something. And Mum following it would have caused a slight risk that someone would be able to find me. And I didn't want any risks at all, however slight. It was just another thing to eat myself up about.

But I'd said I would do it, and so I was carrying on. Days passed, and no other messages came. I was as careful as I could be. I blocked the sender and vetted new followers as much as I could, checking out their posts and who else they followed before I accepted them. Andychop, the_broke_girl, happyhands – boy, do people pick some weird names for their Instagram accounts. But realistically, putting aside the panic, how dangerous could pretty photos of café food be? After a slow start when I really had wondered what the point was, we were up to nearly two hundred followers. I was posting something every couple of days. It was hard to tell if it was making that much difference to the people who came in, but I had to admit it was kind of fun.

I was running a bit late for work, as I'd had to stay behind after a lecture to talk to my tutor. I'd got a B- on my latest essay, which I didn't think was terrible, but he seemed to think there was room for improvement. He had a point. Maybe I needed to try and spend more time in the library. A couple of streets away from the café, it started to rain - I stepped into the doorway of a music shop to shelter while I tried to find an umbrella in my bag. The door opened behind me.

'Hey! Amy!'

Oh god, it was him.

'Hi. Ummm...'

I didn't know his name. I'd been thinking about asking Jon, but how could I bring it up? 'You know that guy who comes in?' 'Which one?' 'The gorgeous one.' Yeah, wasn't happening. Jon would definitely read too much into it. And I didn't need to know his name, not really. But in that moment, I couldn't exactly say 'Hi Gorgeous Guy' so I was a bit stuck. I smiled vacantly.

'I was just looking for an umbrella,' I said, somewhat pointlessly gesturing at the rain.

'Here, I've got one, do you want to borrow it?' he asked. I realised he had a coat on and looked like he was heading out too.

'Umm... Thanks...Umm.' Literally speechless. I took the umbrella. 'I'll give it back to you when you... next time you're in the café? Or I can leave it with Jon for you, in case I'm not in...'

He pulled his hood up and smiled down at me. I tried not to think that he was about the right height to easily put his arm around my shoulders.

'Yeah, no problem. I was going there now for a takeout actually.'

'Oh. Me too. Not for a takeout. I mean, I'm going to work...'

'Perfect then. We can share the umbrella.' Oh god. How awkward. I handed it back to him, mumbling agreement, and he capably put the umbrella up and held it over me as we walked. It's amazing how difficult it is to walk normally when that's all you're concentrating on. He seemed to be managing it perfectly though, and at the same time angling the umbrella so I wasn't feeling the rain at all.

'Hey... you're getting wet. Don't... ummm'

He shook his head and pulled at the collar of his coat. 'I'm fine, this is waterproof.' He hesitated slightly. 'My name's Jamie,' he added smiling.

I smiled back and wondered if he had some kind of mind-reading super-power. I really hoped not. Jamie and Amy, I thought. No chance. I felt like I ought to somehow continue the conversation, but it was difficult with the rain and the umbrella and the fact that I was dying inside. He was talking about how he was flagging and needed a coffee and a flapjack. I think I said something cringeworthy, but I was so grateful when the café came into sight, and I could regain my composure and put some distance between us. I pushed open the door as he shook the rain from the umbrella. Jon looked surprised as we walked in together.

'Oh. Hello! Come in out of the rain.'

He gave me a questioning look as I passed the counter on my way to the staff room.

'Jamie just lent me his umbrella,' I mumbled. 'Well, we shared it, I mean. And he wants a takeout.'

Jon laughed.

'I'm sure he can manage to tell me that himself. Go and get yourself sorted. What can I get you, Jamie?'

'Flat white please. And I'll stay. Given the weather.'

I closed the door of the staff room behind me and took a few breaths. I was ridiculously flustered. I'd shared an umbrella with someone. Big deal. Well, at least I knew his name now.

Pushing my damp curls out of my face, I went back out to the counter as Jon was proffering the card machine. Jamie managed to smile at me, pay with his phone, stick it in his pocket and pick up his coffee and cake all in one smooth move. Jon put the machine back on its charger and melted quietly off into the kitchen.

'No flapjack left,' Jamie said with a mock look of disappointment.

'Next time,' I said, then started to stammer. 'If you come again, I mean...'

He gave me a steady look. 'There'll definitely be a next time. I'll be in on Saturday, I should think.' He hesitated slightly. 'Will you be?'

I nodded. 'Yeah, more than likely.'

'See you then.'

'Enjoy your coffee.'

I felt my heart bumping way too hard in my ears as I tried a casual smile, then the blood that was flushing my cheeks drained away as I looked to the next customer in the queue for the first time. It was Rosie.

'Amy.'

That oh-so-familiar voice. I hadn't heard it for so long. My blood ran cold.

'What are you doing here?' I hissed. 'How did you know where I was?'

My paranoid brain chased around for the connections. There was no way she'd just wandered in. I'd never even told anyone which university I was going to, let alone that I was working in a café there.

How had Rosie found me? The café Instagram. Rosie's message. If she'd somehow managed to work out that was me, then finding the café was easy. I kicked myself, hard. Bloody Jon, I'd known all along that Instagram was a bad idea. From the corner of my eye, I caught Jamie looking at me. There were two other customers behind Rosie, I had to act normal.

'What can I get you?' I said, too loudly, too cheerfully. Rosie had the grace to look surprised and a little uncomfortable.

'Umm, latte please. Amy, I...'

I spun on my heel and slammed the hopper onto the drawer, emptying the grounds from Jamie's coffee with an explosion of noise. Milk slopped from the jug on the side with the force. I jammed the coffee into the machine and started up the milk steamer, risking scalding my arm in an effort to drown out whatever Rosie was trying to say. I poured the milk into a takeaway cup and placed it on the counter.

'One latte to take out,' I announced.

I shoved the card reader at Rosie and, as she leaned in to pay, hissed under my breath.

'I don't know why you're here and I don't know how you found me, but take the coffee, leave and don't ever come back.'

Before Rosie had time to speak, I turned my back on her, speaking loudly to the next customer.

'Sorry, did my banging around make you jump? Clumsy day today, do you get those? What would you like?'

The door opened and closed and I threw a glance over my shoulder. Rosie had gone. But I felt no sense of relief. None at all. Adrenaline raced. Rosie knew where I was. Who else knew?

16
THEN

Maria was torn between offering to come with me and being completely knackered, so I let her off and said I wanted to go on my own. That wasn't strictly true – well, maybe it was at some level. But in reality, the effort required to do that simple thing, leave the house, was more than I could have imagined. I managed to collect my stuff together and put on a coat and shoes, but as I opened the door to leave, it was almost too much. The fear of being seen and recognised in the outside world, where I used to be happily anonymous, nearly overwhelmed me. I pulled the hood of my parka over my face, took a deep breath and forced myself over the threshold.

As I walked down the street, I kept my head down. I felt like I was being watched from behind the front room curtains in every house I passed. I wondered how many of the four people waiting at the bus stop might have seen me naked. Passing the corner shop, I imagined the guy who knew me as the girl who picked up her mum's Sunday paper now seeing me in a completely different light. The thoughts crowded in, threatening to stop me in my tracks, to paralyse me with paranoia and send me back home. But I needed to see Rosie; somehow I managed to keep walking.

Going up the hill to Rosie's house was something I'd been doing nearly all my life. When we first moved, when I was little, she was the one I'd been paired up with at my new school. The one who made sure I knew which was my peg, where to keep my lunchbox, how to choose a book for reading time and what to play at break. She took her role as my buddy so seriously, always repeating to me under her breath what the teacher had just said, as if she thought being new actually meant I needed a translator. After a week or so, the duty side of the relationship fell away and we became firm friends. She and Maria welcomed me into their group without a trace of jealousy or resentment. And so we'd stayed, a trio that worked, our personalities somehow complementing each other so that we got through the usual pitfalls of changing from children to adolescents without a problem. As I walked the last stretch of Greenside to where she lived, my stomach churned with nerves about seeing my oldest friend. Which was ridiculous. I tried to remember if we'd ever had an argument or any kind of misunderstanding. There was nothing – the odd drunken disagreement was always resolved the next day, with vows to never let alcohol, boys or other women come between us. Until now. So it seemed Harry was an exception to our rule. In spite of everything, I wasn't going to let that happen. Rosie meant more to me than any of this. I reached her door, took a deep breath and knocked.

I waited a good few minutes before anyone answered. I was just wondering whether to go round the back, in case she hadn't heard, when she opened it. She was dressed in joggers and a hoodie, much like me, the uniform of a down day, usually associated with PMT or a hangover. She looked tired, and for a minute I wondered if she actually was ill, and that's why she hadn't answered the phone or gone to school. I went to hug her, but she stiffened and moved away.

'Amy, you should have phoned, I wasn't expecting you.'

I was a bit taken aback.

'Well, I'm sorry. I would have, but Maria said you weren't picking up and I needed to see you, to talk about it all. God, it's been awful, I just don't...'

I tailed off. She wasn't responding with anything to show she was actually listening.

'Rosie? You in there?' I asked.

She let out a stream of air as if she'd been holding her breath for a very long time.

'Look, I know what you want to talk about.'

I tried to laugh. 'No shit. Not much else going on…'

She didn't laugh with me. 'Amy, it's too awkward. Harry's my cousin. I'm sorry.'

Wow, straight to the point. Already this wasn't going the way I'd hoped. I tried to be calm.

'Yeah, I know that, obviously I do. But you know what he's done, right? I mean…'

She interrupted, talking in a weird and stilted way as if it was a little speech she'd been practising.

'You need to understand that it would put me in a difficult position if…'

I couldn't contain myself then.

'If what? If he made a sex tape of your best mate and shared it with everyone we know?'

She wouldn't look at me so I carried on, getting louder.

'The entire school, no, by now probably the entire town and god knows what collection of perverts the world over have seen a very graphic video of me losing my virginity. I feel like I've been abused by hundreds of people, not just tricked and manipulated by your precious cousin. What part of that makes it difficult for you?' I felt myself getting redder and redder but I didn't care. I was oblivious to the fact we were standing on her doorstep in full view of anyone who was interested enough to look. Rosie was not.

'Amy, keep it down. People will hear…' she whispered under her breath.

'I don't give a shit about your neighbours; they're probably enjoying the show. Any hidden cameras around? Am I going to find footage of myself causing a scene all over social media next?'

I paused for breath and calmed slightly. 'You could, of course, invite me in so I can yell at you in the privacy of your own home.'

Rosie stood back to let me in. Always worried about what people would think of her, she obviously realised that talking to me indoors was a better option. She steered me into the little front room, scene of so many playdates and birthday parties, her nan's chair now empty in the window, a photo of Toby, her beloved childhood pet on the mantlepiece. She offered me a seat and sat down opposite. Somehow us both sitting there, with memories of all the time we'd spent together in that room, softened me.

'Rosie, look. I get it that he's your cousin, but you're my friend and I really need you.'

She looked at the floor. I wondered if she was feeling the weight of all the years of our friendship too.

'Maria's been amazing. And Mum. But I can't tell you how this is all making me feel. It's like nothing you can imagine. I wouldn't be ashamed that I had sex, I wouldn't even mind too much knowing Harry told his mates all about it. That's what boys do. I'd tell you and Maria. Probably not the full details, he is your cousin. But you know what I mean?'

I tried to catch her eye, to make her smile, but she was expressionless. I wanted to make her understand, just a bit, so I carried on.

'This is so public. It's so embarrassing to have those images, things I wouldn't even want to see myself, that I'd rather just keep in my head... to have them circulating around everyone I know, people commenting, turning me into a joke.'

I started to feel choked again, the images never too far from my brain. I tried to push them away. I spoke more quietly, trying not to cry.

'It's destroying me. And then when Maria told me it was a set-up, a competition! It's so humiliating. I can't stand it.'

Rosie was twisting a tassel of the sofa cushions in her fingers, something I could imagine her mum had told her a thousand times not to do. I finished my speech and waited for her to say something. She took a deep breath.

'Amy, I'm sorry. I don't know how you're feeling, but I can imagine it's horrible. And I should have come over on Sunday. When Maria asked me to. But I couldn't.'

'Why couldn't you? Surely we've known each other long enough to tackle anything together? I don't understand what it is about this that makes it so hard for you to see me.'

She pulled the cushion onto her lap, the tassel-twiddling not enough on its own, like she needed a barrier between us for what she was about to say next.

'When you went upstairs with Harry, Oli seemed very pleased about it and was giving the thumbs up to some of the others. I asked him what was so funny. And god knows why, but he told me about the camera.'

I looked at her in disbelief.

'He told you? So all the time I was up there oblivious and you knew it was being filmed?'

She nodded. To give her some credit, she looked devastated. But it wasn't a time for sympathy. I couldn't believe what I was hearing.

'So your best friend is upstairs, throwing away her virginity and being filmed doing it, and you didn't think it would be a good idea to try and stop this happening?'

I was trying hard not to lose my cool.

'Amy, I tried. Of course I did! I said to him I thought it was awful. I told him I wanted him to delete the video. He said he wouldn't send it to anyone. He said it was just a joke. He promised.'

I started to see red again, blazing, crimson, all-consuming red.

'A slimeball like Oli, who has just confessed to a perverted scheme like that, made you a promise and you believed him? Are you stupid? For God's sake, why didn't you come upstairs and tell me?' Briefly I visualised a much less painful alternative reality where the worst thing that had happened was that it had all been a dare. It made things even worse.

'Rosie, why?'

'I... I didn't want to walk in on you. I thought you'd be embarrassed. I didn't want to see you with Harry.'

I interrupted her, needing to check I had understood.

'You thought I'd be embarrassed? And somehow you thought that would have been so bad for both of us that you let the whole thing carry on, knowing what was happening? Oh my God, Rosie, you could have stopped it all.'

She nodded slowly and put her head in her hands.

'I'm really sorry, Amy, I really am. He said I was just being a killjoy and it was all a bit of fun. He told me no one would see it. When I woke up the next day and saw the link and all the messages, I knew. I knew it was my fault. That's why I couldn't come over.'

I shook my head and bit back my anger. At least she was talking. Her reasons were weird and misplaced, but if I tried really hard, I could understand, just a little bit. I went over to the sofa to hug her. In that moment I thought I had my friend back.

'It's okay. We can get over this. Rosie, you're not the one to blame. In fact, you could really help.' I started to feel another little glimmer of hope.

'You, knowing this, about what they did. It's going to be a way to make things better. You can tell school; they'll be able to do something.'

I felt almost excited. There might be a way out of this mess. Words tumbled out. 'I mean, this is probably a criminal offence, right? I should go to the police, maybe then the video would be taken down for good, and...'

I hugged her tighter in my enthusiasm. But then I realised she wasn't hugging me back. She pushed me away.

'Amy. I'm sorry. I don't know if I can. Sanctions from school, getting the police involved. Harry's hoping for a scholarship to Durham. And his whole group, our year. They'd never forgive me if I took your side in this.'

'Taking my side? Is that how you see it?'

She bit her lip. 'He's my cousin.'

'And I'm your best friend!' I yelled at her. She didn't answer, just sat, silently squeezing the cushion.

'Oh my god, even if this had happened to some other girl, you must see this is wrong? But it was me! Please! Please, Rosie. I need you to help. I need you to back me up.'

She still didn't say anything but I recognised the little sniff she always did when she was trying not to cry. I tried to hold it together.

'It's the right thing to do. The people that did this, they could do it to other people. No one would blame you for doing the right thing. Not in the long run. Even your family. Do they even know what he's done?'

She shook her head and found a small, shaky voice.

'No. And I don't want to be the one to tell them. Harry, Oli, their friends. They wouldn't ever forgive me. I don't want to be involved. I'm sorry. I'm so sorry, Amy.'

My voice was shaking too when I answered. 'And what about me? What if I don't ever forgive you? Does that not matter?'

She wouldn't meet my eye. I got up to leave. 'Just... just please, think about it. For me. Please.'

I waited for her to say something, but she just carried on snivelling quietly into the cushion. There was no point staying any longer. She didn't even look up as I turned and walked out.

I must have looked like a crazy woman, running home, sobbing and trying not to look anyone in the eye. I got back to the house and gratefully fell inside, collapsing against the wall in the hallway as I closed the door behind me. I heard a sound in the kitchen – I'd lost track of time but of course, Mum must be home by now. I tried to get my breath back and make myself look a bit more composed. I couldn't let Mum see quite how bad things were.

'Oh, there you are,' she said cheerfully, coming out of the kitchen. 'Where have you been, darling?'

She came up to me and smoothed my hair out of my face as if I was six. I hesitated.

'I just needed some air.'

I don't know why I couldn't tell her where I'd been. It was a blatant lie that just came out. Maybe I needed to process it all before I talked to Mum about it. Or maybe something in me was protecting Rosie. Not that she deserved it.

Mum didn't seem to notice my hesitation anyway. And if she could tell I'd been crying, she wisely chose not to mention it.

'Good idea. Come on, up you get, I've got things to tell you.'

She steered me into the lounge and I sat down on the sofa. She seemed to have forgotten I'd been there in the room the whole time she and Maria were making plans. She got out her notebook and ran through the action plan with updates. The video had been reported to some helpline she'd found, and she'd checked and the link didn't work anymore. She'd called the school and they were looking into it. She'd found the name of a website where parents and teenagers could get help and advice on dealing with online abuse. I watched her, reading from her list, her glasses halfway down the bridge of her nose, her hair falling out of its ponytail. I watched how she tapped her teeth with her pen in between thoughts, how the ticks on the list gave an impression of progress. I loved her deeply, but I realised she'd never get it. Even if the video completely disappeared, if no one ever saw it again, it wouldn't make that much difference to me now. I'd never be able to trust anyone after this. But trust goes both ways, doesn't it? I thought of my lie about where I'd just been and told myself I was doing it for Mum's sake.

She looked up and smiled, waiting for me to respond.

'That's amazing, Mum. You've done loads. Thank you.'

She looked pleased with the validation.

'I just did what any mum would do to protect their child,' she said, somewhat unnecessarily, as she put the lid on her pen and put the notebook down.

'Come here.' She gave me a quick hug and kissed the top of my head.

'I'm making stir fry for dinner and I got some Ben and Jerry's for pudding. You must feel like eating by now. I'll go and get on with it.'

She gave me another smile as she left the room. The smell of stir fry started to fill the house and I tried to muster up some kind of appetite. She thought we were out of the woods. She thought she could see a way for things to go back to normal. I really wanted that to be possible. I thought that maybe if she believed it, I could believe it too. I made a pact with myself that however bad things got, I couldn't land this on Mum. She'd had enough to deal with, bringing up a child on her own. I remembered the fear on her face when she'd found me in the bath. She didn't need or deserve to be put through any more. I knew I had to do my best to let Mum think I was doing okay, however hard that might be. And maybe, if I pretended hard enough, it would be true.

17
NOW

I wasn't prepared for how totally unsettled I started to feel at work, of all places. Every time I heard the bloody door, I'd spin round instantly. It was never anyone I needed to worry about. But even that jangled my nerves. I had to start counting to ten before I let myself look round. Sometimes I only made it to five. I don't know who I was expecting to walk in, but since Rosie's unwelcome appearance, I felt exposed.

What had Rosie come to say? I kept replaying the scene in my head. I hadn't actually let her speak, so there were lots of gaps that my imagination was keen to fill. And depending on the day, my ideas were wild and various. My biggest question was whether or not she'd looked sorry. But I couldn't answer it because my memory was playing tricks. The whole exchange had taken the time it takes to register the fact that your ex-best friend, who you hoped never to see again, is standing in front of you ordering a latte. Well, plus the time it took to make the latte, but I hadn't been looking at Rosie for that part. So maybe she had come to say sorry. It seemed unlikely. And if that is what she'd wanted to say, wouldn't she have said it in the Instagram message? Rather than just "Hi, how are you?". Which, to be fair, I hadn't responded to. So maybe she was intending to say sorry after that.

But Rosie had had millions of opportunities to apologise. So why suddenly turn up out of the blue like that, now? There must be something else. And the something else was what was tying my brain in absolute knots. Because every possible something else I came up with led to the past and the things I didn't want to remember. Things I'd had done my utmost to get away from. I was so worried that somehow those things might be able to track me down.

Ping went the door. Fuck's sake. 1, 2, 3, 4, 5. And breathe. Just some guy I didn't know with a laptop bag.

I started to make his coffee but adrenaline was still buzzing. With Andrew there every Saturday I couldn't even get away from the door by hiding in the kitchen. He was doing my head in with how cheerful he was all the time, and his cheesy photo-ready grin. And the way he went on and on about where we might have met.

'Were you at the All-Blacks game at Twickenham last year? Did you used to work at Sainsbury's? Do you know my Auntie Margery?'

He seemed to find himself hilarious, and had no need of any response from me, positive or negative. If he was someone who could take a hint, I might have let him know I really wasn't interested in being friends. But you'd literally have to tell him straight, and the last thing I wanted was to cause a scene. Anyway, Andrew wasn't worth it, and my days of causing a scene were supposed to be behind me; the incident with Rosie being a regrettable exception.

I was still cringing about the fact that Jamie had been there for that. Although in the circumstances, I'd been pretty cool. Just that no one actually knew quite how cool I'd been, because no one would understand why an old school friend turning up at your place of work could be so stressful. And how it might turn you into a complete nervous wreck.

I thought I was managing not to let it affect my work. Aside from the jumpiness. And the counting. But I kept catching Jon looking at me thoughtfully. It was unnerving. He was just being kind, but there were only so many times I could say 'I'm fine' when he asked if I was okay. Although whether he did it consciously or not, when Andrew was around, Jon dealt with all food orders and anything else that involved time in the kitchen. Which definitely helped.

'So, what do you think? Is it useful having someone to clear up on a Saturday?' he'd asked me after Andrew had left. I hesitated.

'Well, I think we could manage without. Would just be like it was before, more washing up at the end of the day.'

'Yeah, but then we wouldn't be getting away as early to go off for our crazy Saturday nights out.'

Maybe he had a wild social life away from this place, although it seemed unlikely. And I certainly didn't.

'Very true. Anyway, you're the boss, it's up to you!' I'd said brightly.

Ping. I wondered if I could ask if we could change the sound. Maybe something more bell-like would be less stressful. One, two, three - I was starting the manic counting, and breathing, and trying not to turn round, but Jon jumped in with a cheery, 'Hey, my man! Good to see you' which meant it was someone Jon knew, which on balance probably meant it was someone safe. God, the thought processes were driving me nuts. It was Jamie. I blushed. He smiled at me and Jon gave us a knowing look and disappeared.

'Hiya,' he said. Maybe he's forgotten I'm an idiot, I thought, hopefully. Maybe I can forget I'm an idiot too if he carries on smiling like that. I heard the door again and almost didn't even need to look. Almost. It was no one of any importance. Phew. I turned back to him. He was still smiling. He looked different today. Had he changed his hair? Well, something was making his eyes look even more hypnotic than usual.

'Oh! Hi!' I said hurriedly, suddenly aware I hadn't spoken, that he'd said hi, that he'd been standing there smiling for what felt like ten minutes with me just looking at him. Come on, say something! He had a guitar with him, I noticed. A normal person who knew how to have a conversation would ask him about the guitar.

'Have you had your hair cut?' I said. For fuck's sake! Why did I say that? He looked a bit surprised and put his hand to his hair.

'Uh. A couple of weeks ago?'

'Oh! Right. Um. I thought you looked different.' Nice, Amy. Cool way to not look like an idiot. Oh god. He ruffled his hair and was clearly wondering what to say.

'So, did you want a coffee?' I went on. Or did you just come in so I could stare at you and ask personal questions.

'Yes, latte please.' Thank god, something to do. He was still smiling, I noticed, before I turned my back. That was something. I wondered if the other people in the queue had noticed what a mess I was making of this. I tried really hard not to do anything clumsy. Spilling oat milk everywhere would not have helped.

When I turned back to Jamie, he'd propped the guitar against the counter and was looking at his phone. Probably trying to avoid any more of the awkward conversation. I put the coffee down and he looked up at me and smiled, again, pushing the phone into his pocket.

'Sorry, I was just checking something. I have to drop this off for someone.' He nodded at the guitar.

'Oh right! I wondered if it was yours.'

'No, not this one.' He hesitated slightly. 'I do play, but not that well. I don't tend to tell many people that.' He smiled again. I couldn't speak; the image of his fingers on the fret board of a guitar had turned me temporarily mute.

'I work in that music shop, you know where I saw you the other day? In the rain?' I realised I hadn't even asked him what he did. He must have thought I was so rude. Or just dumb.

'I was going to ask you something,' he said. I widened my eyes and he cleared his throat. I might have imagined it, but the guy behind him in the queue seemed to lean in a bit.

'Umm. I'm going to a gig next Friday. At the Half Moon. Do you know it?'

I shook my head. The queue guy nodded. I shot him a look and he looked away. Jamie went on.

'Oh, I thought you would. It does a big student night on a Wednesday.'

I shook my head again. 'No, I, uhhh. I don't really go to student nights much.'

He looked slightly surprised. 'Oh right. Well, the gig's not a student night. They do live music at weekends. I've been a few times before, it's a laid-back kind of thing. I wondered if...' He stopped and paused like he was waiting for me to say something. Had he just asked me out? I looked at the queue. The guy seemed to have become less interested in eavesdropping and more interested in getting his coffee.

'Uh. Okay. Friday? Uh, yeah. Okay. Why not.'

He looked pleased.

'Great. Do you want me to pay for this coffee then?'

Jesus Christ, I was all over the place. I nodded at him and handed over the card reader. He picked the coffee up and gestured at the guitar.

'Is that okay there? I'll come back for it in a minute,' he said.

It wasn't really in the way but I didn't really want him to come back for it either. And why hadn't I just said I was busy on Friday? I turned to the now very annoyed man in the queue.

'I'm so sorry to have kept you waiting. What can I get you?'

I tried to get on with work and not notice that Jamie was always just at the edge of my peripheral vision. He looked like he'd finished the coffee a while ago and was just sitting looking at his phone. I felt like I needed to go and check what he'd asked me. Had I said yes to a date? Obviously I wasn't going to ask that. He must already think I was stupid, there was no point confirming it for him. The queue had gone and I was going to have to go and clear some tables. I'd faffed around for as long as I could, assuming as he'd finished he might disappear, but there were dirty cups and plates all over so I took a deep breath and came out from the safety of the counter, just as he stood up.

'Oh! Don't forget the guitar.' I said, for something to say, as he put his jacket on. Nice jacket. Maybe that was the difference, not the hair.

He gave me his best smile yet and I felt a bit better. 'No, better not. It's worth more than I earn in a month.'

Blimey. I was glad I hadn't known that when he left it leaning on my counter. I moved to one side to let him past, then went to clear his table. There was a flyer next to the coffee cup.

'Hey, you left this,' I said, picking it up, suddenly needing another reason to talk to him before he left. He turned around, putting the strap of the guitar case over his shoulder.

'That's for you,' he said, reaching for the door. 'See you Friday.'

'Bye,' I called, looking down at the paper in my hand. A flyer for the Half Moon, photos of various indie-looking singers and an address on the front. I turned it over to see if I knew any of the band names. The back was blank, apart from a handwritten phone number and a message.

'See you 8.30,' he'd written.

I pushed it carefully into my apron pocket. So I had said yes to a date. Shit.

18
THEN

The problem with having convinced Mum I was feeling better was that it left me no good reason to miss school. I woke really early with a sense of utter dread. I pulled the duvet over my head, and the desire to stay where I was almost got the better of me. But I remembered I'd made it over to Rosie's the day before. Maybe I could just take it one step at a time and that would be enough.

About seven, Mum carefully put her head round the door.

'Darling! You're awake. Here, I brought you tea.' I tried to smile and took it. I didn't tell her I'd only slept about four hours the whole night. She flung open the curtains.

'You feeling okay for school today?' she said with breezy intonation, the kind of question that isn't really a question. I didn't actually say anything, but she didn't seem to need a reply.

'I'm sure it won't be as bad as you think. I've spoken to Mrs Jameson, she knows the situation, and things will have blown over a bit by now. Yesterday's news and all that.'

She gave me a pale smile and I wondered if she actually believed what she was saying. She surely couldn't expect me to believe it. I sipped the tea.

'I don't think you're right, Mum. But I'm going to school.'

She nodded, looking pleased, and left me to it without attempting to convince me any further. I couldn't really blame her; my aim was to let her believe life could get back to normal. But inside I churned with thoughts of all the people I was going to have to face that day. Not least Harry.

Tapping into some supreme inner strength, I managed to get out of bed and put on some clothes. We were supposed to dress as if for work now we were in the sixth form; I looked at myself in the baggy top and cargo pants I'd picked out for myself. The best you could say was that it looked like a dress down day. I pulled my hair into a ponytail and stared at myself. My face was pale with dark shadows under my eyes. No, I thought. You can do so much better than this. You don't go into battle looking beaten. I ditched the baggy top for a smart shirt, swapped the cargo pants for smart grey trousers, brushed my hair and plaited it neatly and put on my make up. I still felt the same inside but I didn't look so much like a victim. Surely that would help.

I avoided Mum by waiting until I'd heard her cheery 'See you later' before leaving my room. I might have convinced her with my performance, but there was always a chance she'd see how much I was shaking inside. She'd be happier thinking I might have an awkward day ahead, but it would all be okay now the adults were in charge. I wished I could believe her.

It seemed impossible that it was only three days since the last time I'd walked to school. From above it must have looked like an ant hill, sitting there in the valley, squat and sprawling, with thousands of tiny grey figures converging on it from all directions. It took all my strength to keep walking towards it. As I rounded the corner and joined the steady stream of students, I was just waiting for the first comment. I managed quite a few streets before anyone seemed to notice me. Maybe the younger kids hadn't seen it, I thought, trying to kid myself. The more likely explanation was they weren't quite brave enough to say to my face what they'd be more than happy to post online. I stopped at the bus stop near the corner shop to wait for Maria. A couple of guys from my year saw me as they got off a bus. I quickly looked away, but not before I saw them exchange a comment that left them sniggering as they walked past. I shut my eyes and felt it sting, bracing myself for more to come. Across the road I glimpsed two of the girls I recognised from the group of smokers Maria had befriended on Saturday night. Even from the other side of the road I heard their laughter.

'Amy!'

I jumped at my name. It was Maria. I gave her a tight hug.

'I don't think I can do it,' I whispered into her hair. She gave me a squeeze and took my hand.

'You can. I'm here. We're doing it together, come on.'

We'd normally have headed through the main door and straight into the sixth form common room, but by tacit agreement we went in the back way, through the sports hall and the girls' changing rooms.

'Let's sit here,' I said, spotting a little nook under the stairs where we'd be able to hide until form time. 'Heard anything from Rosie?'

Maria shook her head.

'No. Not a word. I messaged to say I knew she'd seen you. Said I thought the three of us should get together, try and work something out. But nothing.'

'Thanks for trying.'

She slid her hands into the pockets of her jacket and looked into the distance, shaking her head.

'I just don't get it. How is she siding with that tool of a cousin and his pervert friends over her best mate? Well, best mates.' She looked at me. 'I'm Team Amy.'

'And what would I do without you?' I said, squeezing her hand. 'But I know. I don't get it either. She almost seemed scared of what might happen if she stood up for me. Getting Harry into trouble could affect his future – what a load of shit. He should've thought of that before he turned star and director of his own porn film.'

Maria smiled in spite of herself.

'Well, we don't need her. We can do this.'

I shook my head.

'Not sure I can. I'm feeling so wobbly. All those eyes on me.' I felt the start of a sob threatening to come to the surface and forced it back down. Maria was looking at me steadily.

'Mate. You got up, you got dressed - you look amazing, by the way. You were so brave - you did the walk from your house to the bus stop on your own. Every little victory makes you stronger.' She paused as the bell rang. 'Into battle?' She looked at me questioningly. I picked up my bag, took a deep breath and stood up.

'Let's do this' I said.

Maria nodded and took my arm, and together we walked down the corridor to our form room.

Instead of Mr Dolan, our usual, slightly dippy form tutor, it was Mrs Jameson, head of sixth form, at the teacher's desk. The rest of the form were standing around or leaning on desks chatting. I swear all of them looked up when we walked in, Mrs J included. A giggle, a few comments under people's breath, but Mrs Jameson stood and took charge.

'Good morning, Amy and Maria. Can you all sit down please? The bell has already gone.'

Maria and I sat in our usual places. I focussed on the floor, not wanting to look up and see who was there, but I felt eyes on me and heard little ripples of whispering as she called the register. When she got to my name, someone responded with 'Oh Harry, yes!' and the pretence of quiet disappeared as everyone laughed out loud. Under the desk, Maria grabbed my hand.

'That's enough!' said Mrs Jameson in her best Professor McGonagall voice. The laughter settled, but I could feel panic starting. I used everything I had to stop my mask from dropping, but it was so hard not to just crumble and cry. The five minutes of form time felt like an endless test of my ability to stay in control. I just wanted to get up and run, to go home and close the door. Maria didn't let go of my hand, and I think Mrs J might have rugby tackled me to the floor if I'd made a run for it. I sat through announcements about arrangements for exam week, a timetable was given out that was supposed to help us organise our revision. Then a notice about our end of sixth form prom. A week ago, exams, study leave, prom — they all seemed so important, such big life events marking the end of our school days. Now they seemed like the biggest hurdles I could imagine between the present moment and the time I could leave school for good. Somehow I knew I had to finish school. I had to do the exams and get out of there. But how I was going to do that was another question.

After an eternity, the five minutes was up. I stuffed my revision timetable into my bag and stood to leave.

'Going to prom with Harry, Amy?' asked Charlie Dobson, self-appointed class clown and general halfwit who would never normally speak to me. I looked at him without answering.

'Just, if you're not, I wouldn't mind a turn.'

His stupid bunch of mates spluttered behind him. I blushed and turned away, leaving Maria calling him a perverted little tosser as I left the room.

'Amy.' Every time someone said my name I tensed up. Mrs Jameson caught me up in the corridor.

'Good to see you back. I just wanted you to know, I had a word with those concerned yesterday and I'm happy that the matter needs no further investigation. I hope you'll be able to get over this and carry on with your studies. You're on track for good grades, don't let this mess things up for you.'

I looked at her in disbelief.

'Let it mess things up? Were you just in that form room or not? And you think it needs no further investigation? Well, that's good to know, Mrs J. Thanks for your support.'

I walked off, leaving her calling my name.

I sat in my usual place in English. There were only eight in the class, and four of them were such geeks I actually thought it was possible they might not have seen the video. I felt guilty for the years I'd spent ignoring their existence. Suddenly I longed to be one of them, with their love of Shakespeare and Sylvia Plath poems the most important things in their lives.

Mrs Barras looked at me kindly.

'If you need some more time for your Plath essay, Amy, we can talk about it.'

I nodded, choking back tears at the kindness. And realising she knew. I'd been intending to do the essay on Sunday, once my hangover and post-party euphoria had worn off. I shuddered at the memory of the afternoon on the sofa and the too-hot bath.

The lesson passed, uneventful. If anyone in there had seen the video, they wisely kept quiet and, although I didn't really take anything in, I felt proud that I'd got through it. It was ten-twenty, that meant I'd made it through a quarter of the day.

Maria met me back under the stairs.

'Hey, how are you doing?'

I nodded. 'Well, English was better than form time. So I'm taking that as a win. How are you?'

'I'm okay.' She paused. 'Rosie's back. She was in R.S. just now.' Another pause as she picked at a broken nail. I felt guilty - it was a nervous habit she'd managed to kick two years earlier, but it seemed to have come back. 'She didn't sit with me. We didn't speak.'

I gave her a hug.

'Oh Maria, I'm so sorry this is affecting you so much too.'

She shook her head and blinked tears away.

'Don't be. She's a twat. But it wasn't the right time to talk to her in class. I guess she thinks it's easier to be "popular" than to stand up to them. I think we should get her on her own, both of us. Try and talk some sense into her.'

I nodded, although after my visit to Rosie's house the day before, there was no way I could see that happening.

'For now, it's just you and me then,' I said, with a watery smile. 'See you at lunch.'

Maria went off to the art block and I took myself to the library, avoiding the sixth form common room at all costs. At least in the library no one could really say anything to me, whatever they were thinking. Also, in the context of a fairly ordinary secondary school, it wasn't an unpleasant place to hang out. The chairs were comfy, sun streamed in through the roof lights and, apart from the librarian, there wasn't anyone there. I found a computer near the back, at a vantage point where I could see the door, just in case.

I fiddled around with my essay for a bit, then ran out of steam about ten minutes before lunchtime, packed up my stuff and headed back to meet Maria.

I took the long route, avoiding the canteen, history department and sports hall, all potential areas for bumping into the wrong people. So I really wasn't prepared for seeing Harry. He was coming the other way down the corridor behind the music rooms. I briefly wondered if he'd ever been near a music room in his life. It crossed my mind he must be avoiding people too, but as he realised who was coming towards him, the look on his face told me the person he was trying to avoid was me.

The last time I'd seen this boy in the flesh, he was kissing me goodbye, the imprint of my body still on his, his hair ruffled from my hands, his taste on my tongue. That was so lovely, he'd said, all the time knowing he'd just tricked me. Seeing him there in the corridor, walking along as if life was normal, rage boiled up inside me – my face flushed, I had to hold myself back from running at him, pounding him with my fists. For one split second, he made eye contact, fixed a fake smile on his contemptuous mouth, and seemed to be wondering if he could get away with pretending Saturday night never happened. But then I guess he thought better of it - he opened his mouth to speak, then closed it again and looked away quickly.

I'd run the first encounter with Harry through in my head a hundred times, and best-case scenario was that I'd spot him from a distance and be able to hide. But having him there in front of me, with his shifting feet and his eyes that looked anywhere but at me, I didn't want to run. And he did, that was obvious, so the last thing I was going to do was let him. I kept on walking towards him as his eyes darted around looking for a friend or an escape route. As I got to him, he said, 'Oh, hi Amy.' I could have spat on him.

'Hi Amy? Are you fucking kidding?'

'I... er ... I don't know what to say. It was...' He tailed off.

'It was what? It was great, thanks for the sex and the help with winning my friends' disgusting competition? It was fun, we made a real fun video that the whole school is now enjoying watching? It was life-changing, no one we know will ever be able to look at us again without remembering us naked?' I paused for breath, not expecting an answer. He looked taken aback.

'I'm not... I mean, it wasn't ...'

'It wasn't life-changing? Oh, I think you'll find it will be. Already is for me, but nothing compared to the life-change it will be for you when I go to the police about it.'

Suddenly he stopped cowering and looked serious, like he was properly paying attention at last. He sounded defensive.

'Go to the police? I didn't rape you. You were the one guiding me upstairs and saying let's find a bed. Everyone saw you, you'll never...'

The memories made me shudder with disgust. I shook my head.

'I'm not talking about rape. I'm talking about you filming me without my consent and sharing it. That's a crime, Harry. Did you and your mates not think of that when you set up your disgusting little camera?'

He was trying to move away from me but there was nowhere to go.

'I saw the picture of you checking it as we walked in. And I know about the dare, the competition, whatever you want to call it. Maria told me. And everyone knows. It's sick. But more than that – it's illegal. So you, Oli and whoever else was in on it should be very worried. Because there's no fucking way I'm only person coming out of this with their life in ruins.'

I was speaking very loudly, with Harry backed up against the door of the nearest music room. I hadn't noticed a small group of people forming behind me in the corridor leading back to the library. When I finished speaking, there was a collective gasp and lots of muttering. I looked over my shoulder – a couple of Harry's mates were in the group, looking uneasy. Seeing people watching made me feel suddenly nervous. But I hadn't really finished. I turned back to him. He looked smaller and younger, all of a sudden. I found some inner strength.

'Nothing to say?' I asked him.

'Amy, look. I'm sorry, okay? I didn't mean this to happen. It was a joke. I mean, I...'

I held up my hand.

'Too late. You're not sorry about how I feel. You're not sorry it happened. If you were, you'd have said it before now. You'd have been there when it all got crazy. You could have stopped it all. You're only sorry for what it's going to mean for you.'

I picked up my bag from the floor where I'd dropped it, turned on my heel and pushed through the crowd of onlookers. As I made my exit, someone patted my arm. 'Nice one, Amy.' Someone else said, 'Well done.' I didn't stop to chat; I left the scene as Harry's mates crowded round him and the hubbub got louder.

Maria was waiting for me under the stairs when I arrived. I was shaking. I recounted what had happened.

'Wow, Ames! Go you. That's amazing. Wish I'd seen it.' She nudged me. 'See, you're stronger than you think.'

I shook my head. Sobs started to rise up inside as the enormity of the scene I'd just caused hit me.

'I'm not. I mean, I wasn't pretending – seeing him there, I was so angry. But now I feel sick. And really? Go to the police? I don't think I can do that.'

She was looking at me very steadily.

'You can, you know. And you should. What they did to you... it's a crime. It's called voyeurism, I think. Or revenge porn. Or some kind of combination of the two. A lawyer would need to work out what...'

'Hey!' I stopped her. 'You seem to know a lot about this?'

Mrs J said there was no further investigation needed. Going to the police had been something I'd thought of when I spoke to Rosie, I'd used it as a threat to Harry, but it wasn't really something I'd properly considered. I was taken aback at how much Maria seemed to know about it. She looked a bit uncomfortable.

'Yeah, well, after Sunday I did a bit of research. And you can get the fuckers for this. Your mum thinks so too.' I looked at her quizzically. 'We talked, you know, on Sunday. You were a bit out of it.'

'I think I would have remembered Mum putting "Get the fuckers" on her list.'

'Well, okay. I looked into it when I got home and I phoned her to see what she thought. I didn't want to put any more pressure on you, but, you know... You should do this. It might help.'

A sudden image of me in a police interview room showing the video to two men in uniform flashed up in my head and the tears restarted.

'I don't think I can. I just want it to go away.'

Maria put her arm round me.

'Hey, it's okay. We don't have to think about it now. Today's been a big deal, you're doing so, so well.'

I leant into her and mumbled a thank you.

'I'm here for you, Ames, whatever you need. And if you do take it to the police, I'll be with you every step of the way, I promise.'

19
NOW

I looked at myself in the mirror: grey, long-sleeved top, slightly baggy jeans, white trainers. A blazer on top, and that would do. I'd left my hair down and my make-up was deliberately subtle. I hoped I looked nice, but not as if I'd made too much effort. Good job no one would see the pile of discarded outfits on my bed. I sent a quick selfie to Mum, imagining how happy she'd be that I was off to a gig. I hadn't told her about Jamie. Obviously. But at least she'd know I was going out.

The room looked like a jumble sale as I closed the door. I'll regret that when I get in at midnight, I thought, slightly optimistically. I was trying to keep an open mind about my first actual night out, but realistically I could see myself back home by ten-thirty, putting tops and trousers back in my wardrobe and making hot chocolate.

It was already quarter to eight. I took the stairs two at a time and sneaked out the fire door at the bottom. There was some tasteless games night going on in the bar downstairs and, by the sounds of it, the drinking had started early. I tried to feel happy that at least this Friday night I had plans. Another reason to try and stay out late: to avoid hearing my pissed up and annoying fellow freshers slamming doors on their way to bed.

As I waited for the bus, I pulled the flyer out of my pocket and looked at Jamie's number for the millionth time. He didn't know I was coming. I hadn't messaged him, I didn't know why. That's a lie. I did. Two reasons. I wasn't sure I'd actually have the guts to turn up. And it was better for him not to have my number in case I didn't.

I got off the bus on the opposite side of the road to the pub and looked across at the small crowd gathering and greeting each other outside the main door. The Half Moon was one of those pubs that had successfully reinvented itself without losing any of its charm. The old Victorian bow window frames were painted a muted grey, and the sign was a cool font with a graphic depiction of a moon that also looked like a face. I couldn't see Jamie. But if I'd wanted him to meet me outside, I should have asked. And at least that took away one of my worries, which was whether I should hug him, and whether a casual hug was even something I could pull off. I hunched and released my shoulders and gave myself a mental shake. Be impressed with yourself, you've made it this far, said my inner motivator, unconvincingly. You can do it.

Ready to cross the street, I stepped to the edge of the pavement, and someone grabbed me from behind, almost knocking me off balance. I let out a little scream and spun round to see Andrew, smiling at his own joke as usual.

'Don't panic, only me,' he said. 'Didn't want you to get run over.'

'What the fuck did you do that for?' I said, shaking his hands off me. 'I was not about to get run over. Do you think I don't know how to cross the road?'

'Woah, calm down. Only a joke. Blimey, you're prickly.'

What a twat, I thought, turning away.

'So, what you doing here? Night out?'

My God, he really did not know how to take a hint. 'None of your business really, but I'm going to a gig. Over there.'

As I waved my hand in the direction of the Half Moon, I saw Jamie spot me, smile and start to wave back. Well, at least that put a stop to any possibility of me not turning up.

'Oh I seeeee!' said Andrew, drawing the word out for comic effect. I'm sure he winked but I didn't look at him again.

'Have a lovely time, see you at work!' he called after me, sarcastically, as I crossed the road.

It was easy to forget about him as I walked towards Jamie. He was wearing his nice jacket over some cool jeans, and as wide a smile as I'd ever seen.

'Hey, you made it!' he said, pulling me into a loose hug that felt completely natural and made me wonder what on earth I'd been worrying about.

'Yeah, I'm sorry, I should have called, I wasn't sure until today...' I mumbled as he let me go. He waved the words away.

'It's cool, you're here. That's all that matters.' I smiled dumbly at him, and then noticed two other guys standing awkwardly next to him.

'Oh! Hey, Bill, Harvey. This is Amy. She works at Common Grounds.' They nodded and said hi, and how they'd been meaning to come in sometime. Jamie started to wax lyrical about the food and the coffee and I suddenly wondered if I'd got it all wrong. Had he actually asked me on a date? He was with two friends, maybe I'd totally misread it. I wasn't sure if that made me feel more or less nervous.

'Shall we go in then?' Harvey said. I looked through the windows – inside were lots of tables with people eating trendy piled-high burgers and posh chips served on slates. It didn't look much like a music venue – if I'd got there on my own I'd almost certainly have turned away. And that might not have been the only reason. Jamie must have noticed my look of confusion.

'The music's upstairs,' he explained. 'Must be a bit annoying for the people having dinner, all the guitar fans pushing past them while they eat. Here...' He opened the door and stood back to let me through. I followed as the boys strode confidently past me and wove through the bemused diners. When we reached the back of the room, Jamie glanced over his shoulder at me and put a hand on his mate's arm.

'Harve, you go on up. Me and Amy will get a drink down here and see you up there.'

Harvey gave a knowing nod and he and Bill disappeared, guitar chords leaking into the room as the door opened and closed behind them. Jamie turned to me. 'That okay? Just thought we won't be able to talk very easily up there.'

I nodded, thinking that might not be a bad thing given my track record for sounding like an idiot whenever I tried to talk to him. We found standing space by the bar, away from the tables and the steady flow of people heading for the gig. He seemed totally at ease here in this busy pub, as he bought us drinks and explained that the guitarist from the band was a customer and Harvey and Bill were work colleagues, which was why they'd come together. I wondered again if I'd got the wrong idea about this being some kind of date.

'I'm not on commission by the way,' he said, taking a swig of his beer, confusing me again.

'Sorry?'

He laughed. 'I mean, that's not why I asked you to come.'

I smiled and sipped my coke, but his mind reading powers were definitely stronger than I was comfortable with.

'So, you're not in a band?' I asked quickly, keen to be the one asking the questions.

'No. I used to be, at college. I did sound engineering in Brighton - was always happier behind the desk in a studio than performing to be honest. But it's hard to get a job in music production. Unless you know someone.' Another swig of his beer. 'Well, I knew someone who owns a music shop, so...'

I smiled. 'The rest is history?'

He laughed. 'Yeah, I guess. That's why I'm here. It's a nice enough place to work, but no offence, it's not Brighton.'

'None taken,' I laughed, trying to remember what lies I'd told him when he'd asked where I was from. I was about to ask another question when a funky bass kicked in upstairs and we heard a loud cheer. Jamie winced slightly and bit his lip.

'My God, it's starting and all I've done is talk about me! Again.'

I really hoped my relief wasn't as obvious as it felt, although I had started to feel we were having a normal conversation for once. Probably because I hadn't really said anything. I finished my drink and nodded towards the door. 'Shall we?'

'Yep, let's go,' he said. I felt the light pressure of his hand on my back as he steered me round the unfortunate diners, who had really chosen badly if they wanted a quiet night out.

The upstairs room had a totally different vibe, like we'd been catapulted from civilisation into – well, hell is a bit strong. But somewhere hot, dark and churning with people. A warm haze hit me as we got to the top of the stairs, a fug of bodies and dry ice and vapes. There was a large guy in a Black Sabbath t-shirt with a pierced lip on the door. When I held out my card to pay for a ticket, he grabbed me by the wrist – startled, I went to pull away, but he gave me a hard stare and stamped a dark mark on my hand. I felt silly, what exactly had I thought he was going to do? I tried a self-deprecating eye roll, but he'd moved on to Jamie and wasn't looking. There was no point trying to speak – what from downstairs had sounded like music I'd probably enjoy was screaming at me now I was in the same room.

Jamie leant into me and said something but I couldn't hear.

'What?' I shouted back. He held me by both shoulders to shout into my ear.

'I said we won't get to talk much now!'

I nodded, wondering why I'd come. The whole space was crammed with people pressed up against each other. I could barely see the band, although it was obvious which end of the room held the stage because of the sense of forward motion. For a few moments, we hovered by the door. I thought about suggesting going back downstairs, or maybe trying to head for the bar, although that didn't look very possible either, it was crowded in all directions. Jamie was rocking on his heels, either he liked the music or he was impatient to get nearer the stage. He turned to me again and got in as close as he could.

'Do you want to go to the front? I think the sound will be better further forwards.'

If I thought he'd hear me, I might have suggested it was hard to imagine the sound being any worse. But I just gave a little shake of my head, which I hurriedly changed to a nod when I realised the answer he wanted was yes.

Jamie squeezed my arm gently and moved ahead of me, turning to smile back and give me a nod of encouragement, inviting me to follow. He forced his way through, moving people to one side, twisting sideways and leading with his shoulder, making it look easy. But the crowd seemed to close in behind him and I didn't know where or how to follow. I tried to call him back but there was no way on earth he'd hear above the din. My feet wouldn't move, I was rooted to the floor, held back by the wall of people and noise. A smoke machine hurled out a fog of dry ice, lights from the stage started to flicker and dance, and heat built up inside me, hotter even than the mass of bodies in front of me. I pulled at my blazer, at the neck of my top, shaking, sweating, trying to get some air.

'You alright love?' pierced lip guy yelled at me. I nodded. I wasn't. Jamie had completely disappeared. Harvey and Bill were nowhere to be seen. They probably hadn't even noticed I wasn't there. I'd been so stupid, thinking this was some kind of date. I knew I shouldn't have come, I knew I shouldn't have come. What made me think I could do it? Come somewhere like this, be comfortable in a room with all these strangers. I had to get out.

'Tell my friend I've gone!' I yelled at pierced lip guy. He shrugged, not hearing a word, as I ran for the door, the stairs, the cold of the evening air.

20
THEN

Somehow or other I got through the rest of the day. I sneaked into Mrs Jameson's office and left a note on her desk saying, "After the events of the morning, I will not be attending registration". I could imagine her face when she read it, but I didn't care. Maybe tomorrow I'd be able to handle it. History loomed after lunch – I'd usually sit with Rosie, but I just turned up late, sat at the back and kept quiet. I don't know if she looked over at me at all as I managed not to look her way and excused myself two minutes before the bell so we wouldn't be walking out together. No way old Mr Forsythe was going to query a girl's request to go to the toilet.

I'd had about as much school as I could take by then, so I decided to duck out early, texting Maria to say sorry for not waiting. Emojis of a thumbs up and a hug came straight back – she was obviously concentrating hard in class. I turned the phone off and dropped it into my bag. Unlikely anyone I would want to hear from was going to message me now.

No one really used the main school entrance, apart from for exams and prize-giving, so I headed out that way expecting a clear route off the premises. I'd forgotten I'd have to pass the head's office. At the precise moment I swung through the fire door into the lobby, he was coming out of his office door. Mr Jake Turner. Head of our school. A vain, figurehead of a man far more interested in progressing his own career than wasting his efforts on his students. I wasn't a fan. He looked straight at me, then tried to make as if we weren't the only two people in a completely empty entrance hall. A flash of anger lit me up – there was a reason he was pretending he hadn't seen me and I wasn't about to let him off.

'Mr. Turner,' I called out, watching him try to reverse into his office without me noticing.

'Ah, Amy.' He looked up as if seeing me for the first time, then glanced at his watch. Perhaps he thought he could get away with questioning me on why I wasn't in class. I didn't bother to let him try. For the second time that day, anger was making me brave. 'I'd like to speak to you, please,' I announced, striding towards him. He hesitated for a split second, then pushed open the door to let me into the office.

'I guess you can imagine what I want to talk about.' I tried to maintain the confidence I'd had in the lobby, but sitting in the chair he'd pointed me towards with him behind his big desk, the power shifted and I felt smaller. His eyes narrowed and he clasped his hands and set them down on the tidy pile of papers in front of him.

'I believe Mrs Jameson is dealing with the matter of the sixth form party, if that's what you mean.'

I reached inside for the anger to fire me up. 'What I mean is, the school don't seem to be taking any action against the people who shared a video of me without my consent.'

I'd avoided the word "sex", but I was still dying inside at having to raise this with him. Still, I'd got this far. I pressed on.

'I seem to be the only person suffering here, and yet I did nothing wrong. I want to know what penalties the boys responsible will face.'

I was proud of myself for managing to use the kind of language I thought he'd relate to. I waited. He unclasped his hands and tapped the side of his desk.

'The sixth form were spoken to yesterday with regard to the risks of using social media. I believe you were absent…'

'I heard,' I said, prickling. I opened my mouth to say something else but he raised his hand slightly and continued.

'As the events of the weekend took place outside of school and, as I understand it, you were a willing participant, the school leadership are satisfied that no further action is required.'

My brain tried to decode the jargon and I abandoned my attempts to speak his language.

'What? So that's it? You'd not going to punish them? Oli. Harry. You think I'm as much to blame as they are?'

He cleared his throat. 'As I've said, leadership are satisfied this is not a school issue. Now, if you wouldn't mind, Amy, I have another meeting shortly.' I stared as he got to his feet and made his way to the door, opening it in a gesture of dismissal. As I didn't seem to have another option, I picked up my bag and left, without finding any words. As I left, I turned to say something along the lines of 'Thanks for nothing, you arsehole,' but he'd closed the door on me. I stood for a second, stunned, then headed for the door.

I got back home and let myself in. As I closed the door, an enormous wave of relief flooded over me, and I sank to the floor. It was exhausting. The whole thing was exhausting. It hadn't even lived up to the horror I'd imagined, but I was completely drained. I sat there, back to the door, wondering how the hell I'd got through it. I ran the events of the day through my mind, as if I'd been watching it all from a distance. Apart from twat face Charlie in form time, there hadn't been that many direct insults. Most of my classmates were as brave and funny as you like online, but not quite so keen to speak up to your face. But the shame I felt was crippling. Every time I walked into a room, I felt everyone looking at me. I could almost see the thoughts floating out of their heads, circling round me and calling me names. Seeing me like I'd been in the video – drunk, flirty, naked. And even if they weren't thinking about me, even if their brains were full of History or English or French, or what they were going to have for lunch, it didn't actually matter. Because I was thinking it about myself.

I dragged myself to the kitchen to make a cup of tea, more from habit than because I actually wanted one. I stood and waited for the kettle to boil and thought about the encounter with Harry. Fuck's sake, I'd been so stupid. I had caused such a scene when what I really needed to do was to keep my head down. So many people had witnessed it. Me facing up to him, making him cower, threatening him with the police. You should be worried, I'd said. It was illegal, I'd said. And Harry had certainly looked worried. I'd had a glimmer of hope. But then, Mr Turner had quashed that. If the school thought there was nothing to be done, why would the police care?

I poured the water onto the teabag and watched as it infused. I could still go to the police. Maybe even without Rosie. Enough people knew what had happened. Wouldn't look good for the school, would it? Maybe that was why they were keen to stress no more action was required. I stirred the teabag and squeezed it, then left it on the side on top of the spoon. But there'd be lawyers, statements, evidence. Loads more people who would have to watch the video. I shook my head to clear the images from my brain. That fact alone was enough to make me doubt that I could.

I took my school bag and mug of tea up to my room. It was a state. I hadn't made my bed and there was stuff everywhere. I swept my hand across the dressing table so I could put the tea down, knocking a couple of lipsticks and an eyeliner onto the floor. I kicked some stuff out of the way and my foot caught on the black top, still in a heap where I'd dropped it, drunk and happy, on Saturday night.

I looked at it. It looked like some artefact from a parallel universe where going to a party and having sex with a boy you like seemed perfectly reasonable things to do. It was so small, and so tight, its halter straps nothing more than flimsy bits of string, designed to show off breasts, shoulders, bare neck. I picked it up as if it was radioactive, as if its very fibres might be infected. Carrying it carefully at arms' length, I went downstairs to the kitchen. I had to get rid of it. What was I doing wearing a top like that? I needed it out of the house.

I lit the gas on the hob and held it over the flame. As I watched, the flames licked around the hem, and the black synthetic fabric sizzled, then caught light. Jumping back from the heat, I chucked the burning top into the sink and watched as it started to flame. I wanted to stand there and watch the flames spreading, watch as the blind over the sink caught light, watch as it burnt the tea towels hanging next to it, feel the heat increase until it was so intense that the worktops and the cupboard doors would start to burn, until the whole kitchen would be on fire. How would it feel to be surrounded, fire and smoke and heat out of control, no escape?

A sudden scream jerked me out of the daze and I sprang forwards and turned on the tap, transforming the flames into a plume of acrid black smoke. The smoke alarm continued to screech at me as I opened the window. Leaving the remains of the top in the sink, I walked out of the kitchen and shut the door so I could no longer hear it.

Sometime later, lying on my bed, I heard the door and Mum called, 'Hello'. I listened as she took off her coat, changed work shoes for indoor clogs and made her way to the kitchen. She gasped as she opened the door. There was a pause and I waited for the inevitable, then I heard her footsteps on the stairs.

'Darling!' She came into my room, her face a picture of concern, a wet, black mess of fabric in her hand.

'What on earth? I found this in the sink and the kitchen stinks of burning.'

There wasn't really an explanation. I shrugged.

'It was an accident,' I said.

She raised an eyebrow. 'Strange kind of accident that meant your best top ended up burnt and in the sink.'

'Sorry, Mum. I just...' I bit my lip. I couldn't let her think I was losing it. I thought of the scalding bath incident, my promise to myself not to give her any more reasons to worry. Her life didn't have to stop too. I had to make her believe I was going to be okay.

'I felt angry and I wanted it all to go away. The top was a reminder of what happened.'

She looked sceptical.

'Okay, I understand that. But maybe just putting it in the bin would have done the trick?'

I tried to smile.

'I'm sorry Mum. It's... it's been quite a day.'

She dropped the charred, wet bundle onto the floor where it started to seep into the carpet, and came over to sit on my bed.

'It's okay, darling. I understand. Come here.'

I let her fold me into her arms. For that moment I felt safe.

'So, do you want to talk about today?' Mum asked casually as we sat down to eat. 'How was it?'

'Alright really,' I lied.

I gave her the edited highlights – walked in with Maria, form time was a bit of a nightmare, English was okay. I didn't tell her about seeing Harry. I didn't tell her about Mr Turner. She listened attentively and smiled as if to remind me she'd said it would all be okay once I got there. Luckily she didn't say that out loud. Having spent my life as an open book with Mum, suddenly I was hiding things. It made me feel distant and I hated it, but when I heard her whistling happily as she cleared up, I knew I was doing the right thing.

'Do you want tea, Amy?' she called. I was thinking about whether to put the TV on or maybe try and do some work on my essay.

'Yes, okay, thanks.'

She brought it through and sat down on the chair. Her notebook was still there on the coffee table but she didn't pick it up.

'So. Have you seen Rosie yet?' she asked, too casual.

'Um. I...' I thought about it. Who was I protecting? Rosie? Because she certainly didn't deserve it. I decided to come clean. Well partially.

'Yeah, I've seen her. She's being... unhelpful I guess.'

Mum put her head on one side.

'Unhelpful?'

'Yeah, I mean, not that she's spreading the video or anything nasty.' I actually had no idea if she was or not. I'd believed Mum when she told me the link wasn't working any more, but I hadn't been able to bring myself to check any of the other places it might have been. Rosie had fucked up badly, but I was pretty sure she wouldn't have shared it.

'Yeah, she's just... well, she's sort of siding with Harry.' My voice sounded rational and calm, but I was digging my nails harder and harder into my hand as I spoke. 'I asked her to help, as she knows what happened. She's refusing to back me up.'

'That doesn't sound like Rosie. Do you want me to call her mum?'

'No!' I shouted, the calm instantly destroyed. 'No! I really, really don't want that. How do you even know her parents are aware of what's going on? That would be an awful thing to do.'

Mum looked hurt.

'Amy, I'm only trying to help,' she said, looking a bit teary.

I relented, fighting to get the calm voice back. I didn't want to betray how I was really feeling.

'I'm sorry. I didn't mean to snap. It's just that this whole thing is so difficult. I know I should report it. But it's so much easier to try and pretend it didn't happen.'

She nodded, sniffing. I got up and went over to give her a hug.

'All I want is for you to be okay,' she said into my shoulder. That was such a simple thing to want. But it seemed so impossible. I held her there for a few seconds too long, so she couldn't see the tears starting.

For the rest of the evening, me and Mum caught up with a drama we'd been watching on iPlayer. I stared at the screen, the actors were well-known, the story was good, but I wasn't concentrating. There was too much going on in my head and my stomach. Mum seemed to quite like it, although maybe she was just staring at it too.

'You staying up for the news?' she asked.

'No, I think I'll say goodnight. I'm knackered.'

That was true at least. School had really taken it out of me; I was exhausted.

My phone was still turned off in my bag, but as I brushed my teeth and got ready for bed, destructive little thoughts started crowding into my head. Normally after school I'd get a load of messages - snapchats, new stories on Instagram, the usual, all from my friends and the people I'd just spent the whole day with. Ridiculous how much there was that needed communicating once we all got back on our phones. It was hours since I'd looked at mine. What would they have been talking about today? My mind played tricks. I remembered the speed of the wildfire as it spread on Sunday, Maria constantly pushing away notifications and trying to shut it down. I remembered everything I'd seen on Monday, the comments and frozen moments from the video. It might all have started again. What if someone had filmed me confronting Harry? I had to check, even if it was something I didn't want to see. I picked up my phone.

The social media apps were all littered with little red circles. Notifications of more torture. My stomach knotted, regretting dinner. I took a deep breath and wondered where to start. Which one of them would be the worst? And should I start with that one, or work up to it? I let my finger hover, and accidentally touched the screen. All the little icons started vibrating. And suddenly, I knew what to do. I didn't need this anymore. I didn't need to see. I tapped on WhatsApp. Remove WhatsApp? my phone asked, incredulous. I hovered over "Delete app". I took a breath. Tap. Tap. Gone.

The other apps shimmered. Snapchat. Tap. Tap. Gone. I felt a strange sensation, like I was standing at the top of something, about to jump. I went through all of them, every little icon that meant someone could reach me. Instagram, Facebook, Messenger. I felt a rush of something good. Liberation.

I flicked onto Messages. There was still nothing from Rosie.

Quickly I typed:

Hi. Please can we talk again? I really need your support.

I watched. Delivered. Read. Nothing.

Something inside me gave up and I knew. I couldn't report it. I couldn't talk it all over with new people, again and again. Either with or without Rosie. I looked at the other texts. There were still lots I hadn't replied to. Some of them offering support, some of them just checking how I was. Suddenly I felt outraged by all these people and their concern. What right did they all have to send me a text, ask me how I was? I barely even knew some of them. They hadn't just seen me in the video, they thought it was okay to contact me about it. I had become some kind of grotesque public property. I wanted all of it and all of them to go away. I had another brainwave. I'd change my number. I'd give it to Maria, and Mum, and that was it. And until then, I'd just do without a phone. I could shut the world out.

I went to text Maria to tell her I'd deleted everything, just in case she was trying to contact me. Just as I started to type, a new message appeared.

Amy, I need to talk to you.

My heart stopped dead and suddenly my plan seemed flimsy and pointless. It was from Harry. I deleted it, turned the phone off and went to bed, with the very faint hope that at some point, maybe, I might be able to fall asleep.

In the morning when I woke up, the idea of school was almost more than I could handle. But I had to keep it up. Mum had to think I was doing fine. I thought of Harry's message. Fuck him. Whatever he wanted to talk to me about, it was too late. I pushed the evil butterflies back into the pit of my stomach, hauled myself out of bed and got ready for school. I'd managed it once. There had to be a way.

Over the next couple of days, I worked it out. The nook under the stairs became the unspoken meeting place for me and Maria. We'd sit and compare notes on how our days were going, briefly mentioning if we'd managed to avoid Rosie and Harry but mainly focussing on lessons and non-controversial topics. She was a rock. When it seemed like it was all going to overwhelm me, when the paranoia and the humiliation was getting too much, I knew I just had to get back there, and she'd be waiting for me after every lesson. When I had free periods on my own, I could hide in the library. The booth at the back was secluded, and no one ever bothered me. In lessons, I felt a level of protection from the staff, who had definitely all been briefed to keep an eye on me and not let anything get out of control. Mrs Jameson had emailed to say that, as long as I needed to, I could sign in at Reception instead of going to form time. I wasn't sure if Mum had said something to her, or whether she'd taken her own initiative, regardless of Turner's unwillingness to take any action. But I didn't really want to know. I felt safer just following the strategy that let me stay under the radar.

Having no social media was a weird kind of bliss. I hardly used my phone at all and managed to get it through to Maria that whatever might be going on, I'd rather not know. Rosie never replied to my message. I blocked Harry's number, and texts from anyone else I just deleted without reading. The only time I really got notifications at school were messages from Mum. They were always upbeat emojis and statements of encouragement peppered with exclamation marks – the language of self-delusion. I was happy to play along with it.

On Thursday break, I stayed behind a few minutes in English, having got properly absorbed in a piece I was writing.

'Amy, this is great,' Mrs. Barras said, reading over my shoulder.

'Thank you.' In the midst of everything that was going on, I felt proud of my ability to write anything at all, let alone something my English teacher thought was great.

'You know, I've been meaning to ask you. Have you applied to study English?'

I nodded. I had. It had been a no-brainer for me, although a bit of a fight with the careers adviser who thought I should choose a career path first and the degree subject later. Not the way I saw it. English was my thing and that was what I wanted to study. I'd think about a job sometime later. But I hadn't given it any thought since the party. I'd almost forgotten there was anything I was good at.

When I left the classroom, there were still a few people milling around in the corridor, including some young girls who looked at me with the kind of recognition usually reserved for a minor celebrity. I brushed past them, not wanting to think about how they knew who I was. As I rounded the corner, I saw the back of Rosie's head as it disappeared downstairs. My first instinct was to turn on my heel and head in the other direction. But that wasn't going to get me anywhere. I raced to catch her up.

'Wait!' I said, putting my hand on her arm. She turned suddenly and pulled her arm away.

'Why are you sneaking up on me?'

'I wasn't, I...' She knocked me off balance with the ice of her reply. 'I just wanted to know... I messaged you... have you thought about...?'

I couldn't even get the words out, but I knew. She shook her head.

'There was a reason I didn't reply.' She carried on walking downstairs, not looking at me. 'I don't want to talk about it anymore. I told you.'

She stopped and turned suddenly, making me jolt to a stop one step above her. Something in her eyes was hard to read, but her words were very clear. 'I can't help you. I'm sorry.'

She carried on down the stairs and I let her get away.

I dragged myself off to the library, all of it churning around in my head. The video, the shame, the embarrassment, the feeling of people looking at me everywhere I went. Harry getting away with it, Rosie letting me down. If there had been even a glimmer of hope that somehow Harry and his friends would be punished, Rosie had pretty much extinguished it. Without Rosie on my side, any delusion I'd had that I might, one day, report it to the police disappeared. I felt powerless, that my life was out of my own control.

In the library I pulled the revision timetable I'd got in form time the day before out of my bag. There were twenty-three days to go before my first exam. I thought about my conversation in English, Mrs Barras waxing lyrical about my ability, and I let myself drift away to a future where I was studying English all the time, somewhere no one knew me. A plan started to form. Getting away from here was my way out. I could do this. Twenty-three more days, that was all. And some of it was study leave so I wouldn't even need to leave the house. All I had to do was get to that point in the future where I could put all this behind me. It was like emerging from a fog and seeing the path you've been looking for stretching right there in front of you. I knew exactly what I needed to do – focus, work, get those A levels and then take myself off to university where no one would know me. I would be anonymous. I could start again.

I started to fill out the timetable with all the available days and hours I'd be able to study. I felt a sense of purpose; I had a list of things I could do myself, tasks to tick off, steps I could take in the safety of my own home that would get me to my goal. I could hide from all the things that were difficult and soon, I'd be able to escape. I had a plan.

21
NOW

'How was the gig?'

Obviously that was the first thing a beaming Jon said when he opened the door to me the next morning.

'Umm, it was... loud,' I said, deciding to go for minimal but truthful answers. The grin faded slightly.

'Oh, right. I really meant...' But before I could get my coat off and before he could tell me what he really meant, the door flew open behind us. Jamie. Flustered, slightly wild-looking, his hair squashed down on one side of his head and looking as if he'd just got out of bed. Which, given it wasn't quite nine in the morning, was probably true.

'Amy! Oh thank goodness you're okay. I didn't know where you'd gone.' He reached out but stopped short of touching me as I shrank away.

'I'm... fine,' I mumbled, still sticking with the minimal answers.

'I was so worried,' he said, almost in a whisper, his arms dropping to his sides. Jon clearly didn't have a clue what was going on, and they were both looking at me for some kind of explanation. This would be a really good time to quit the minimal answers and say something, I thought.

'I'm sorry. I'm fine, honestly. It was just very... loud. And I lost you. And so, I... I just left.' I shot Jon a sideways glance and he turned his hands upwards and shrugged his shoulders as if to say, 'What the fuck?'

'But I came back for you!' Jamie said, reaching out to me again then thinking better of it and awkwardly folding his arms. 'I found the others, realised you weren't behind me and went back to the door. You can't have waited more than a couple of minutes.'

Is that all it was? It felt like a lot longer than that. But there wasn't much point arguing about a technicality. I couldn't stand how his face was screwing up, how his fists were clenching.

'You could have messaged me! I was so worried. And I didn't have your number.'

'I… um. I said to the guy on the door…' It was hardly fair to blame pierced lip guy, who clearly hadn't heard me, but it was all I had.

Jamie was shaking his head. 'He didn't say anything.' A sigh escaped through the side of his mouth, a sound of resignation. 'Well, at least you're okay,' he said quietly.

I stared hard at a tiny mark on one of the floorboards as if it might tell me what to say. The silence was deafening. Jon cleared his throat.

'So! You look tired mate; can I get you a coffee maybe?'

'Yeah, yeah thanks, that would be good.'

Selfishly, I thought how I'd much rather he'd said no and just left. I hated myself, so for punishment, I said, 'Please. Let me get it. It's the least I can do.'

They both looked slightly taken aback, but Jon took my coat and went to put it away while Jamie just nodded. I left him standing there and went behind the counter, not asking what he wanted, just starting to steam the oat milk. I needed to say something, something with a bit more substance, something to explain what happened, that it wasn't him, that I really would have loved to stay and chat, just the two of us, that it was all the other people, and the heat, and the noise. And that I hadn't been on a date since the night my best friend's cousin took away my virginity and, with it, my self-confidence, self-belief and ability to trust anyone I would ever meet. But I just gave the milk an extra few seconds to prolong the noise, poured it onto the coffee and carefully placed a teaspoon on the saucer.

'Thanks,' he said, not looking at me. I wanted to die at how uncomfortable I was making him.

'Jamie... I...'

He looked up, not even hopeful anymore. Just confused and hurt and probably wondering why on earth he'd even bothered with me. I pulled at the sleeves of my jumper and fixed my eyes on the countertop. 'It's just, I'm not really into gigs. Or pubs. I... I don't go out much. So I probably shouldn't have come.'

I dared to lift my eyes to look at him. He looked completely crushed. My heart hurt.

'Sorry,' I said, uselessly.

He picked up his coffee.

'Oh, hey, no worries. Maybe some other time.'

He walked away. I'd forgotten to ask him to pay. I just left it.

I fiddled with the milk jug and stared at the countertop. Jon had a go at chatting to Jamie, but there really wasn't anything to say. Jamie downed his coffee faster than I'd ever seen someone drink a latte. It must have been too hot. I felt responsible for him burning his mouth too. He got up to leave, gave me a little nod and walked out.

'Bye,' I said, weakly, as the door shut. 'Sorry.'

The whole morning was awkward and quiet for a Saturday, just when I needed to be rushed off my feet and distracted. All I could do was stand at the meticulously clean counter going over and over what I'd done and trying to think of a single reason why Jamie would ever come in again. Jon sat near the front doing some paperwork. Wisely he didn't ask any questions, but I'm sure the admin was just a way to stop himself from grilling me.

'Can I do some salads or something?' I asked as it neared lunchtime and the usual rush hadn't materialised.

'All done,' he said with a hollow cheerfulness. 'I'm all over it today.'

I slumped onto my elbows and he took pity on me.

'Do you want to go and do some sorting out in the staff room? I'm nearly done here; I'll give you a shout if it gets busy. We've got a delivery on Monday, good opportunity to do some rationalising. I know you've always wanted to get me organised.' I tried a smile and failed, but at least I had something to do.

As I stacked boxes of napkins and straws and lined all the oat milk cartons neatly on the shelves, I mulled over just how spectacularly I had stuffed up the chance of a date. It was very clear now; it had been a date. I'd tried to justify my swift exit to myself by thinking no one would have noticed, but Jamie's worry-stricken face that morning showed me I was wrong. And how he looked when he got up to leave. Like a man who'd given up. No one could blame him. I'd given up on myself. Unbidden, a thought of Harry popped into my head. Swanning around Durham just like he did at school, untouched by what he'd done. I shoved at some crates of olive oil on the floor with my foot, stubbing my toe. There was no point thinking about Harry. There was no point regretting that, when I had the chance, I did nothing. There was no point wondering, for the millionth time, what it would take for me to get a fucking grip and start living my life. There was no point...

My mantra of despair was interrupted by Andrew arriving. Bloody hell, I'd lost track of time, I'd normally make sure I was nowhere near the staffroom or the kitchen at twelve.

'Oh hello!' he said, in his usual grating and cheerful voice. 'Let me look at you, any signs of a late night?'

I turned away, although I'm sure the kind of sleepless night I'd had was not what he was implying.

'How was the gig?' he carried on, slinging his jacket carelessly over the pile of boxes I'd just tidied.

'It was fine,' I said. Back to the minimal answers. Although he had no need of details, he was perfectly capable of inventing his own.

'I'd have come if I'd known, looked like a good line up. Wouldn't have thought it was your thing?'

'What do you know?' I turned on him. 'You don't know anything about me. You're always trying to ask personal questions, like you think we know each other. So you recognise me? So what. We're not friends, okay? Leave me alone.'

He looked a bit stunned, as well he might. He'd only asked about my evening. But I didn't feel bad for venting my anger on him. He left without saying anything else, and I cursed him as I picked up his jacket. He might be good at clearing up a kitchen but he didn't seem to be able to hang a jacket on a coat hook. It was one of those thin, windproof training tops that sports teams wear, with what I assumed to be his nickname, Chopper, emblazoned across the back. Andychop, his Instagram name. That made sense then. Wonder what he did to earn that one, I thought disparagingly. Then I noticed the badge on the front and my heart stopped. Windermere Rugby Club. That was six miles from my home town.

I couldn't drag my eyes away from the logo. Was there any way he could have a rugby top from Windermere if he wasn't from there? Maybe he'd just borrowed it... But that was clutching at straws. Somehow, in all his ridiculous questioning, he'd never mentioned where he was from. And he didn't have a northern accent that was particularly noticeable. More that kind of unidentifiable poshness that could be from anywhere in England. But from that first moment in the kitchen, we knew we'd seen each other before. I knew it, and so did he. If he was from Windermere, then it was scarily possible that we had.

Work did at least pick up a bit over lunchtime, but I felt sick the entire shift. I tried to stay out of Andrew's way, treating the kitchen like some kind of hot zone where I'd spend the shortest amount of time possible – dropping off plates, grabbing food orders, all at top speed. It was amazing there weren't more casualties in the broken pots department. Unsurprisingly, Andrew didn't bother with his usual attempts at conversation. Maybe I should have been more blunt with him earlier on. What with that, and me and Jon still skirting around the elephant in the room, it was tense all afternoon. Not at all what I wanted from my time at work.

Three o'clock came round eventually, thank god. Andrew appeared with his jacket, slinging it over his shoulder, said 'Cheerio,' to Jon and headed for the door. I managed not to look as he called 'See you,' in my general direction. But I didn't feel much sense of relief.

It was the jacket. It was too much of a coincidence that we recognised each other and we were from the same part of the country. Maybe it was something innocent, like he'd come in for a pizza sometime. But would either of us have remembered that? It was another major worry to add to my ever-growing list. I wondered about phoning Maria again. But we hadn't talked that much lately, not about anything big and important. I thought of how she brushed off the message from Rosie. I hadn't even phoned to tell her Rosie had turned up. Maria felt far away, and busy, and immersed in her new life. I didn't want to bother her with my worries. And I definitely wasn't going to tell Mum. No chance. Mum was happy believing her daughter's life was settled and normal. It was better that way.

It all went quiet again towards the end of the afternoon. About four, Jon came out from the kitchen and looked at the clock.

'You could knock off early if you want,' he said.

'Oh, okay.' My heart sank. Even with the awkwardness and the lack of customers, I'd take being at work over an extra hour alone in my room.

Jon went out to the tables and started tidying papers and magazines that had been read and left out. I fiddled about, pretending to do something useful when in fact there was nothing left to do. I probably should go home. The last customers left and Jon called a cheery goodbye.

'We might as well call it a day,' he said, turning the sign to "Closed". I made a noise that was meant to be agreement but came out as a bit of a sigh.

'Well, that didn't sound too good!' he said. He gave me one of the knowing looks that I was beginning to get a bit wary of. 'Were you hoping someone else might come in?' he asked, pointedly.

'No, I...'

But he wasn't going to let it go.

'Look, it's none of my business. But what the hell happened last night? I thought you liked him, Jamie. I mean…'

'No, you're right. It isn't any of your business.' I shocked both of us with my offhand tone. 'I'm sorry, Jon. That came across as rude.'

'It did a bit! I'm only trying to look out for you.'

'I know. And I'm fine, honestly. He seems like a nice guy but, I'm not really looking for a relationship, so…'

'To be fair to him, he only took you to a gig. I think there are a few more stages you'd need to get through before anyone was calling it a relationship.'

I tried to smile, but it was too much effort.

'Yeah, I know. But it wasn't the right time.'

Jon nodded, trying to look as if he understood. I knew he didn't. I didn't really understand either, but that was the way it was. Jon carried on tidying chairs and tables. I'd normally have offered to help sweep up. But somehow, I thought I should just go.

'Okay if I get off then?' I asked.

'Yeah, yeah. No problem at all. I'll see you next week.'

'Saturday? Sure. Call me if you need me before then.'

He tipped an imaginary hat.

'Will do. Enjoy the rest of your weekend, Amy.'

I thought of the four walls of my room, my laptop, Netflix, the constant sound of the students around me enjoying their lives.

'You too,' I said, picking up my bag and heading to the door.

22
THEN

At last it was Friday of that week back at school, that hideous nightmare of a week. Still early days. Making it back home at the end of the day was a massive relief every single time I did it. And then I'd spend the evening with Mum, trying to be cheerful and pretending I'd forgotten about it all. But every day was one more cross on my countdown calendar, one step closer to being able to leave, one more painful day I wouldn't have to live through again. I was sticking to my plan and I felt like I was managing the situation as best I could. Maria and Mum had obviously had a chat and decided to leave the idea of me going to the police for a bit, as no one had mentioned it for a couple of days. I guess, in the grander scheme of things, by the time I walked home on Friday, some kind of calm had descended.

Until I found Harry waiting on my doorstep.

I turned the corner, music on loud in my headphones, looking forward to shutting the door on the world and the week, and there he was. Sitting on my doorstep like he had some kind of right to be there. Larger than life, in blue jeans and a navy Adidas hoodie, looking like any eighteen-year-old boy might look while waiting for the girl whose life he'd just ruined. I ripped my earphones out and stormed up to the house as he stood up.

'What the fuck are you doing here?' I hissed, more aware of my neighbours than I had been of Rosie's.

'Amy. Please. I really want to talk to you,'

'You think I give a shit about what you want? Get out of my way, you're trespassing.'

I tried to muscle past but that was pointless; he played first team rugby, I was never going to be any kind of match for him, even with the anger that was fuelling me. He just put an arm out and stopped me getting past.

'Please, Amy,' he said. I looked at him properly for the first time – and thought I saw something soft in his eyes.

Seizing on my momentary hesitation he spoke again, his arm still barring my way but with less force. 'Look. I want to explain. I know you went to the head. And people have been saying stuff all week. But I want to tell you my side of things. Please, just ten minutes. Then I promise I'll leave.'

For a moment I paused. Maybe I should have sent him away. But he'd got me. I did want to hear his side of things. Because I really didn't know how anyone could have done to me what he did.

'Alright. You can come in. But I'm texting Maria to tell her you're here.'

'Fine. Whatever you want.'

I had a flicker of feeling for this boy in his casual clothes. Rosie's cousin. That boy who used to tease me at her birthday parties. I quickly shook it away and unlocked the door.

'Here, you wait in the lounge. I'm making tea, do you want one?'

'Yeah, please. One sugar.'

Having a conversation with Harry in my house about how he liked his tea was too surreal. I went into the kitchen and put the kettle on, then messaged Maria.

Harry's here. Call me in fifteen.

She was straight back to me before the kettle had even boiled.

Are you mad???? What are you doing???

It's okay. He wants to talk, that's all. I'm fine.

Okay, if you think you know what you're doing... Just be careful. I'll call in a bit.

I turned silent mode off, put my phone in my pocket, and took the tea into the lounge. Harry looked huge and out of place, Mum's favourite cushion forcing him to perch on the edge of the sofa. I caught sight of her notebook still next to the TV. Thank God it hadn't been open on the table.

'Thanks,' he said as I put the tea down.

I sat on the chair in the corner and looked at him. What I would have given, just a week before, to have Harry alone in my house. When he was still an exciting idea and a promise of things to come. I looked at him, feeling a strange sense of detachment. A load of unbidden thoughts ran through my head. We've been naked together. We've touched each other. You fingered me. I sucked your cock. Are you thinking about that too? I thought. But it was impossible to tell what he was thinking.

He picked up his tea and shifted uncomfortably on the grey upholstery.

'You said you wanted to talk. You've got ten minutes.'

He put the tea down and looked at the carpet. I waited. I'd given him enough of a helping hand. He cleared his throat.

'So, the party. Oli's party...'

I laughed, a cold laugh I didn't really recognise.

'Oh that one? Like there was any other party you might want to talk about.'

'Yeah. Okay, look. This is hard, okay? I think maybe, maybe you think I did it all on purpose or something. Took you to that room for the video, the... the...'

'Competition?' I offered.

He rubbed the back of his neck. 'Yeah, that. I mean, I'm not going to lie.'

Well, that was something.

'I knew about it. I knew the camera was there and all that. But I didn't have anything to do with the video being shared. Honestly, I was as surprised as you were...'

I stopped him with a raised hand.

'I don't really think surprised covers it. And anyway, no. You weren't. Because you knew there was a camera in that room. All I knew was that you and me...'

I couldn't even say it to him.

'Amy, I promise you. I didn't do it on purpose. I didn't want it to happen that way. Yeah, I knew about the camera and I found it funny about the competition. I know you think it's disgusting. And now I think about it, you might be right.'

I lifted one eyebrow, trying to maintain my composure.

'You have to believe me, I didn't want it to be me and you in there. I like you too much. I've liked you for ages. Rosie warned me off you. And she was probably right, I mean, look what's happened.'

My brain was trying to keep up. Was this meant to be some kind of apology? I hadn't heard the word sorry. He was looking at me from under his eyelashes, trying to gauge if he was winning me over. I didn't know what to say so I let him carry on.

'So yeah. I wanted you to know that. I really liked you. Like you, I mean. I still do. You know, it was great, Saturday night. The thing with the camera, well, could we just forget it happened? Because it wasn't like I planned it. It was kind of an accident. I mean, you were the one leading me into that room. So that makes me think that maybe you like me too? And I was thinking, you know, maybe we could put it behind us? Start properly...'

You really can feel so angry that the blood rushes to your head. I couldn't listen to any more of his shit.

'Are you insane?' I snapped. He stopped mid-flow and looked up at me, startled.

'Forget it happened? Do you have any idea what this has done to me? I feel like the whole school, the whole town, raped me in that room that night. You were just the other person in the frame. You are out of your mind.'

He was trying to shrink away from me, but the cushions stopped him, he just looked even more out of place. I was incandescent.

'If you think this is some way to get yourself off the hook, to stop me from "making a fuss" or whatever you want to call it, you are wrong. You, Oli, the rest of your seedy gang. You're all in the shit. I thought you were supposed to be intelligent? Do you really think

you can come round here and, what? Ask me out? Did you think if
you told me you actually really like me, I'd just say, hey, I like you too.
Forget the whole video incident, let's have sex again before Mum
gets back. Fuck you, Harry.'

My phone rang. Maria.

'Your time's up,' I said as I answered it. 'Hi Maria. All fine. Harry's
just leaving.'

I hung up the call and stood, signalling for him to leave. He stayed
seated for a second or two, twisting his hands together. But when he
got up, his face had hardened.

'Okay. I'll go.' His voice sounded cold. 'But I wouldn't bother
going to the head again if I were you. Or the police. You'd have to
prove that you didn't know about the video. And I'll just tell them
you did. You won't have a leg to stand on.'

I hesitated, my righteous anger ebbing away slightly.

'What do you know about it? There were loads of people who
knew what was going on.' I had a flash of inspiration. 'Rosie, for
example.'

He smirked and I felt nauseous.

'Oh yeah. Rosie. My cousin. Well, I think you can rest assured
she's not going to give evidence against me and my friends. She
knows how to keep a promise.'

He sounded really threatening. But even more worryingly, he
sounded like he knew what he was talking about. Rosie's strange
look as she walked away from me sprang into my head.

I didn't speak as I followed him to the door. My heart was racing.
He suddenly turned back towards me as I thought he was about to
walk out. I recoiled as he got closer.

'You've got a lot more to lose than me. That video still exists.
People still have it. And it would be so easy for someone to share it
again. And in places where you really wouldn't want to look. So I'd
think long and hard about how much of a fuss you're prepared to
make, if I was you.'

He turned away and I managed to shove him out the house and shut the door behind him. I listened to his footsteps on the drive as I leant my head against the hard, cold wood of the front door.

23

THEN

When Mum got in an hour or so later, I was still sitting in the lounge, staring at the wall.

'Hello,' she called brightly up the stairs to where I would usually be, in my room, getting ready for work.

'I'm in here.' I called. She poked her head round the door and looked surprised to see me still in school clothes.

'Oh! You know it's five already? I can take you in if you're running a bit late, do you want a lift?'

She phrased her reminder as an offer of help. I'd noticed all week she'd been speaking to me like this, as if she didn't want to upset me about anything. Perhaps she thought nagging me for needing a lift when I could quite easily walk was more than I could take. I didn't reply.

She clocked the two mugs on the table.

'Has Maria been over?'

At the third unanswered question she pushed the door open fully and came in.

'Amy, what's the matter?'

She sat down on the sofa in front of me, moving aside the cushion that Harry had been leaning on.

'I'm not going to work today,' I told her, curling more tightly into my chair. 'I called them. Said I wasn't feeling up to it.'

I thought back to the way Suzanne had hesitated slightly when I'd phoned to make my excuse. I felt sure she knew exactly why I wasn't feeling up to it.

'Oh. Right.' Mum frowned slightly and bit her lip. 'I thought… I mean, you've been doing so well. I thought you were doing okay…' She tailed off. I couldn't really blame her for believing the act I'd been pulling off all week, but somehow it still annoyed me that she'd been taken in so easily.

'No, I'm not okay,' I said. 'And I just can't face work. Imagine you're out for a pizza and you realise your waitress is someone you've seen in a video having sex.'

Mum looked stung by my directness. I sounded a lot more aggressive than I really felt, but I had Harry's words stuck in my head. As long as anyone still had it on their phone, the video was ready to go again whenever someone felt like sharing it.

'Darling. I understand,' she said, soothingly. It was the worst tone of voice she could have used. 'But you can't live your life in hiding. And honestly, I think most people who have seen the video will just feel sorry that it happened to you.'

I hunched my shoulders in disbelief and made a noise somewhere between a hoarse laugh and a cough.

'You think they'll feel sorry for me? Is that supposed to make me feel better? I hadn't even thought of that one. Let me add pity to the list of emotions that strangers might feel about me.'

'Amy, please.' Mum looked tearful, but I couldn't stop. Suddenly I wanted to hurt her a little bit, like I was hurting.

'You say you understand. No, you don't. You can't possibly. I feel so dirty, so ashamed. In my brain I know I didn't really do anything wrong, but when I think of that video, that shitty, awful, wonky camera shot…' I exhaled, trying to get the image out of my head. 'I can't look at myself in the mirror because all I can see is what everyone else has seen – me naked, us on the bed, his hands all over my body.'

Mum sucked in her breath. I looked at her properly for the first time for days. Worry lines I'd never noticed before were etched deep around her eyes and across her forehead. I realised I wasn't the only one who'd been putting on an act. I softened.

'Sometimes,' I said quietly, 'sometimes I... I don't think I know how to carry on.'

She rushed over and scooped me awkwardly into her arms.

'Amy, no. Don't ever say that. Nothing is that bad. I can't bear it. I can't bear to think of my little girl in so much pain.'

I leant into her, trying desperately to find the comfort I'd always felt with her arms around me. It wasn't there.

'Every time someone looks at me, I imagine... I wonder what they're thinking about me. I feel so humiliated. Each day has been awful... an ordeal to get through. Then sometimes for a moment I forget. Or I get a flash of feeling strong. But it doesn't last.' I inhaled her familiar smell, breathing deep, the next wave of tears threatening to come.

Mum rocked me gently, stroking my hair. I think she was trying to comfort herself as much as me.

'Darling, I thought you'd been doing so well. You've managed school all week. That must have been so hard. But you did it.'

I shook my head.

'I did it by hiding as much as I could. I've never spent so much time in the library. I haven't been anywhere near the canteen, the common room or my form.'

'But you've found a way. That's amazing. You're so brave.'

'I'm not brave. Not at all! All I can do is hide. I just want to get through to the end of school and finish my exams. Then I can leave.'

'Shhh, shhh. I'll talk to school. I'll see what they can do to help.'

I thought of Mr Turner and his firmly clasped hands. I didn't bother telling her it was a waste of time. There was the slightest pause in the rocking, and she kissed my head, gently, then asked, 'What did Maria say? When she called earlier?'

I hesitated. Might as well tell her the truth for once.

'It wasn't Maria. It was Harry.'

Mum pulled away, her hands gripped my shoulders just a bit too tightly, her face a picture of confusion.

'What? Harry was here?'

I shrugged and she let go.

'He was on the doorstep when I got home. He wanted to talk. Tried to tell me none of it was his fault and we could start again.'

'He said what?' Mum looked like a cartoon character doing "outraged". I almost laughed.

'I know. And when I said no, he gently reminded me he still has the video so I'd better not make a fuss.'

'He said what?' She was on repeat. 'Amy, that's blackmail. Well, it's something illegal. Actually I think it's called "threat to share".'

My turn to look confused. She stood up and went to get her notebook, speaking as she went.

'I've been in touch with a brilliant girl at an organisation called the Revenge Porn Helpline. They've been helping to make sure the video has been removed everywhere. Already they think they have got it down. Well, eighty percent sure. So that's great, isn't it?'

Call me glass half-empty but I immediately wondered where the other twenty percent might be. Mum carried on, talking excitedly; she had so much information to tell me, so many ways to help, phone numbers, websites, people to talk to. All I could think about was that video still out there, somewhere. Even if it was just on Harry's phone. Or Oli's. Or whichever depraved bastard set it all up in the first place. It was still there and I didn't see how a helpline or a counsellor or even going to the police was going to make the slightest bit of difference.

Mum stopped talking, looking up expectantly, her glasses pushed onto the top of her head. Her hair had caught in the catch as it always did. She was waiting for me to say something.

'That's all really... helpful.' I fished around for the right word, not wanting to offend Mum for everything she'd done, but feeling numb.

'I just...' I tried to visualise myself talking to a policeman to tell them what had happened. The pictures wouldn't come. I shook my head.

'I just don't think I can, Mum. Talk about it anymore. Tell someone new. It's too much.'

'But they'll help you. There are more and more cases of this every year, the chances of him being prosecuted...' She was off again. She sounded like she'd swallowed a leaflet of facts about revenge porn and was reciting it back at me.

I shook my head, cutting her off, I couldn't listen anymore.

'Mum, I just can't. Please don't ask me again. I hate what they did to me, I hate that everyone else is just getting on with their lives and I feel... I feel destroyed. But I don't think I can do anything. It's exhausting. I can't keep trying. Without Rosie, no one will believe me. And even if they did, standing in a court, telling everyone what happened... No.'

I caught a flicker of disappointment as she closed the notebook.

'Okay darling. We don't need to talk about it now. I just want you to feel better.'

She put the book down and came back to me, wrapping me in her hug.

'Mum, all I want is for it to go away. I want to feel like I did before it all happened. But I don't know if that's ever going to be possible.'

'Whatever you want. I'll support you. Whatever you need, we're in it together. If you did want to report it to the police, I'm here for you. But if what you want is just to get through to the end of term and go off to uni, I'll help you do that. In any way that I can.'

I felt her breath shake and she lowered her voice to a whisper.

'But don't ever, ever say that you can't carry on. Nothing is that bad. We can do this, you and me.'

I think she believed we could. Curled up there in my chair with her arms around me, I almost believed it too.

24
NOW

It had been a long, lonely week, and despite knowing Andrew would be there, I was dying to be back at work. Every day I'd hoped Jon might message to ask me to help out, but he hadn't. I hoped that was because it wasn't busy, and not because I'd snapped at him. I had apologised. Well, sort of. Jon didn't seem like the kind of guy to hold a grudge, but it didn't take much for me to start overthinking. I'd messaged a few times and he'd been his usual friendly self, so I'd come in hopeful that the awkwardness could be forgotten. Jamie was another matter entirely. I'd gone to text him probably sixteen times a day. But I didn't dare. I'd blown it. And sending a message he would probably ignore was more than I could take.

I arrived ten minutes early and had to knock. Jon came out from the kitchen and unlocked the door.

'Well, well! You're early. That is a surprise.' He said it kindly, with a big smile.

'I'm full of surprises,' I said. 'So, you've managed a week without me. What kind of chaos are we looking at today?'

He laughed, I laughed, the normal, easy-going banter resumed. It was going to be alright.

I managed to not speak to Andrew when he arrived, and he didn't make any attempt to catch my attention. I shuddered slightly to see the legend "Chopper" emblazoned across his jacket as he went into the staff room. Jon slipped quietly into his intermediary role, doing the food orders and delivering them to tables, allowing me to stay away from the kitchen. Maybe I'd been worrying about nothing.

Maybe Jamie would come in shortly and ask for an oat milk latte, and everything would be okay.

The milk fridge had suffered from a busy early morning, and probably from a few days of Jon on his own. I was crouched down behind the counter trying to sort it out, when I heard the doorbell go, sparking the usual rush of adrenalin. With an extra spike. On balance I probably didn't want Jamie to come in after all. Oh, come on, just count and breathe. One, two, three, four... I stood up as slowly as I could manage, turning towards the door gradually, fighting the crazy urge to spin round instantly to see who it was.

'Hello stranger,' said the most familiar of voices as I stood up.

'Maria! Oh my god! What are you doing here? Why didn't you tell me you were coming?'

I shoved the fridge shut with my foot and ran out from behind the counter.

'Wouldn't have been a surprise if you'd known.' Maria smiled and I swallowed her up in a hug.

'Oh, I can't believe you're here. This is amazing.'

The hug made us laugh and cry at the same time. Out of the corner of my eye, I saw Jon come to the counter and I let her go. He looked a bit surprised but he was smiling.

'Well, well, this isn't the kind of scene I'm used to,' he said, one eyebrow raised. 'So, do I get an introduction?'

'Jon, this is Maria. My best friend,' I said, grinning. 'Maria, this is Jon.'

'Your best boss?' he asked.

'My only boss. But yeah, he's not bad.' I beamed at him, then turned back to my friend.

'Wow! I just can't believe you're here. And that I'm working!' I looked round at Jon, who was watching us thoughtfully. 'Jon, I don't suppose...'

'Sure. Take a break. Not too busy at the moment. Have some time with your friend and catch up.'

I steered Maria to the table at the back while Jon made coffees and brought them over. I felt like a customer again. Just a normal teenage girl having a drink with a friend. I hardly stopped to ask myself why that should feel so strange.

'So, what on earth are you doing here? You look amazing by the way. Love your hair.'

Maria's trademark blonde hair was streaked with pink. She put a hand through it.

'My flat mate's a trainee hairdresser. I let him experiment. I think I like it…'

'It's great! You look great. And nice jacket too.'

'Borrowed.' She shrugged.

Maria chatted away, telling me all about uni life. I listened attentively, wondering why I felt so out of touch and thinking how long it was since we'd last seen each other. I wondered at the things she was telling me – the flat mates who did her hair and lent her their clothes. The friends she'd made on her course. I felt a pang of emptiness for my own solitary life. But this is what I wanted, I reminded myself, quickly shaking it off.

'So you still haven't told me why you're here. To what do I owe the pleasure?'

Maria raised an eyebrow. 'Mate, you talk like an English student.'

I laughed. 'Can't imagine why!'

'Well, I was passing. I'm with another friend, and we were so near to you, I thought we'd drop in.' Maria twirled the packet of sugar she wasn't using between her fingers.

'Oh right! I thought you were on your own.' It seemed a bit of an odd explanation. Not a special trip to see me then. I felt a bit deflated but rallied. 'But that's fine. It'll be a bit cosy, assuming you're staying over?'

'Um. Yeah, we could. We were playing it by ear really.'

The door opened and a family of four came in, followed by Gladys and one of her cronies. I glanced over to the counter, caught Jon's eye and nodded.

'Look, I should probably go and help. But we'll see each other later, right? Come back in a couple of hours, I'll be finished by four-thirty.'

'Yeah sure.' Maria finished the last of the froth from her coffee with her finger. 'Great coffee! Is there anywhere to visit or anything?'

'It's not exactly known as a tourist hotspot.' I laughed. 'But there's a nice park you could wander round.' I gave her directions and picked up our cups as I stood up.

'I can't tell you how good it is to see you,' I said. An expression I couldn't quite read flickered across Maria's face.

'You too, Ames. It's been way too long.'

We hugged again. Maria left and I took the cups back to the kitchen on my way to help Jon with the sudden rush. Andrew was coming out with some clean plates. He paused and I stood to one side to let him pass, but he was looking straight at me with a slight smile on his lips. A knowing smile that flipped my insides around.

'That girl you were with,' he said, deliberately. 'I recognise her too. I think I've just remembered where I know you from, Amy.'

25
THEN

I woke up early, that feeling in the pit of my stomach you get when you know there's something you don't want to do that day. The split second of unexplained tension before you realise what it is. First day of exams. I looked at my revision timetable, pinned to the wall, big crosses in purple felt tip marking the countdown. The twenty-two days were up. It was now.

Mum came in with a cup of tea.

'Alright, darling? All ready?'

I pulled myself up to sitting and took the tea.

'Guess we're about to find out.'

Mum sat on the edge of the bed.

'You've worked so hard, you must know everything there is to know inside out and back to front. I even know most of Macbeth off by heart now!'

I smiled. Mum had been diligently testing me with my revision cards.

'Thanks for all your help.'

'My pleasure. Good luck.' She left me to get up and get ready.

She was right, I should have been pretty well-prepared; I'd spent hours and hours in my room, looking at schoolwork and revision notes. But I wasn't sure how much of it had gone in. And I wasn't at all sure I had what it would take for me to walk into an exam room.

I met Maria at the bus stop as usual. She pulled me into a hug.

'You look like shit,' she said helpfully. I laughed in spite of myself.

'With friends like you,' I said.

'No, seriously. You need to start getting more fresh air or something. You're white as a sheet.'

I hadn't really bothered with make up for weeks, and my hair needed a cut so I just had it scraped back in a ponytail. Since the start of study leave, I hadn't really been out. The early days of dressing to be brave and not look like a victim didn't last very long. I'd stopped spending any time in front of the mirror, it was too hard to look at myself.

'Oh well, nothing I can do about it now.' I shrugged. 'Come on, let's walk. Before I change my mind.'

We went into the school through our usual back route, avoiding the main corridors, and made our way to the nook under the stairs. My heart was racing and it was nothing to do with the actual exam.

'Maria. I don't think I can do this,' I said shakily. She chewed her lip.

'Ames. You can. And you have to. If we're getting out of here, we need to get our A-levels. If you don't walk into that exam room, that's step one of the plan right out of the window.'

I sighed loudly. She was right, I had no choice.

'We've got to go to the main entrance and wait outside the hall. Everyone will be there but it'll be five minutes, max. Then they'll let us in and you'll be so preoccupied with emptying the contents of your brain onto the page that you'll stop thinking about anyone else.' She caught my look. 'And I promise you they won't be thinking about you either.'

She grabbed my hand and pulled me to my feet. 'Come on. It's time. Get your game face on, we're doing it.'

As we walked towards the hall, I could see everyone from our year crowded round, all standing in little groups, each holding a couple of pens and a bottle of water. Some had rulers and calculators sticking out of their back pockets. There was a buzz of anticipation, people sharing last minute panics and thoughts about what would come up, freaking each other out about how much or how little they knew. I hesitated at the edge of the crowd and Maria tightened her hold on my hand.

'Come on, we're here now,' she said, pulling me forwards.

That was fine for her to say. But she didn't really know how I was feeling. As we made our way through the group, the conversations stopped – heads turned, and I could feel everyone looking at me. I kept my eyes on the floor but I felt their whispers as I passed. Maria's hand was steady, I focussed on breathing and carried on walking, trying not to hear, trying not to imagine what they were saying. It was so long since I'd seen them all together like this, in a pack, outnumbering me, surrounding me. Memories of comments these people had posted about me came flooding back as I saw faces I'd managed to avoid for weeks. They all seemed to be looking and leering. I felt hot, so hot, and dizzy, but at least the blood now pounding in my ears was starting to drown out the whispering.

'Amy?' I jumped. It was Mrs Jameson. She wasn't trying to hide her look of concern.

'Are you okay, dear?'

I managed to nod.

'Don't worry, natural to feel a bit nervous. You'll be fine. I'm sure you're well prepared.'

Jesus Christ, she still didn't get it. I managed a wobbly half- smile and she patted my arm and moved on.

'Stupid bitch. Can't wait to see the back of her,' said Maria under her breath. I looked at her gratefully. She understood much more than I gave her credit for.

We stood against the wall, waiting for our names to be called.

'Amy Henderson!' shouted Mrs Jameson.

'Good luck,' Maria said, giving my hand a last squeeze. I let go, feeling like a child being left on their first day at school. I moved forwards, through the churning sea of people, gripping my pens and my bottle of water like a life raft. At the door, Mr Dolan thrust a numbered envelope at me. He was standing there with a book of raffle tickets like a cloakroom attendant. I looked at him blankly.

'Your phone, Amy,' he said, as if speaking to a four-year-old. 'You have to give it in.'

'I… I haven't got it,' I said. He looked sceptical. I thought for a horrible second he was going to suggest searching me, but he obviously thought better of it and let me through.

A school hall has a certain smell that never goes, soaked into the faded velour curtains and the gaps between the floor tiles. The ghosts of old school dinners made me feel nauseous as I looked around at the rows and rows of identical desks. I felt hot again, my neck prickling, overwhelmed with a sense of not knowing where to go. I stood paralysed in the centre of the room, as everyone else managed the simple task of finding their own place. An invigilator took pity on me. She squeaked over to me in her supposedly quiet shoes.

'Your name, dear?' she asked. I told her, and she guided me forwards, to the first row of desks, right in front of the stage. I wondered at the many times I had stood on that stage, with a roomful of people looking at me, watching me sing or speak or collect a prize. Now these things all seemed ridiculous, impossible feats of bravery that I couldn't believe had ever actually happened.

'Do you want to take your seat, Amy?' The invigilator was still hovering at my shoulder. I turned to answer her and saw hundreds of faces, all turned in my direction. If I sat, I'd be trapped in their gaze, unable to run away. I tried to breathe through it, but I could feel panic rising. In for four, out for six. She continued waiting, ever more impatiently, for me to sit down. The desks directly behind me were still unoccupied, but as I dithered, I saw two very familiar figures heading my way. As they got nearer, they exchanged a silent nod of encouragement, then looked to where they were going to sit. To give them their due, they both paused, ever so slightly, as we all realised the same thing at the same time. Rosie and Harry were going to be sitting behind me.

'Amy, please sit.'

I sat down and stared straight ahead, my eyes fixed on a patch of sunlight on the stage curtains as I breathed hard, in for four, out for six. Squeak, squeak, squeak – the invigilator walked to the middle of the room and started to go through the instructions.

'You are now under exam conditions…'

Her words were distant, as if I was hearing them from the end of a tunnel. I looked up at the clock – the length of this test is two hours, she said. Two hours in this room. With all these people. With Rosie and Harry within touching distance. My hands shook as I picked up my pen. All around me, I could hear the rustling of papers turning over. The sound was too loud, too echoey. I looked down at my exam paper, crisp and white on the scrubbed wooden desk, and the words started to wiggle and swirl as if the paper was rippling. The pen fell from my hand and clattered to the floor. The heat in my head became too much to bear, the edges of the room started to blur and everything went black.

'Amy! Amy!'

'Stand back, all of you, give her space. Please sit back down at your desks.'

'No, I'm staying with her. Amy? Amy, can you hear me?'

Maria's voice and face swam into focus through the blur. The floor was hard under my head, I was looking at the underside of a desk, complete with remnants of years old chewing gum and pen marks.

'Amy! You're back. Bloody hell, mate, you scared me!'

'Maria Whittaker, please can you return to your desk? This is an exam. We will look after Amy.'

'No, I…'

I took her hand.

'S'okay.' I managed to say.

'You sure?'

I nodded. She gave me an uncertain smile and moved away. The sense of wooziness was starting to leave me and was being replaced by crippling embarrassment. I had just fainted in front of my entire year at the front of the exam hall. As if I hadn't given everyone enough reasons to notice me this year. I closed my eyes, I wanted to die. When I opened them again, Mrs Jameson had taken Maria's place in my line of vision.

'Amy. According to the rules, you ought to try and carry on with your exam, but I am prepared to make a case for you to sit it in the privacy of the head's office. I will supervise you. Do you think you can get up?'

She helped me into a seated position. My head felt a bit light but I thought I could probably stand, with help. I held her arm and she lifted me to my feet. Everyone watched as she guided me out of the room, holding my exam paper, pens and water bottle. I couldn't have felt any more mortified. If any of the looks I'd felt coming in my direction before the exam had been figments of my imagination, now I was in no way imagining it. They were staring, shamelessly, some with pity, some with thinly disguised disdain. I didn't look at Harry. Rosie had the decency to look away as I passed her. Maria gave me a weak smile.

In the head's office, it was cooler and private. Mrs Jameson opened a window and sat me down at the table where many a student had seen out their detentions over the years. I felt like a freak.

'How are you feeling?' she asked, properly worried. Maybe she wasn't such a bitch after all.

'I'm okay. I'm sorry, I don't know...' She brushed my protestations aside.

'We've asked a lot of you, I can see that now. Don't worry, for the rest of your exams I'll give you special compensation and you can sit in a room on your own. For today's though, you'll just have to do your best. You should still have plenty of time if you get started now.'

I thanked her and turned the paper over. Name, candidate number, centre number. I hadn't managed to write anything yet. I filled it all in and tried to concentrate on the first question. I understood each of the words on their own, but the way they formed into a sentence made no sense to me at all. I took a deep breath and tried to calm myself. I read it again. I knew I had to write something. Mrs J was sitting at the head's desk, trying to look as if she wasn't watching me. I wrote a few words. I stopped. I wrote a few more. I stared at the wall. I read the second question to see if that was any easier. I didn't understand that either. My brain tried to take itself back to the hours of study, to visualise all the cards written out in coloured pen, to search vainly for some kind of answers. I wrote what I could, and somehow the time passed. But when she said, 'Please put down your pen, the time is up,' I'd already been sitting there, not writing, for some time.

'Well done, Amy,' she said, taking the paper off me. 'You can go.'

I could hear the hall emptying, voices jabbering, relief, worry, excitement all echoing around the stairwell of the school.

'Would it be okay if I just waited here for a bit?' I asked.

'Of course. Take as long as you need. I just need to go and put your paper with the others.'

I sat and watched through the window as the rest of my year flooded out. Rosie seemed to hang back as she got to the gate, then Harry grabbed her arm and pulled her along with him. I shuddered and looked away. There was a knock at the door and Maria poked her head in.

'You okay?' She was frowning and she looked really tired.

I nodded. 'I'm so sorry, that must have been so distracting for you.'

She shook her head.

'Hey, honestly, it was fine. As long as you're okay. I didn't have a clue about question three though,'

I managed a wobbly laugh.

'There were three questions? If I have even passed that paper I will be amazed,' I said.

'Everyone's gone, shall we get out of here?'

I nodded, picked up my stuff, left the safety of the head's office and the now quiet school building and headed for home.

26
NOW

The smile curled on Andrew's lips. I pressed myself to the wall; if he didn't move I was completely trapped. I desperately wanted to get past. Maybe if I didn't hear him say it, I could get away from him and never see him again. I'd have to quit my job. The best thing in my sad, little life. But at that moment it felt like a worthwhile sacrifice.

'Excuse me, I need to get through,' I said, trying not to look at him. He moved very slightly, not getting out of my way at all, just placing himself where I couldn't avoid looking at him. A flicker of disappointment crossed his face.

'Did you hear me? I said I've remembered. Where I know you from.'

'I heard. But I don't really care. So if you could just...'

He stood back ever so slightly but not quite leaving enough room – to pass him I'd have needed to brush against him. God, no.

'Oh really? You don't care? I don't think that's true, is it? I think you know exactly how I recognised you, and you care rather a lot. Wasn't a gig we both went to, was it? It was a party. Oli and Hugo's party. Remember now?'

Hugo? I tried to locate a face for the name. My hands were sweating, my pulse beating in triplets. I fought to stop myself clapping my hands over my ears, anything to stop hearing what he was about to say.

'Hugo's my mate,' he said, answering my unasked question. 'We played rugby together. He's at Loughborough now, haven't seen him for a while. Used to hang out a bit though. He's Oli's brother,' he added, as all the pieces fell into place.

'Please,' I said, pushing into him. Images of a sticky dining room floor crowded with dancers, a jam-packed hallway, groups of people I'd never seen before or since all crowded into my head as I dived towards the kitchen. I needed some space. But he followed me in.

'I knew I recognised you. All this time I've been asking. And you've never shown any interest in me. Now I get it. You didn't want me to remember.'

Oh fuck, oh fuck. I moved towards the sink, but he was so close to me, I couldn't breathe.

'But you remember me now? Probably not. And don't flatter yourself, not sure I would have remembered you either. I had a lot to drink that night and there were a fair few good-looking women there.' He dropped his voice, and I felt his breath on my ear. 'It's only because I watched you in that video afterwards. More than once. That's where I know you from.'

I slammed the cups into the sink, slopping soapy water all over the floor, twisted round and somehow pushed past him. I ran, out of the heat of the kitchen, out of the fire door and down the couple of steps into the car park. I flopped against the wall, gasping for air like I'd just run a marathon. I could hear his voice coming through the kitchen window. Was he on his phone? Oh god, who was he calling? His jokey tone grated on me even more now I knew who he was. And what he knew. I sank to my knees, arms round my head, protecting myself from the impact as my closely guarded secret shattered my world.

Oh god, don't let him tell Jon. I sobbed, a futile prayer, the idea of my boss seeing those images crippled me. It was like it was happening all over again. I felt like I did that Sunday when Maria turned up with my phone. The horror, the shame, the humiliation. The rising panic. The sense of losing control as the number of views went up and up. That sure and certain knowledge that, whatever Mum said and whatever I hoped, I was never going to escape this.

I could hear Jon's voice in the kitchen now. I strained to hear what he was saying. Didn't sound like more than a couple of short questions and answers. Probably wondering where I am, I thought miserably. He's already let me have a long break to see Maria and now I've disappeared when I was meant to be heading back to help him. Oh god. I had to pull myself together somehow and get back to work.

I shuddered, trying to stop the sobs. In for four, out for six. How to cope in moments of stress, that's what I'd looked up on YouTube. Breathe, breathe. Try and clear your mind. God! That fucking video. That fucking arsehole, Harry. With each in-breath, I tried to force all the feelings back into the depths of myself where I'd tried to keep them hidden for so long. Jon couldn't know. And somehow I had to stop Andrew from telling him.

The fire door swung open again. Jon.

'Amy?'

'I'm here,' I called, my voice trembling.

'Oh, there you are! I thought you were missing in action. I...'

He stopped speaking as he got to the bottom step and found me crouched in a brace position against the wall.

'Whoa! What happened? Are you okay?'

I wiped my face with the back of my hand and tried to smile. It must have been wholly unconvincing, and I didn't dare speak when the sobs were so close to the surface. He crouched down beside me.

'Are you ill? God, how did this happen? You seemed really happy half an hour ago.'

I managed to nod and took a deep breath to stop my voice from shaking. It almost worked.

'I'm sorry. I think... well it was all a bit much for me I guess. Maria showing up like that.'

Jon looked very confused. Who could blame him? In a matter of minutes, I'd gone from a state of euphoria with Maria to a sobbing wreck, and now I was trying to tell him one was a direct result of the other.

'I mean. It was lovely. To see her. Of course it was. Just...' Did someone once say the best way to lie was to include a bit of the truth? Maybe not, but I thought I'd try it.

'Just... I haven't ever mixed my two lives. Home and here. I mean. There's stuff in my past that... well, that I'd rather forget. So seeing Maria here, in this world... I guess it brought back some unwelcome feelings.'

I looked at Jon properly, wondering if there was any part of what I'd just said that was credible. I was surprised that he was nodding, his expression one of empathy and understanding.

'Kiddo, you are speaking to the right person there. I know exactly what you're saying. No need to explain further. Do you want the rest of the day off? Take a bit of time out?'

I shook my head vigorously. It must be nearly three, Andrew would be leaving soon anyway and the very last thing I wanted was time on my own.

'No, I'll be okay. I'll just go and wash my face. Then I'll be fine.'

Jon looked relieved. He patted me on the shoulder, then stood up and put his hand under my elbow, guiding me to my feet.

'You sure?'

I nodded. 'Let's go back inside.'

With Jon there beside me I found the strength to walk past Andrew. I didn't take my eyes off the floor as we went through the kitchen.

'Hey, there you both are!' he said falsely. I ignored him and prayed with everything I had that he wasn't in a mood to say anything more about his recent realisation in front of our boss.

27
THEN

I didn't tell Mum the full extent of the disaster that was my first exam. But someone must have done, because for the rest of them she insisted on driving me in and picking me up. I suspected Maria, although maybe school had called her. I didn't ask. But either way, without consultation and without making a fuss, she just said, 'I'll take you in tomorrow, Amy.' And that was it. No further discussion.

Nothing was as bad as that first one. Mainly because Mrs Jameson was as good as her word and somehow got me special dispensation to sit in the head's office on my own. God knows what she told whoever it was who had to give permission – I hoped she'd gone with a general concern about mental health, rather than anything too detailed. Which was true enough – my mental health was, still is, a bit of a concern. Blacking out in an exam hall was pretty dramatic. But there was much more to it than that. Bit by bit, my world got smaller and smaller. When I look back, I don't know why I stopped fighting. How I felt in those early days, an anger against Harry and the others and what they'd done. Thinking there was a way to get justice, to make someone pay. That anger somehow died, replaced with an overwhelming shame. I gave up trying to make contact with Rosie. When I was anywhere near her, we just didn't look at each other. I seemed to see Harry wherever I went, always strutting around looking confident and relaxed. Sometimes he acknowledged me with a nod, more often than not he didn't. I hated him. But I had to accept that there was nothing I could do. I wasn't strong enough.

Mum was amazing – she managed all the practicalities of dealing with the video. I didn't really ask how. Whenever she started to try and talk to me about it, I shut down. I didn't want to hear that there were searches you could do to find images. Or key words that would give you an alert if it popped up anywhere. I didn't want to think about the possibility it would ever pop up anywhere. And it didn't matter if it did or not, the damage was done. I was already defeated. Mum didn't give up, but each time I told her to stop talking about it or refused to take whatever action she was suggesting, she looked just a little bit more crushed. I didn't have it in me to do it for her. I don't think I realised how much she did without me. We didn't talk all that much, at that time. Probably I should have talked to her. Or been more open with Maria. But I was trying to protect them from the worst of it.

And sometimes it was bad. I had nights when I couldn't sleep, dreams where naked images of me were on billboards and advertising hoardings, where people were pointing and laughing at me in the street. I'd wake sitting bolt upright, sweating, my heart racing. I'd try to calm down and get back to sleep, telling myself they were only dreams. But the way those dreams made me feel – ashamed, dirty, worthless – I couldn't shake those feelings when I woke up.

So I got through the exams. Eight written exams and a French oral. Eight papers with my name and candidate number and my best stab at the answers to the questions. I don't know what it was but the knowledge I had seemed to refuse to come out. I'd look at the paper and every time I felt the same sensation – the words became detached from their meaning and my brain wasn't able to decode what the question was asking me. I'd read it, over and over, but I just couldn't make sense of it. So I'd write what I knew, in the hope that some of it would overlap with what I was being asked. Even then I could only concentrate for a few minutes at a time, then I'd have to pause and stare at the wall for a bit, like I needed a mental screen refresh before I could carry on.

When exams were all over, I just went into myself. I stayed at home, often in bed, curtains closed, trying not to think. Mum would come in, let the daylight in, bring me tea and toast, suggest things I might want to do. And I wanted to do them, for her sake. I wanted to go into town with her and get a coffee and look for new trainers. I wanted to go for a walk with her to get some fresh air. I wanted to try, to make myself be normal again. I just couldn't. I was detached. Down. I felt hopeless, literally without hope. I didn't want to see anyone. And the more I thought about my goal of getting away, doing the exams, being able to leave, the more I felt like I'd screwed up. Those offers I'd had from uni, two As and a B from York, three Bs from De Montfort – they'd seemed so doable. Now, I wasn't even confident I'd passed. Well, probably English. But History and French? I shuddered at the memory of the French oral exam where every word I ever knew dried up on my lips as she asked me to discuss, of all things, the negative impact of social media.

So, six weeks somehow passed without me earning any money or doing anything to prepare me for leaving home. Most days I didn't even make it out of my room. But they went by regardless, every day just like the day before, and the one before that. And then it was Thursday. The seventeenth of August. Results day.

Maria had phoned on the Wednesday to see if I wanted to go over to hers for our pre-exam results vigil. We'd established it at GCSEs – pizza, crap horror film, late night, and then a walk to school together to find out the real horror. Of course, there had never been any real horror – we'd all done well. All three of us. Me, Rosie, Maria.

'So, what do you reckon? *Dead by Dawn* or *Halloween II*?' she asked. When I said I didn't think I'd be coming over, but thanks for asking, she sounded resigned to it, like she'd been before prom, and on every Saturday she'd invited me to do something with her. I wondered if she was going to get together with anyone else instead, but I couldn't even muster up any jealousy. Who could blame her if she did? As best friends go, she was a great one and I was a wash out. The thought did nothing to make me feel better.

The sun woke me. Of course it was a lovely day. The kind of day where you'd get your results and take them off to a pub garden and spend the afternoon with your friends, celebrating or drowning your sorrows. I wouldn't be doing either. I wished I'd opted to get them sent to me. I turned my face to the wall and tried to forget about it.

I must have dozed off because I jumped when Mum came in, tea in hand, smile fixed on her face. She pulled back the curtains with a flourish, forcing me to blink in the daylight.

'Alright lazy bones. Here's some tea.'

She put it on my bedside table, wincing ever so slightly at the untouched tea and toast she'd brought me the day before. I didn't say anything but she sat down on the bed regardless.

'So! Results day!' she carried on brightly. Whenever she spoke to me, her sentences always sounded like they were peppered with exclamation marks, full of enthusiasm and energy. It must have been exhausting for her.

'Are you meeting Maria? Do you want a lift into school? I can take you, I've said I'll be in late today.'

I still didn't say anything. Well, I might have grunted. But I wasn't buying the act. Pretending I might have made plans. Being all cheerful. I rolled over, my back to her. I thought that would be enough of a signal that I didn't want to talk. But it seemed that Mum had had enough of not talking. She cracked.

'Amy! For god's sake. Get up! This is enough.' Startled, I turned to look at her. She was ranting, words spilling over themselves, a catalogue of reasons why the soft touch wasn't working. How she'd more or less given up her life to keep an eye on me, how selfish I was, how I was doing nothing to help myself, how we just couldn't go on like this. She looked really tired, now she wasn't putting on a smile anymore, but her anger gave her energy and she was almost shouting. I let her carry on, stunned.

'This is what you wanted, you said. To get your A-levels. Go to university, get away. But look at you! You haven't been out of the house for weeks. How on earth do you think you can leave home when you can't even get out of bed to go and get your results?'

She looked at me in desperation, but I couldn't find any words, so she stood up abruptly and left the room.

I guess it sounds harsh, what she was saying. A child psychologist would probably have a fit. But in a really weird way, I think that's what I needed. She had been pussy-footing around me – we both knew it. And it wasn't helping. I'd spent so long on my own in that room that I'd lost sight of my goal. In my head, I'd failed everything so there was no point. But something in Mum's anger got through to me. I had to try.

I got up and followed her out of the room. She was on her own bed, hugging a cushion to her, staring into space. She looked so alone. I realised we hadn't hugged for weeks. I started to cry.

'Mum. You're right. I haven't tried. I just couldn't face it. I'm so, so sorry.'

She opened her arms to me and pulled me into her. We rocked together on her bed, both crying now. It was hard to get the words out but I managed it.

'Please will you? Drive me into school? I want to go in and get my results.'

She pulled away and looked me right in the eyes and nodded.

'Of course, my darling. Whatever you want.' She smiled slightly through her own tears and smoothed my hair from my face. 'Can I suggest a shower before we go?'

I managed to shower, wash my hair and put on real clothes. I had to change twice, my jeans hung off me. Six weeks of cold tea and uneaten toast hadn't done me any favours. But I did my best. I put on a skirt and t-shirt and Converse high-tops, pulled a baseball hat on and got into the car. Mum reached over and squeezed my hand.

'Ready?'

It was all very well being proud of myself for getting out of the house. As we got closer and closer to school, my shaky sense of purpose started to ebb away, until I was left with a churning stomach and legs that didn't remember how to move. My hands were shaking, I didn't really trust myself to speak, let alone open the door and get out of the car. As we neared the gates, I pulled the hat down over my eyes.

'Mum,' I said quietly. 'I... I can't. Could you go in for me? I'll just wait here.'

Mum didn't answer, just pulled into the staff carpark and stopped the car. I kept my eyes down, not wanting to see the flurry of my year coming out with their results slips. There were way too many people I didn't want to run into. A tap on the window made me jump. I turned to Mum in disbelief, but she was smiling. I turned around – there was Maria, pressed up to the window, pulling a face. She stepped back to let me open the door.

'Well, fancy seeing you here,' she said.

'Have you got your results?' I asked. She shook her head.

'Course not. I was waiting for you. Had to watch *Dead by Dawn* last night on my own. I'm not going in there on my own too.'

I looked over at Mum. She gave me a nod.

'I'll be right here, darling,' she said.

Hanging tightly onto Maria, I walked towards the main entrance of the school. We must have looked a right pair; Maria was practically holding me up, my legs were so wobbly and unsure of themselves. I could see the window of the office where I'd sat all my exams. I sent up a quick prayer that the hours I'd spent in there hadn't been wasted. As we got to the steps, I ground to a halt, my feet refusing to carry on.

'You're okay. You can do this,' Maria whispered, holding me tighter. I took a deep breath and tried to move forwards. I was feeling light-headed; god forbid that I fainted dramatically again. I tried to focus on putting one foot in front of the next and not think about all the people inside the building who may or may not be looking out of the windows at me. My hands started to sweat as Maria guided me through the door. I hesitated again, but she put one hand on my back and steered me to the left, towards the head's office.

'Hey! Shouldn't we be going up there?' I gestured at the staircase to the common room, from where I could hear sounds of excited chatter and the odd whoop.

'Uh-uh.' She shook her head. 'Not us. We're special.'

She led me into the office. Mrs Jameson was there with two named envelopes, one each.

'Amy. Maria,' she said, handing them over as if we were just the next in a long line of students, when we all knew that everyone else was upstairs. They must have had it all planned, Mum, Maria, Mrs J. They must have worked it all out for me. I wasn't sure whether to feel loved or betrayed that they'd been plotting behind my back. But I looked at my friend, standing there, waiting to open her own envelope until I was steady enough to open mine, and I knew.

'Thank you,' I whispered. She nodded, silently. There was a moment of quiet, broken only by sounds of joy from above us.

'So? Are you going to open them then?' asked Mrs J. I laughed. Of course. The results. I'd almost forgotten that the sheer act of walking into that school wasn't the main reason I was there.

'It's okay, you know. Three Cs.'

Maria was back at mine. Mum had given us a lift and gone off to work, leaving us to work out what happened next. Maria had done well – two As and a B, enough to get her first choice, Edinburgh. I was staring at the paper in my hand, trying to see if staring long and hard would make it change for the better.

'Honestly, Ames. Three Cs. For what you've been through, I think it's a fucking triumph.'

I nodded. I kind of agreed. But still. Neither York nor De Montfort were interested in me.

'You could get school to phone them, maybe?' she suggested. 'Tell them what you've been though...' I cut her off with a shake of the head.

'No way. I've had enough special treatment. And I don't want anyone at uni to know anything about it. It's fine. There are always other spaces you can get through Clearing, right? Chuck me the laptop.'

Somewhere or other on the UCAS form was info about Clearing. I hadn't paid it much attention before, but I logged into my account and started clicking around. Lists of courses and unis that still had places available. I tried to work out where I could find what I needed. Maria picked up her phone and did some scrolling. I'd just managed to find a list of unis offering English when she said, 'Would you fucking believe it?'

I looked up. She was fuming.

'Fucking Harry. Three As. Into Durham. With a rugby scholarship. How is that okay?'

I shrugged.

'It's not okay. It's shit. But that's Harry all over, isn't it? Coming out on top whatever happens. At least I didn't see him today.'

Maria looked confused.

'I thought you'd be mad. Don't you want him to suffer for what he did?'

I shrugged again.

'I've told you before. There's nothing I can do now. I wasn't able to go to the police. I just want to forget about it.'

That bit was true, I did want to forget about it. But of course it bothered me. Of course I wanted him to suffer for what he'd done. Everything about the fact that Harry was still just living his life as if nothing had happened was testament to everything that was shit about the world. But I was the one who could have put a stop to that. And I just wasn't strong enough. So for my own sanity, I had to try and pretend. Maria looked unconvinced by all the shrugging.

'I'll never forget about it. But good for you. And at least you know which area of the country to avoid, I guess.'

I nodded.

'If I never see that boy again it will be too soon. Look here. This one. Three Cs. I'm going to call them.'

28
NOW

The tiles were cold against my cheek and I leant there, wondering how long I could reasonably stay in the bathroom. Jon was being amazingly kind for someone who had no idea what was wrong with me. Surely he was going to run out of patience soon, with my strange behaviour and disappearing acts. And while I was trying and failing to pull myself together, safe in the toilet where no one could see me, Andrew was out there on his own with Jon, telling him God knows what. It was like a game of Russian roulette. I put my head in my hands and searched for some kind of inner guidance.

I thought leaving home would be enough. Maybe I should have changed my name. Dyed my hair. Moved abroad. But deep down, there was almost a sense of sick inevitability. Somehow I'd always known this would happen, one day. The problem was that I'd never quite worked out how I would handle it when it did.

I stood up, testing my legs, wondering if they'd hold me, and caught a glimpse of myself in the mirror. I looked shocking – as well as the red eyes I'd clearly been dragging my hands through my hair and I was all blotchy.

Knock, knock.

'Is there someone in there?'

Bollocks. Decision made for me.

'Yeah, just a minute,' I called back. I smoothed my hair as best I could and dried my face with a paper towel. It wasn't great damage limitation but it would have to do. I checked the time. Nearly three. Thank God for that. Andrew would be leaving. I opened the toilet door and made a beeline for the counter, hoping that surrounding myself with customers and noise would give me a similar level of protection to a locked toilet door. Andrew wouldn't be able to say anything to me, that was the main thing for now. I gave myself a little shake and tried to get back into waitress mode.

Jon looked up from serving coffees and motioned to me to stay where I was.

'Amy, you can stay out back for a bit if you want?' he suggested quietly. 'Until you're feeling better?'

I was caught, wanting to hide but knowing who was in the kitchen, but then Andrew appeared from the staff room, holding his rugby jacket. I nodded gratefully at Jon and hovered, my face towards the wall so I didn't catch Andrew's eye.

As he passed me, he reached over and tapped my shoulder, gently, ever so gently, but his touch ran through my arm like an electric shock and I twisted round to look at him.

'See you next time, Amy.'

I looked straight into his eyes and he gave me a sick, pervy wink that hit me right in the stomach.

I spent most of the hour and a bit after Andrew left doing nothing. I watched him leave, taking the back route through the car park, his jacket gradually disappearing round a corner in the direction of the uni. Then I carried on standing there, unable to move, looking at all the people coming and going, in groups, in pairs, on their own. Looking at their phones, chatting, wandering along with earpieces doing a good impression of talking to themselves. Connected people, people with somewhere to be, someone to meet, things to do. I felt a pang of emptiness, wondering what it was like to be one of them, with their friendships, their relationships. But that wasn't what I wanted, was it? This life where no one called, no one made or cancelled plans – that was my choice. I didn't have anyone following me, liking me, sending me snaps. I thought I'd protected myself. But in spite of the contactless, connectionless life I'd managed to live, it had found me out. That fucking video had come back. If you could say it had ever really gone away.

As it started to get dark outside, I pulled out some tired-looking celery from the fridge and started to chop it. Andrew had left the kitchen spotless, there were no real jobs, but I needed something to do. Jon could turn it into soup. Or one of his Waldorf salads, keep the old folks happy. I really didn't care. It was just a way to stop pulling at my sleeves, trying to think of any possible way that this wasn't going to end in disaster. What was Andrew doing right now? Messaging someone - *Hey mate, you'll never guess who I'm working with. Remember that video you sent me? Yeah that one. You still got it?* I died inside. It was all happening again. It was never, ever going to stop.

I heard the doorbell, Jon greeting someone, girls' voices. Maria! Oh, thank God. Maria. I'd almost forgotten. I started to shove the celery into a Tupperware. It was like Maria had turned up just when I needed her. Like a guardian angel. Enough keeping it all in. Maria was here and this had all happened, and what better person to talk to. I really didn't know how or why I'd stopped telling Maria everything.

'Hey! It's twenty-five past four.' Jon poked his head round the door frame. 'You want to call it a day? Your friends are here.'

He looked a bit confused at the debris of the chopped celery and the burgeoning Tupperware.

'I thought maybe soup tomorrow?' I said, by way of explanation.

'Yeah, sure. You get off, I'll finish up.' He took the knife off me with a look of slight relief. 'You okay now?' he said with a sideways glance.

I nodded. 'I will be. It's great that Maria's here. She's my best friend. I...'

'I know. Someone to talk to. You go and have a lovely evening.' He stopped what he was doing and turned to face me, looking me straight in the eyes. 'But, you know, if you ever need to talk, I'm quite a good listener.'

I looked away and gently bit my lip. I imagined how pathetic I looked, with my too-long sleeves, my blotchy face still red from the crying.

'Thanks. I do know. Thanks.' I didn't know if I should say anything else. He probably did mean it. But I'd never, ever tell him. Still, it was nice of him to offer.

'So go! They're waiting.'

They! Of course. Maria had a friend. Oh, well, she'd just have to sit and listen or watch Netflix. I really needed to offload.

I dashed out into the café, on the way to the staff room to grab my bag and coat.

'Maria! I'll be two seconds,' I called over. Maria stood up, and so did her friend. My legs lost the power to move and my mouth fell open. Maria's friend was Rosie. Maria was there, in the café, with Rosie. I turned to stone. Maria quickly came over to me, leaving Rosie standing awkwardly where she was.

'Mate. Stay calm. It's not what you think. We can explain. We can explain everything.'

I wanted to lash out, to hurt her, to show her how she'd just torn me apart.

'We? Since when did you and Rosie become "we" again? What the actual fuck? How could you do this to me?'

Jon appeared, drawn by the raised voices. 'Girls? Is everything okay?'

I turned to him. 'No. Everything is not okay. Please, Jon. Please get them out of here.'

Shaking, I turned and marched back to the kitchen. I couldn't hear what they said, there were a few seconds of quiet murmuring, then the door opened. And closed.

I gave it a minute then ventured back into the café. The sign was turned to "Closed" and Jon was standing at the door, watching the empty street where Maria and Rosie had walked away.

'They've gone,' he said.

I nodded, but I was still shaking, my veins bursting with adrenaline and an overwhelming sense of betrayal. Jon motioned to the nearest table and pulled out a chair.

'Amy. Please. Let's talk.'

I shook my head, vigorously. 'I'm fine. I just need to go home.'

I stumbled into the staff room, leaving him hovering in the middle of the empty café, and grabbed my stuff as quickly as I could.

'Amy, really, I...' Jon moved towards me as I crossed the floor, but I was pulling on my jacket, slinging the bag over my shoulder, heading for the door, anything not to look him in the eyes.

'I'm fine. I'll see you next week.'

And I walked away, turning left out of the door where the others had turned right.

29
THEN

Having spent so much time holed up in my bedroom, leaving it felt like much less of a wrench than I'd anticipated. The weeks between getting my place at uni and actually going had felt like a waiting game. I was ready to go. Nervous, yes. But ready.

I looked around. Mum had insisted I take my favourite duvet cover with me, so the bed had travelled back in time to when I was about ten and everything I owned was patterned with pink butterflies. One wall was bare – I'd taken down my Banksy poster to put up in my new room. Something to make it feel like home. I'd left everything else more or less as it was, tidy now, the dirty cups and plates all back in the kitchen since I'd been managing to eat with Mum most days. It all looked a bit off balance – one empty wall and the rest of it cluttered with a lifetime's accumulation of posters, old birthday cards and photos, like a shrine to my school days. The crossed-out exam timetable was still stuck to the pinboard. I tore it off, screwed it into a ball and chucked it in the bin.

The doorbell went and I heard Mum say hi, then she called up the stairs.

'Amy! Someone to see you.' I heard Maria's laugh and pelted down the stairs.

'Hey! I thought you were off today too.' I gave her a big hug. 'Come in.'

'Yeah, we're going in an hour. But I wanted to say goodbye in person. As you didn't make it last night.'

I looked at the floor. There'd been leaving drinks at the New Inn, just a small group, Maria had said. Nothing to make me feel uneasy. Which was code for "Rosie won't be there". Of course I hadn't gone, although I'd told her I would try.

'Thank you,' I said.

She rubbed my arm. 'No need.'

'Girls, go into the lounge, you don't need to stand on the doorstep,' Mum called from the kitchen. 'Who wants tea?'

We both said no to the tea but moved into the lounge as she suggested. Maria followed me in and we took up our usual places, me curled on the sofa, her on the chair next to the fireplace.

'I got you a little present,' she said, putting a brown paper gift bag down on the coffee table. My hand flew to my mouth.

'Oh! I haven't got you anything. I didn't think. I feel awful.'

She shook her head, dismissing my apology.

'Ames, it's fine. You've been somewhere else these past few weeks, don't worry about it. I'm just so pleased you're really doing this. It's the new start you need.'

I nodded, although the butterflies in my stomach were going crazy. I hoped she was right.

'You going to open it then?' she asked, pushing it towards me. I picked it up and took out a frame, wrapped in tissue paper. I looked at her quizzically.

'Just so you don't forget about me.'

It was a collage of pictures of me and Maria, each photo pegged onto strings in a wooden frame. One in school uniform, maybe year seven, lying on the playing field one sunny lunchtime. A selfie in front of the mirror in the toilets of our favourite bar. The two of us in shorts and bikini tops on a beach in Bournemouth on a weekend away the summer before. And one of us in impossibly short dresses and Christmas hats, arms around each other. In that one there was a stray arm just to one side of me where she'd cut Rosie out.

She was watching me closely as I looked at it. I just didn't know what to say.

'Don't you like it?' She sounded worried, disappointed in me again. I burst into tears and ran over to her for a hug.

'You're kidding. I love it. It's just, all these memories... They already feel like so long ago. And you've been here all this time and I've wasted so many chances to make new ones.' I sobbed on her shoulder. 'I'd give everything I have to go back to the day before Oli's party. To tell Harry I wasn't going because I had work and an essay to write. To not feel like I've felt for the last three months.' I flapped my hand at the photo frame. 'To have more times like these. Happy times.'

She nodded.

'Me too, Ames. More than anything. But we'll have them again. It's a new start. You can come to Edinburgh and I'll come and visit you too. We can do it.'

I gave her a big hug and pulled away.

'Yes. We can do it.' I smiled. But I didn't really believe it.

She left shortly afterwards, a text from her dad reminding her they needed to leave. She hugged me and Mum, and we promised to FaceTime every day. Mum closed the door and looked at me.

'Okay then? Time for us to do the same.'

'Yep. Just let me get my stuff.'

I took the photo frame upstairs – the case was already full to bursting, I was going to have to fit it into my rucksack. I opened the top – there was my old teddy, Mum must have put him in without me knowing. I took him out, tucked him into the pink butterfly bed, carefully squeezed the frame in between a couple of towels and I was done. Ready to go. I gave the room a last glance and called for Mum.

'Ready. Can you give me a hand with the bags?'

My heart was thumping as I closed the door but I tried to hold on to the thought that this was what I had been waiting for all this time. Escape.

It took us more than three hours to get to my new home. I felt quite chatty when we first set off, me and Mum on a little road trip, butterflies in my stomach that could just have been excitement. But as we got nearer, the reality hit. The outskirts of this unfamiliar town seemed like a huge metropolis to me and I got quieter and quieter. Mum shot me a few side glances, and started chatting more and more, using that fake cheerful voice she'd had all summer. At that moment, I didn't mind it so much. At least it meant I didn't really have to speak.

'Look, there are lots of other cars laden with stuff, do you think they're heading to uni too?' she asked. I shuddered. People in cars that shortly I might meet in person. I nodded and mumbled a kind of reply, but my brain was racing. I'd avoided all of the Facebook groups and other "getting to know you" type stuff that the university had suggested. But I suddenly realised that most other people had probably connected with someone at least, been chatting, following each other on Instagram. Working out if they shared any friends or knew anyone in common. A familiar sense of dread started to creep through me, silencing the butterflies.

King's Campus was modern and dynamic and, to me, terrifying. We were just one of hundreds of little families, parking up, dragging their cases and bags through the quad next to the hall, girls and boys all my age, probably a bit nervous too. But not in the way I was. I bumped my case along, avoiding the eyes of everyone else who seemed really happy to say hello to each other. I could feel Mum watching me as she hoisted the rucksack up onto her shoulder and tried to balance it with the box she was carrying.

We got to my block, which was round the back of the main accommodation. The dad of the family in front of us saw Mum struggling with her box and paused to hold the door. She gave him a smile.

'Thank you. I hadn't realised I'd have to carry all this stuff such a long way!'

'Oh, that's nothing. We're on our second trip.' He nodded up the stairs to where a boy and his mum were manoeuvring a big duffle bag. The dad let the door go once we were through and picked up a couple of holdalls.

'I got the heavy ones,' he said. 'Tells me he's brought some books, I suppose that's a good sign.'

He was one of those over-friendly, over-confident middle-aged men who looked like he enjoyed a bit too much red wine. I disliked him, but Mum seemed happy to chat as we all headed up the same staircase.

'Yes, Amy's been reading a lot already, I think she was thinking she might have better things to do when she got here.'

Oh right! Is that the parental chat of the new student? How little work you thought your kids might do once they were let loose into the world of university? I was surprised Mum was entering into that. Surely she didn't really think I was there for a wild social life?

I was even more surprised when she said, 'Have you had a long journey?'

My face flushed. Was she about to tell him where we'd come from? I tried desperately to catch her eye, but she wasn't looking my way, she was listening to the boorish dad talking about motorway numbers I didn't recognise and how congested they'd been. Luckily he was much more interested in hearing himself speak than asking Mum any questions, and we got to the top of the stairs before he finished.

'Mum!' I hissed, as she stopped to let him open the door. She turned, surprised, a look of worry on her face. I frowned and shook my head, a silent warning to her to shut up that I hoped she'd be able to interpret. But the dad had already moved on, towards an open door, presumably his son's room. He dropped any fake interest in the conversation, chucked a 'good luck' over his shoulder and went in. Mum looked at me, confused.

'What's wrong? I was just being friendly.'

I shook my head again. 'Just don't,' I said, shortly. She looked stung. Luckily my room was through the next fire door, so we had the distraction of finding the key and getting in.

It was small, characterless, the walls bare, a single bed, desk and chair the only furniture, apart from a built-in cupboard that served as a bookcase and wardrobe. The window looked out onto a grassy bank and path that lead to the dining hall in the main building. More students with their families were walking down the path. People seemed to be approaching from all sides. I felt like I was in the centre of a boiling cauldron, all these people bubbling around it, gradually getting pulled in.

'It's nice!' Mum said, resuming the cheerful voice and starting to open the box, get out mugs, a kettle. It wasn't nice. At best it was okay, slightly too small, with no redeeming features. The walls were painted breeze blocks – the last resident had obviously had them covered in posters as there were bits of sellotape at the top where it was too high for the cleaner to reach. I hated it.

Mum was unpacking like a demon.

'Here, let's get your bed made, that will make it feel more like home. And put your poster up. I've put the mugs on that shelf there, there's a plug next to it so you can use the kettle. Will be nice to have your own means of making tea, you can invite friends in too, although I'm not sure where they'd sit! Should have thought, you could have brought that beanbag. I guess the kitchen is further down the corridor, the showers and stuff are just next to you, did you see them on the way past?' She carried on talking, incessantly, anything to hide the growing inevitability that any moment she was going to have to leave me here. I let her help with the duvet cover, but then I took her hands gently.

'Mum. Thank you. For bringing me. And… everything. But you can go now. I think I can take it from here.'

She tried to smile but her eyes were wet, her lip trembling in that way she had that always reminded me she'd been a child once, too. She hugged me, so tightly that I could feel the stifled sobs in her breathing. I tried to hold it together. I didn't want to be crying when she left me.

'Okay, darling.' She pulled away, taking a deep breath and trying to smile again. 'I'll get off then. Long drive home.'

I nodded and smiled weakly.

'Drive safely, Mum. I'll talk to you later.'

She kissed me, and I let her leave, closing the door behind her so I didn't have to watch her walk away.

Alone in my room, I sat on the bed. I took in the solid walls, the grey, office-style carpet, the slight chip at the bottom of the full-length mirror, the back of the door. I had a sinking feeling as I realised how much time I was going to be spending in there. Half-heartedly, I carried on unpacking, putting the books Mum thought I had read onto the shelves, underwear and socks into drawers. I wished I'd thought of sellotape for the poster. There must be a shop on campus where you could buy things like that, I told myself, knowing even as I formed the thought that Banksy would be sitting rolled up in the corner for some time before I managed that.

I pulled a towel from the rucksack and Maria's present fell onto the floor. Seeing our faces in the context of that cell of a room was too much for me. The lid came off the emotion I'd been trying to hold in all day and I sobbed. The Amy from before the party smiled up at me as my tears fell onto the photo frame, and I had that feeling of despair that almost feels like relief, the sobs coming from a place deep inside me that I had been trying not to acknowledge. I wanted so much to forget everything that had happened to me. To find the bits of my memory where I kept the shame, the humiliation, the paranoia and to erase them. Cut them out so they were no longer a part of me. Then maybe I could go back to being me as I was before. Someone who had fun, who laughed, who had friends, people she fancied. Someone who could talk about their dreams and hopes and the plans she had for the future and actually believe she might carry them out.

There was a knock at the door. I jumped. Who the hell was that? I held my breath and tried to be silent. Another knock.

'Hey! Room 16? Is anyone there?'

My heart slowed down a little bit. It was just someone being nice.

'Ummm... yeah. I'm here.'

'We're going down to dinner, do you want to come?' A gaggle of voices, some laughing, a buzz of general excitement I didn't share.

'Uh, yeah, I'm not quite ready, I'll be down in a minute.'

'Okay!' The voices moved away. I peered through the spy hole – there was a group of about ten or twelve of them, moving towards the stairs. I didn't want to go. I looked in the mirror, smoothed my hair down. My eyes looked red and puffy. I didn't want to meet people looking like a cry-baby. And I wasn't all that hungry.

I checked the door again a minute or two later; the corridor was empty. I picked up the kettle and went to the bathroom – Mum was right, it was just next to my room. No one there, what a relief. I scampered back to my room and put the kettle on. Mum had brought four mugs in preparation for the friends I'd be asking in for tea and a chat. I wondered if she really thought that would ever happen.

As I waited for the water to boil, I looked again at the photos of Maria. I wondered what she was up to now, in her new halls in Edinburgh. Not hiding in her room, I was pretty sure. And I was totally convinced that Harry would already be strutting around in Durham, flirting, drinking, making himself at home. Why had I let him do this to me? Reduce me to this pathetic girl who couldn't even take up an invitation to go down for dinner. I tried to imagine myself walking into a crowded dining room, picking up a plate, finding somewhere to sit. Everyone looking up at me, the girl who was late. I couldn't do it. I had missed my chance; I should have gone with the ones who'd knocked.

I took the lid off the biscuit tin that Mum had filled for me and my fictitious future afternoon tea guests. There was a note, folded over, "Amy" written on it in her turquoise scrawl. I unfolded it.

You've made it! I'm so proud of you darling. I'll miss you so much, but I'm sure you'll have an amazing time with lots of new friends. You're so brave. Never forget how much you've achieved to get to where you are.

All my love, Mum

I felt a stab of pain – for Mum, for Maria, for me. The me I should have been, the one who would have been in the dining room now, eating macaroni cheese and making new friends. The note fell from my hand and the teabag stewed in the mug as I looked out of my window. I could see light spilling from the crowded dining hall, where the other freshers were making a start on their new lives.

30
NOW

On balance, I'd decided that after the previous weekend's dramatic exit it would be better if I arrived at work late. It didn't seem that busy when I walked in, and it was never a problem if I was late anyway, but Jon noticed. I mouthed him a quick 'sorry', but I could tell I hadn't got away with it. He was going to want to talk. But I didn't want to. When he'd messaged to see if I could do Thursday, I'd even contemplated turning it down. In some moments in the last five relatively sleepless nights, I'd even contemplated never coming in again. But then what did I have left? At least Andrew wouldn't be in on a Thursday.

I hung my bag and my coat up in the cloakroom. My phone lay in my pocket, notifications all off so I couldn't see the unopened messages and voicemails I'd had from Maria. I didn't want to hear it. There was nothing, nothing she could say that could explain how she'd dared to bring Rosie back into my life. Clearly it must have been Maria all along – how else had Rosie found the café on Instagram to send that message? Maria must have told her where I was, there was no other explanation. The betrayal was total. I didn't need to hear her try and explain.

Within fifteen minutes of being in the café, I'd dropped a tray, tripped over the food bin and scalded my arm. I was livid – with myself, the bin, the milk frother and the whole fucking world. I stomped off to the kitchen, hoping Jon hadn't noticed. Although that was unlikely, he probably felt like an angry bull had just charged at him.

He followed me in a few minutes later, finding me sweeping up broken pots, cake crumbs and potato peelings with an ice pack strapped to my arm.

'So, are we okay? That was quite an entrance.'

He flipped the bin open for me, and I tipped the contents of the dustpan into it angrily, narrowly avoiding dumping it all onto his feet.

'Oh, sorry, Jon, I...'

'Hey. It's okay.' He put his hand on my ice-free arm. 'Look. I'd really like you to tell me what's up. After last Saturday. I've been worried. And you seem really rattled today. Wanna talk about it?'

Did I want to talk about it? Well, no, not really. I shook my head, not trusting myself to say anything. He watched me for a minute, dodging some more debris from the dustpan as I carried on clearing up the mess. As someone who didn't talk much about himself, I thought he might just leave me alone, but it seemed he wasn't going to let it lie.

'You know, I'm not trying to be nosy, but it really does help to talk to someone, when there's something wrong. And even if I'm not the most sensitive person on the planet, I can't help noticing that things haven't been so good for you lately.' He waved at the still messy floor and my damaged arm. He seemed to think my lack of response was an invitation to carry on.

'I only cause a scene of devastation on this kind of scale when there's something really bothering me. Or on the morning after the night before, assuming the night before was largely lost in a bottle of whiskey. And you don't drink, or so you tell me, so my conclusion is that there is something bothering you.'

I looked at him, then down at the shards of ceramic and sticky jam smudges on the floor. My arm was still throbbing under the ice pack and suddenly it was all too much. I started to cry – not the noiseless, pretty crying like they do in films – full-on snot, tears and an instantly red face.

'Whoah! Hey, it's okay. Here, let me get you some kitchen paper.'

He gave me the tissue and I sobbed into it, half-heartedly wiping away the snot. But I couldn't stop. There was too much to cry about. Maria, Rosie, the friends I didn't have. The future I couldn't imagine. Jamie. Andrew. The video. The video. The fucking video. What was I going to do? The sobs threatened to overwhelm me, until he put his arm round me and guided me over to the fire door.

'Come on, let's go out here. We'll hear if anyone comes in, you need to cool down a bit.'

Gulping air seemed to fuel the crying even more. Jon passed me more kitchen towel and waited until I was able to speak.

'Jon, I'm sorry. I know, I haven't been myself. And it's just been a shitty, shitty week,' I managed after some prolonged blubbing. 'I'll be okay. In a minute.'

He looked unconvinced.

'Okay. Well, that would be good. But they don't sound like the kind of sobs that have only been brewing for a few days, young lady. That sounds like deep, unadulterated, long-term misery. And believe me, I know very well what that sounds like.'

I vaguely registered that he had just told me something about himself. But it was the wrong moment. Knowing my boss had reasons to be miserable was something I'd have to think about another time.

'I just... it's...'

The effort of finding words to describe why I was standing in a car park, clutching kitchen paper to my face and falling apart was too much. I cried with renewed vigour, the lid well and truly off and everything spilling out. Jon gently took hold of my shoulders and turned me towards him.

'Alright. Listen. So, this is what we're going to do. You're going to stay here and compose yourself. Then probably go and wash your face. No offence, but you look awful. I'll go front of house for today and you can stay in the kitchen, out of the way. Then when I close up, we'll sit down and you can tell me what's been going on. Deal?'

Deal. I felt so grateful. I was wrung out. I'd had enough. Someone else taking charge was just what had been missing from my life. I managed a nod and a huge, snotty sniff. Jon gave me more kitchen towel, rubbed my good arm, then quietly retreated and left me to it.

I somehow managed to get the sobs under control with the help of the kitchen paper, gulps of air and months of practice. I flipped the camera on my phone and checked myself out; Jon wasn't wrong – blotchy, puffy and red-eyed. I looked like shit. I took a huge breath, sighed it out, went back into the kitchen, splashed my face as instructed and tried to get a grip.

Jon was as good as his word, handling all of the front of house stuff. Each time he came in with an order or some pots, I managed a smile, and each time it seemed to get easier to act normal. He must have put in a demon shift - I was pretty busy with salads and toasties, but I stayed on top of everything that came my way, and it was good to be distracted.

As the day wore on, it started to feel like the whole snotty fire escape incident had been a dream – a bad one, but one we'd both probably rather not have to deal with.

'You okay?' he asked, quickly dropping off a couple of food tickets as the lunchtime rush was in full swing.

'Uh-huh.' I looked at the tickets. 'What does this say? Bacon and what?'

'Brie,' he said. I gave him a smile that was meant to be reassuring as he left me to it, but he still looked worried. I was starting to feel uneasy about the whole thing again. I'd promised to tell him what was wrong. Or he'd promised to listen to me later. Or something. But one way or another, I had a feeling getting out of the shift without any kind of explanation just wasn't going to be possible this time.

From about three-thirty onwards, the rush dropped off. I got the kitchen tidy and wondered if he'd buy it if I put the tears down to tiredness and suggested going home early. Sometime just after four, the door opened and closed, Jon called goodbye to the last customer and then I heard the click of the lock.

'I'm calling it a day,' he shouted through to the kitchen. 'Don't know about you but I'm knackered.'

Oh. No chance of getting away then. I thought how relieved I'd felt just a few hours earlier at the idea that someone else was taking control. I pulled myself together and walked out into the café.

Jon was behind the counter, making drinks. He'd turned the music down and stuck a notice on the door.

'What's that?' I asked, pointing to it.

'Says "Closed for staff training".' He gave a wry smile. 'Thought that just about covered it. I'm having a coffee. How about a hot chocolate after all that crying?'

'Oat milk?' I asked. He rolled his eyes.

'Of course. I have been listening to you for the past two months you know. Here you go.'

I took the hot chocolate, feeling very wobbly. Jon proceeded with caution.

'So... What was going on earlier?'

'Jon, I don't know if I can. I...'

'Look, Amy. You're a great member of my team, don't get me wrong. But lately, there've been a few times when I've felt you were... well, distracted would be one way of putting it. You're never completely unprofessional or anything, but I've been feeling we should probably have a chat.'

Shit! Was he going to sack me? That wasn't what I was expecting. But he hadn't finished.

'It's none of my business, what goes on in your personal life. Until it affects your work. I've been meaning to try and talk to you about it since that day with Jamie. But you didn't seem to want to. But today was something else. So I'm offering to listen.' He sat down at the nearest table and indicated me to join him. 'You don't have to tell me what's up. But I think there's more to you than I know and it's starting to affect our working relationship. Don't worry, it will stay between us. Whatever it is. But let's see if it's something I can help with.'

Reluctantly, I walked over and took a seat. The hot chocolate smelt good. I took a sip and closed my eyes. For a second I was back at home with Mum. In pyjamas on the sofa in the lounge, with troubles that were never too big to be solved with a hot drink and a cuddle. I opened my eyes and took a deep breath.

'It's quite a long story.' I hesitated. Jon waited, patiently. 'Well, here goes. It all started when a boy called Harry invited me to a party.'

PART TWO
FROM NOW ON

31

You know how it is when you wake up from a really deep sleep; your emotions kick in, while your brain fumbles around to piece together what happened to make you feel like that. That's how I felt after telling Jon. I slept ten hours straight and woke up the calmest I've felt for... well... since the party.

It wasn't easy telling him. At times I dried up. I've never said it all out loud before and sometimes it was just too hard to form the words. Too painful. But I tried to give him the whole story – the days up to the party, that night, and everything that happened afterwards. It was like reading aloud from an old diary. But Jon was the best listener I could have imagined. No interruptions, no annoying questions, just the occasional gentle prompt when I stumbled, and patient pauses as I pulled myself together before carrying on.

When I was crying in the kitchen and he asked me to tell him what was going on, it felt like a lifeline I didn't know I needed. But in the time between that and us sitting down to talk, I'd shoved a lot of the feelings back down into their usual hiding places. At the end of the shift, if he'd given me the option, I'd probably have left it. Picked up my stuff, headed back to hall, spent another evening alone avoiding life. But he hadn't. Thank God. Now I've done it – I've actually talked, and yes, I have to admit, I'm feeling... better. Only the tiniest bit. Like when it's been grey skies and rain for days on end and you get the first glimmer of light. That's funny – Jon as a glimmer of light. Makes him sound god-like.

I told him almost everything. The party, the video, the run in with Harry. My summer of depression, how Mum and Maria had got me back on track. The end of my friendship with Rosie. I told him about starting at uni, how running away hadn't been as easy as I'd thought. How lonely I was. The fact I hadn't been home at all because I couldn't face seeing anyone who reminds me of what happened. Even Mum. He just listened, and made more drinks, and brought some food about six o'clock when I was still talking. His eyes filled with tears at times, and he dug his fingernails into his hand when I told him about the video, gulped down his coffee, as if steadying himself. I pretended not to notice. I'm used to my own pain, but his reaction nearly broke me.

It was nearly eight by the time I stopped talking. In spite of the hot chocolate and various snacks, I was drained. Jon tried a smile, but it was a very faded version of his usual one. He put his head on one side.

'So you haven't told anyone all that before?'

I shook my head and gave a little laugh. 'Wasn't the way I thought I'd be spending my evening.' Then I gasped and put my hand to my mouth. 'God, you didn't have plans, did you? It's nearly eight o'clock! I'm so sorry. I...'

He shook his head, his eyes soft.

'I didn't. But even if I had, this was more important. You've done so well, you know. Let me get you an Uber. I think I laced my coffees too much to drive you home, and I'm not letting you walk on your own.'

The knocked-back coffees suddenly made sense. He fussed around, getting me an Uber, clearing up our mugs and plates, checking things were closed, cleared, turned off. All I could do was sit there, exhausted, staring at the table until the car arrived and I got up to leave.

'Thank you. For listening. I think you were right. I... I did need to talk about it.'

He took me by the shoulders and looked straight into my eyes.

'You don't ever need to thank me. I said I was here for you and I am. But now you need to go home and sleep.'

And yet again, he was right.

That was two days ago though, and now I'm on my way to work and I can't visualise what it will be like to see him again. He knows everything about me. More or less. Ouch. Maybe professional therapy would have been a better idea. At least I wouldn't have to go back two days later and work a shift in a café with a real therapist. God, I really hope he doesn't start acting all weird with me. Our relationship has always been relaxed with lots of friendly banter. If that's changed, it will be yet another thing in my life that fucking video has ruined.

Ding ding! Jesus! I jump out of the way of a cyclist furiously ringing his bell. Shit, concentrate, nearly got run over then. I can't work out what I'm feeling. Nerves. But that's ridiculous, to feel nervous about Jon. It's just that all those layers of protection I wrapped around myself have been there a long time. Peeling them back feels weird. I really hope he won't be too nice. I really, really hope he won't hug me or anything. I just want everything to be as it used to be. So if I just act normal, maybe he will too.

But there's something nagging at me. Something I held back, and I don't know why. When I got to Andrew's part in the story, I glossed over it. It's not like I have any reason to protect Andrew. I never liked him, even before he worked out where he knew me from. But now I'm kicking myself. In an ideal world, I'd never see Andrew again. But obviously I couldn't ask Jon to sack him. And actually, apart from recognising me and being a bit annoying, Andrew hasn't done anything wrong. So if Jon knew the full picture, we'd all have felt awkward. Well. I would. You can't sack an employee for recognising someone. Sadly. So I'm going to have to see him at work today. I just hope and pray that he hasn't still got the video. Oh God. I can't even think about the possibility he might show it to Jon. I'm going to have to deal with Andrew. Somehow or other.

I'm a couple of minutes early. I bang on the locked door, trying to make Jon hear. My stomach flips over when I see him approach, but then he meets my eyes through the glass and gives me a big smile. Not the faded one from the other night. I smile back, hopeful of normality.

'You're early!' he says, opening the door. 'Didn't realise you telling me your life story was going to mean I'd get a whole new you.'

I widen my eyes at him, and there's a split second of silence, then he asks, 'Too soon?' We both crack up laughing. It's going to be okay.

'Don't, in any way, get used to it,' I say, taking off my coat. I look down at myself, then back at Jon, shrugging. 'Forgot my apron again!'

'That's more like it,' he says. 'There's one in the staff room. And can you grab some coffee beans while you're at it?'

We get to work, people start coming in and it's all fine, but as lunchtime looms, the more I wish I'd told him about Andrew. I don't know why I didn't. The other stuff I told him was worse. Maybe if I grab Andrew, have a quiet word, tell him how awful it all was, back then. How much it affected me. How thinking about the party and all that is just too... No. I can't see that happening. That slimy grin when he realised how he knew me, that pervy wink when he said goodbye. I don't think appealing to his better nature is the right way. I'll have to have another think.

I'm in the kitchen and I hear the door and a 'Hey, what's up?' from Jon. I look at my watch – eleven fifty-five. Oh shit. I quickly calculate that I have time to get to the counter while Andrew's hanging up his stuff. I abandon the cucumber I was slicing and bundle into the café, narrowly missing Jon, who is coming the other way.

'Whoa! Blimey, steady on!' He puts his hands up in front of him to stop me crashing into him.

'God, sorry! I'm so sorry.' Nice way to act normal.

'I was just on my way to see if you wanted to swap and go onto drinks for lunchtime, but by the speed you were running, I think I can assume the answer is yes.'

I manage a smile and quickly turn my back as Andrew emerges from the staff room.

'Hi, Amy,' he calls over. I nod without looking at him, and notice Jon give me a quick look before they head into the kitchen together. I strain to hear what they're saying, but the music is too loud.

Just after two, the lunchtime rush drops off and Jon comes out, pulling on his jacket. I have a heart sink moment. Where's he going?

'Amy, you okay if I just pop out for half an hour? I need to get some keys cut.'

Half an hour. That means half an hour on my own with Andrew. I swallow hard, and hope maybe Jon will read my mind and stay here. He looks at me carefully.

'That okay?'

It's not, but I nod.

'Promise I won't be long, just need another set. Can't see it getting too busy now, anyway. I'll be back before you miss me.'

I nearly say no, actually, it's not okay, please can you not leave me? But he's already out of the door.

Half an hour. Maybe this is my chance to talk to Andrew. But I'm not ready, I haven't decided what to say. And anyway, there are customers on four of the tables. Someone might want another drink or something. Better to stay out of his way for a bit longer, I'll speak to him another time. It's been easy enough avoiding him so far, and I can definitely manage not to go into the kitchen. It'll be fine.

Except, shit.

He emerges from the kitchen wiping his enormous hands on a tea towel, small beads of sweat on his forehead. I try not to cower.

'So Amy. How's your week been?' As usual, he doesn't seem to need an actual answer, but he's getting closer to me even though I'm backing away.

'Have to say, mine's been quite good. After our little chat last week, I was feeling quite nostalgic. Got back in touch with a few of our mutual friends. They send their regards.'

He laughs at his little joke. His words make me feel sick.

'They all remembered you really well. Couldn't believe it had taken me so long to recognise you. Seems like you were a bit of celebrity back home.'

Oh god, I want to run, but he's in my way. I glance quickly round the café. No one at any of the tables seems to be paying us any attention. He's so close to me, I can't stand it. But at least he's keeping his voice down.

'It does seem mad now, that it took me so long to place you. Not going to lie, I remember some nice times I spent with that little video. Not sure why I didn't keep it, to be honest.'

Urgh! My skin crawls. With every fibre of my being, I need him to stop talking. I put my hand up to stop him moving any closer.

'Please, Andrew,' I whisper. That stops him, and he looks genuinely surprised.

'Wow. Do you know, I think that's the first time you've used my name since we met? I don't know why you couldn't have been a bit more friendly.'

I'm fighting all my instincts, wanting to cry, to scream, to do anything at all just to get this to stop. He moves closer still, dropping his voice to not much more than a hideous whisper. Small beads of sweat trickle down his temples. He smells of cheap aftershave, unwashed hair and washing up liquid. He smiles and it is so much worse in close up.

'You're not really how I thought you'd be. Video Amy seemed like a fun girl. With nice tits, I remember. But you. You're so unfriendly. You seem to think you're better than me. Never wanted to work out why I knew you, did you? Wonder if Jamie would like to know a bit more about his new girlfriend. I mean, if you and me were friends, I wouldn't do that. But I've given you the chance and you don't seem interested.'

With each word he's getting louder. The people on table two look up. I need him to shut up. I hiss at him in a low whisper, hoping he'll take the lead and lower his voice again.

'What are you talking about? You're trying to force me to be friends with you by threatening me. Are you that much of a saddo that you have to blackmail people to be your friend?'

He puts his hand on his heart in mock pain.

'That hurts. But if that's the way you want it.'

He pulls his phone out of his pocket and leans right in so when he speaks I feel a spray of spit on my cheek.

'Lucky for me I wasn't the only one who enjoyed looking at your video. Didn't take many messages to find someone who still had it. Did you think it had gone away? That would have been a real shame. I can send it to you if you like? Oh wait, I don't have your number, do I? But I do have Jon's...'

I pounce, grabbing for the phone. The momentum catches him off guard and he lets go. The phone flies, arcing into the air and over the counter. Andrew dives after it, knocking a milk jug flying onto the floor where it smashes into little pieces. The phone lands a couple of metres from table two, where the customers have abandoned any pretence of not watching the show. Everyone in the café looks on as we scramble from behind the counter, both desperate to be the first to pick up the phone where it lies, shattered, on the floor.

Suddenly, the door opens and Jon walks in.

'The keys didn't take as long as I thought,' he says calmly, dropping them onto the counter. 'Good job, it seems.'

He looks at the broken pieces of jug, the pool of milk that is gradually spreading to where the phone lies on the floor, and then from me to Andrew and back again.

'Would one of you like to tell me what's going on here?'

Andrew picks up the damaged phone and shoves it into his pocket. I can't look at Jon, so I look at the mess on the floor. The customers are all suddenly really interested in their phones and their drinks and their own conversations. Jon points to the kitchen.

'Andrew, get back in there. Amy, can you please clear up this mess? Then I want a word with both of you.'

Miserably, I clean up the milk and the broken bits of jug. A couple of ladies I don't know very well smile sympathetically at me as they get up to leave. The couple on table two move their feet as I mop and avoid my eye when I thank them. I dread to think what they just heard. I try to remember at which point in the conversation Andrew started to raise his voice. Thinking about him makes me sick. And now he's in the kitchen with Jon, telling him god knows what. Maybe I should hurry up and get in there. But actually, do I want to know? If Jon sees the video, I'll leave. There's nothing else for it. And I'm sure Andrew will be very happy to show him.

I wrap paper towels around the smashed china and push it into the bin, then take the mop and quietly move towards the kitchen. I can only make out Jon's voice. No laughter, no testosterone-fuelled banter. Jon just sounds angry. Carefully I lean the mop against the wall and tiptoe closer, straining my ears.

'... and if you think in any way that I would want to see something like this, you are mistaken.'

God! He has tried to show him the video. I lean a bit closer. Andrew's talking now, really quickly.

'Sorry, boss, it was just a bit of fun! I mean, it was a joke, you know? Everyone was laughing about it at the time. It didn't mean any harm. God, I can't believe you're all so uptight about it.'

I suck in my breath. A bit of fun? Is that what he thought it was? My face and neck tingle with all-too-familiar shame and humiliation, but Jon is speaking again. He's lowered his voice; I take another step closer.

'I can't really believe I have to spell this out to you. But it seems that I do. Let's imagine shall we, Andrew, that someone shared a video like that of you. Or someone you love. You don't have a girlfriend, do you? Sister then? Mum?'

'Boss! That's out of order!' Andrew sounds horrified, Jon's struck a nerve.

'So you can't imagine a video of your mum or your sister being shared around your mates, but one of Amy was just a bit of fun?'

Andrew is stammering, I can't catch his words. Then Jon says, 'Give me your phone. Unlocked. I know the screen's shattered. You can still do it.'

My hand flies to my mouth. He can't see it. I want to stop him, but my legs are paralysed.

'So where is it? I want you to delete it in front of me. And all the messages connected to Amy. Right now. Do it now.'

I gasp, then kick myself for being for so loud. Andrew's mumbling again, I hear him cross the floor, Jon says okay. Then before I have time to get out of the way, Jon storms past to the till. I stand back against the wall, narrowly avoiding falling over the mop, as Andrew follows him out. Jon thrusts two twenty-pound notes at Andrew.

'Here. Your pay for today and next week. I won't be needing you anymore. Consider yourself lucky that no one is going to report you for sexual harassment.' Andrew hesitates, looking as if he might be about to try and put up an argument. I hold my breath.

'Go. Get your stuff and go. I don't ever want to see you here again.'

I don't look at Andrew as he walks past me, collects his jacket and heads for the door. As we watch him leave, he looks back as if to say goodbye, then thinks better of it and walks out, the cash in one hand, his broken phone in the other. I sink to the floor and put my head in my hands.

32

I've never seen Jon angry before. Not like he was with Andrew. A rage that was quiet but all the more terrifying for that. He calmed down after Andrew left, but something's still not right. He's back to smiling and joking with me. Just acting normal. Oh! That's it. He's *acting* normal. Not being normal. Oh fuck. And that scene with Andrew, in front of all those customers. A part of me dies inside. I thought my days of causing a scene were meant to be over.

So when I emerge from the staff room at the end of the day, I'm not surprised to find a repeat of the scene from two days before - the "Closed" sign on the door, and Jon making drinks. He looks at me over the counter with raised eyebrows.

'Hot chocolate?'

'Oh, I was just going to head off...'

'Don't try and tell me you have somewhere to be. We're not done talking,' he says, with a stern voice he's never used on me before. No point arguing. He pulls a small bottle of cognac out from under the till and sloshes some into his coffee.

'You want some?' he asks, holding it up. I shake my head. Although if there was a time to start drinking again, maybe this was it.

'Have a seat,' he says, carrying the drinks over. I sit at the same table as before. Might as well pick up where we left off.

Grateful for something to do with my hands, I pick up the hot chocolate and look at him with lowered eyelids. I feel like I'm about to get a telling off. Jon takes a deep breath.

'I'm just going to ask you straight out. Why didn't you tell me about Andrew?'

I slurp the chocolate to delay answering. Too hot. Brilliant. Burnt tongue to go with everything else.

'Don't know,' I say, uselessly. 'I regretted it from the minute I woke up the next day. I was scared of...'

He cut in.

'Me seeing the video? Is that it? Honestly Amy, do you really think I would have wanted to see it?'

It does seem like a ridiculous fear, now I look at him, giving me his time again, picking up my pieces, making me hot chocolate, trying to make things better. Miserably I shake my head.

'How could you think that of me? I would have just dealt with him!'

There didn't seem any point explaining that I'd hoped I could sort it out myself. As if asking Andrew nicely not to mention it again was ever going to work.

'I'm sorry,' I said. It was Jon's turn to shake his head.

'You are such a conundrum. I finally get you to tell me what's wrong, you tell me all that stuff, stuff that I am still trying to process. You leave me wondering how on earth I can help you. And you leave out the one little bit of the story that I actually could do something about.'

I sigh. 'I know. It doesn't make sense. I'm not good at... at trusting people. I've got used to living like this. Not talking to people about it. I somehow thought if I came here, if no one knew, that I could start again. That I could forget. But it wasn't like that.' I hesitate. 'To be honest, meeting Andrew, feeling that I knew him from somewhere. It's happened so many times before. It's almost a relief this time that I was right. It justifies all the time I've spent hiding, worrying, wondering. I was right. I can't ever get away.'

Jon sips his coffee and deliberately sets it down on the table before he speaks.

'I can't begin to imagine what it's been like for you. The whole thing, it makes me so angry on your behalf. That you've suffered like this. And the people who did this to you got away with it.'

I draw circles on the table with some spilt sugar and wait for the next bit. You should have gone to the police; you should have made a complaint. I rehearse the old arguments in my head. But he takes a different approach.

'But here's the thing. What if you could turn what just happened into a positive?'

I jerk my head up and raise an eyebrow sceptically. 'I'm listening, but it will have to be good.'

Jon puts his hands flat down on the table and leans in towards me.

'The thing you've been worried about all this time has finally happened. People in your new life finding out about your past. Yet here you still are. You dealt with it.'

'I think we'd have to say you dealt with it...' Jon dismissed me with a wave of his hand.

'We dealt with it. Doesn't matter. But let's face it, he didn't really do much. Turns out he didn't even have the video on his phone.'

'What? Are you sure?'

Jon nodded. 'Yep. As far as I could see, it wasn't there.'

I frown. 'But he threatened me with it? Said he was going to show it to you if I didn't...' I shake my head.

Jon shrugs. 'He showed me all his messages. No one had replied. Almost felt sorry for him. Maybe everyone has moved on.'

'So what are you saying? You think the video isn't out there anymore?'

'I don't know. It might be. The internet's a big and scary place. But my point is, that's not something you or I can control. The only thing you have the power over is how you let it affect your life.'

I breathe in deeply and deliberately and hold my breath. I try to remember how I used to imagine life at uni, before the party. I think about the people I pass on campus every day, wandering around laughing, chatting, in groups of two, three, more. I used to think I'd be part of that. Not be the girl from the video anymore. That a new start would mean friends, maybe a boyfriend, the kind of life most people my age take for granted.

'And you think that's a choice? How it has affected my life?'

Jon looks at me, steadily.

'I think you can make the choice to change things. If that's what you want.'

I bite my lip. That's easy to say if it's not you that has to make the changes.

'And what does your mum think? About this stuff with Andrew.'

I can't look at him. 'She… she doesn't know.'

Jon is about to take a sip of his drink, but he puts it down heavily.

'You haven't even talked to your mum? But I thought you said she was brilliant about it all, when it happened?'

I pull at my sleeves and look at the floor. 'Yeah, but I think it's just better if she thinks it's all okay now. She thinks I'm fine. I don't want to worry her.'

In my head I replay recent calls to Mum. Mainly her talking, not me. Conversations about work, updates on friends I vaguely know, some concert she'd been to, coffee with a colleague. Suggesting she could come and see me, stay in a hotel or something, me saying I was quite busy, I'd send some dates. Suddenly I feel awful about the way I've been with Mum. Jon shakes his head.

'I'd be surprised if she's not worried. But that's up to you. So, who do you talk to? What about your friends here? Do they know what happened?'

I press my hands deliberately down on the table and look at them as a change from the floor.

'I don't have friends here. Not really. I've kept my distance. It was just…' I try to find the right word. 'Easier, I guess. There's no one I trust. Well, there was Maria. But I don't even trust her anymore.'

I dare to look up at him. His hands are in his lap, he's looking down at them, twisting his thumbs round and round. I give a little laugh, trying to lighten the mood.

'You must feel really honoured that I trust you,' I say brightly, not feeling it. He gives a kind of half-laugh, half-sniff and looks at me, hard.

'I know what it's like not trusting people. Not being able to talk. But with you, I don't really get it. Something happened to you. Yeah, it was shit. I can see how it would make you feel terrible about yourself. But it wasn't your fault.'

Is that an opening for me to try and get him to talk about himself for once? There's clearly something to say. And it might be a way to get the heat off me. I start to open my mouth, but spend too long thinking what to say, so he carries on.

'You don't seem to realise what a great person you are. So lovely, so funny. And from what you've told me, you had really great friends. But what I see is you living this... half-life. You push people away.'

I squirm, pressing my lips together and sitting on my hands. There was more than one reason why telling Jon my problems hadn't been a great idea. He's undeterred.

'Your mum. I don't know her. But I know mums. They worry. Her daughter doesn't go home, won't have her to visit, has very little to report on her exciting life at uni. That, on top of the fact she knows what you went through. Take it from me, she knows you're not fine. So you might think you're protecting her but I'm sure she'd rather know the real picture.'

I puff out my cheeks. This is tough. Jon doesn't seem to believe in pulling his punches. 'Okay, are you done? Because...'

'No, not yet. There's Maria. Your best friend, right? Loyal to the core, always had your back. You told me that.'

I nod, thinking briefly of the photo frame of the two of us, now face down in my wardrobe.

'So she comes in here and you won't even speak to her.'

I shrug. 'Because she was with Rosie. She betrayed me like everyone else.'

This time Jon shakes his head vehemently. 'I don't believe that for a second. Do you? Everything you said about Maria doesn't make sense if that's the case. She must have had a reason to forgive her.'

I have to admit I'd thought of that myself. It floored me, the two of them turning up. I felt so hurt, so shocked. Maybe I had overreacted.

'Don't lose Maria over this. You need to call her. They made the effort to come here, they must have something to say. And then you need to talk to your mum. Now this is all out in the open, it's time you realised who's on your side.'

I drag a finger through a drip of hot chocolate, smearing it across the table.

'I just don't know, Jon. It's all opening up old wounds. I've been fine.'

'But you're not really fine, are you?' he says. 'Take Jamie, for example.'

For the ten thousandth time, I see the image of Jamie walking away from me. I lean back in my chair, hugging my arms around me.

'He's got nothing to do with this,' I say, quietly.

Jon raises a hand. 'Okay. Maybe it's none of my business, as you said before. But I think he does. I think it's all part of the same problem. And as the only person in the world you seem to trust at the moment, I feel it's my duty to tell you what I think.'

I'm starting to feel a bit under attack from all the straight talking. But his expression softens slightly and he gives a lop-sided smile.

'You need to talk to the people you love. You know you do. I'm good, but you can't just put all your trust into a middle-aged barista. Even one as wise and good-looking as me.'

33

A half-eaten bowl of noodles sits congealing between my laptop and a pile of notes for a part-written essay. I tap my fingers on the desk, stand up to take the bowl to the kitchen, then put it back where it was and sit down again, looking at my watch. Still only five to eight. Maria said they'd call at eight. For reasons I can't now remember, I've agreed to a FaceTime with both of them. Jon said the effort they'd made to come and see me, Maria all the way from Edinburgh, suggested what they wanted to say was important. I've spent a lot of time wondering what that might be, but Jon persuaded me to stop guessing and just talk to them. So in about four minutes and thirty-five seconds, I'm going to find out.

'I'm sure it's the right thing,' Jon said as he dropped me off. He insisted on a lift, assuring me he'd only had a dash of alcohol in his coffee. I did believe him, but I'm so emotionally exhausted I'd probably have agreed to anything. In fact, maybe it would be better to talk to Rosie and Maria when I'm not so tired. I pick up the phone to start composing an excuse when the chirpy tones of an incoming FaceTime interrupt. It's 7:57. Maria knows me too well.

'Hey! How you doing?' Maria beams at me from the screen. She's cross-legged on her bed, a jumper and a couple of cushions next to her and in the background, a wall covered in photos.

'I'm okay. Bit tired but...' I get straight to the point. 'Look, I'm sorry I've been ignoring you. I just didn't know what to think. You and Rosie. It was...'

Maria waves her hand in a dismissive gesture.

'It's okay. You're here now.'

I give her a tight-lipped smile. 'I just wasn't ready. It was too much of a shock, I...'

'Oh, Rosie's here!' Maria says. 'Hang on, I'll let her in.'

I bristle. I haven't finished. I'd have liked to talk to Maria first, I should have said that earlier.

The screen splits into three and Rosie appears. There's a lamp or something casting a shadow across her face, and she's a bit hunched over, with a wide necked jumper pulled right up to her chin. She looks uncomfortable. Or maybe just cold.

'Hi!' Maria says. 'So look. This is a bit awkward. We might as well get that out there. And let's skip the Hi, how are yous, when are your exams and all that shit. We need to talk.'

In spite of myself, she makes me smile. Maria in charge. Maria chairing this peculiar FaceTime summit.

'Go on then,' I say. There's a slight pause, then Rosie starts to speak.

I lean back in my chair, watching my ex-best friend talk. She's looking down, occasionally flicking her eyes to the screen, but I can't tell if she's looking at me or seeking Maria's support. Her accent seems to have softened already in the few months she's been away from home, although she was always a bit posher than the rest of us. My mind flicks back to our last proper conversations: that afternoon in her front room; at school, when she brushed me off on the stairs, told me she couldn't help. I pull my knees up to my chest and wrap my arms around myself. It's hard to concentrate on the here and now when the memories haven't really stopped stinging.

'...so Maria said I should maybe get in touch and see what you thought.'

Rosie's looking at the screen. She seems to want me to say something. Bollocks, I wasn't listening properly.

'What I thought about what?' For god's sake, concentrate!

'When I sent that message. On Instagram.'

My brain clicks into the present. 'Oh. Well, I couldn't work out how you'd found me.' I shoot a look at Maria who looks sheepish. 'I was annoyed, I guess. I thought no one knew where I was.'

'Well, when you didn't reply – and I completely get why you wouldn't – I thought maybe if I turned up it would be easier.'

I bite my tongue.

Maria chips in. 'Can I just say that I didn't know she was going to do that. I'd have stopped it.'

'That's why I didn't tell you.' Rosie shrugs. 'But you'd have been right. It was stupid.'

I remember the pure shock I felt when I saw her there. 'Yeah, it was stupid. So what did you want anyway? Can't believe you came all that way for me to make you a coffee.'

Rosie looks up, her eyes slightly wider, like she senses a change of tone, a gentle joke. But I don't crack. I'm not forgiving anyone until someone actually says sorry. And maybe not even then. Rosie shifts in her chair and pulls the sleeves of her jumper over her hands.

'I just... I miss you. And it took me a while but...' I wait. 'I wanted to say sorry.'

She wipes at her nose with the heel of her hand, still wrapped in the jumper. She looks tearful, which isn't a normal thing for her. It's a start. But one little sorry really isn't enough.

'Go on, Rosie,' Maria says. 'Tell her the whole thing.'

I'm expecting to hear that she hadn't wanted to go against Harry for the sake of her family. Or, if she's really honest, that she thought sticking with me would have made her unpopular. I'm not at all ready for her to say what she does say.

'They blackmailed me too.'

'I'm sorry, what?' I ask.

She bites her lip and huffs.

'Go on,' Maria urges her.

'I should have told you. And it's still me being weak. So if you don't want to forgive me, I still get it. I did know what was going on, and I could have interrupted and stopped things, and I didn't. And believe me, I will never, ever forgive myself for that, whether you do or not. It was shitty.'

Well, that's something, I think.

'But afterwards, I was fucking livid with Oli. And with Harry. They were being such dicks about it. And I could see how upset you were. School were useless. I think Harry's dad had a word with the head, to be honest.'

The old rage starts to build up in me, but I nod and keep listening; she clearly hasn't finished.

'The day you saw Harry at school, he came to me and told me what you'd said. And I was annoyed with him. I said yeah, actually she's right. It is something we could go to the police with.' She pauses. Maria is looking at her hands.

'And?' I ask.

She shakes her head, as if sending away the memory. 'He tried the whole "but I'm your cousin" thing and I told him to stick it. I told you, I'd warned him if he got with you and messed you around, he'd have me to deal with.' She hesitates again, before sitting up straight and speaking more loudly. 'But that night... that night he sent me a text. A... a nude. Of me. One I'd sent Oli, ages before.'

'You sent Oli a nude?' I'm gob-smacked. I thought she used to tell us everything. Clearly not.

'Yeah. Don't. I regret it more than I can say. It was kind of a joke one, but even so. Harry said if I helped you, they'd send it to my mum, the school, etc. You know the deal.'

'I do indeed,' I say, grimly. I feel a new level of disgust for Harry. And I'm trying to work out if this makes it better or worse, what Rosie did. Or rather, didn't do. I can't decide.

She starts to cry and drags a hand through her hair.

'I was so weak, I'm so sorry. I... I couldn't admit it to you. Or to Maria. I knew I was being the worst coward, the worst friend. I was caught, and they knew that. I just wish I could have been brave and suffered the consequences. When I saw you in that exam, when you freaked out right in front of me... It was awful; I tried to come back, to come and see you were okay. But Harry stopped me. He reminded me he still had it, the video. And the photo of me. I didn't want to make things worse.'

I try and imagine if anything could have made it worse. Rosie moves and the shadow across her face deepens. She's mumbling now, something about Harry, about the police. 'If going to the police is what you want…'

I shake my head. 'It's not. I decided that a long time ago.'

She looks at me from under her fringe. 'I've been trying to think of a way to apologise. To see if you can forgive me.'

'So what? You decided to get to me through Maria?' Rosie opens her mouth, then closes it again. They both look slightly uncomfortable. Maria interjects.

'Mate, it was my idea for us both to turn up. I can see now it wasn't a great one…'

'No shit. The only way it could have been worse was if you'd brought Harry with you.'

'Don't be mental. I'll never, ever forgive him. And even less so now…' She waves her hand, I'm guessing it's at Rosie although on the screen she might be waving at anything. She carries on. 'And anyway, he's… he's leaving the country.'

In spite of myself, I'm interested. Harry in another country is a damn sight better than Harry closer to home.

'What do you mean? I thought he was at Durham with his nice little scholarship.'

'Tell her, Rosie,' says Maria.

Rosie bites the inside of her lip.

'He, um… He's been kicked out of uni. For sharing sexual images.'

Adrenaline shoots through me and heat flushes right up into my brain.

'Oh my god! Of me? The video? No, please…'

'No! No! Stop! Listen will you?'

It's hard to interrupt on FaceTime but Rosie is flailing her arms around and shouting. 'Sorry! God, no, not of you. Or me. Another girl. Well, I think he shared some nudes or something. But then, he and some mates set up some hideous group, all sharing nudes of their girlfriends and trying to get more and more explicit photos.'

She shudders. 'Sick.'

I shrug, the heat subsiding and my pulse going back to something like normal.

'So your cousin's a sick fuck. It's not news to me, Rosie.'

Rosie puts her head in her hands.

'I know. I always did. I was so pathetic to do what he said. And I lost my two best friends over it.'

I snort. 'Well, forgive me for not feeling that sorry for you.' I pause and look at Maria. 'And anyway, it seems like you've got one of them back.'

I want to hurt them both, but Maria doesn't flinch. I have the feeling she's been expecting it. Neither of them say anything, so I go on. 'So you think this stuff about Harry is going to make a difference? Don't get me wrong, I'm sorry for the other girls affected, I'm happy he's not going to be around anymore. But honestly? He did what he did and I'm still living with it. Your sick cousin is still the only guy I've ever had sex with. Because of him, I still don't want to let anyone into my life. Because how can I ever be sure they won't make me feel as worthless as he did?' It feels good to say it out loud, stuff I've been bottling up. 'And to be honest, Rosie, you siding with him... That was one of the worst things about it all.'

Maria is rubbing her eyes and Rosie looks devastated.

'Amy, I'm more sorry than you can ever know. I'll do anything for you to forgive me. But I know it's a big ask.' Rosie puts her head in her hands. There's silence – I wonder if the screen has frozen, then Maria speaks.

'Oh, god, this is so hard to do over FaceTime,' she says. 'This is why we wanted to see you in person.'

I look at them. She's right, they're hard to read, each on their little screen. Maria carries on.

'Ames. We'll never know what it's like for you. Yeah, what's happened to Harry maybe doesn't make much difference to how you feel about him. But we thought maybe... maybe it might make you think again.'

I huff. 'Think again about what? I don't need any encouragement to think again about that fucking video. And I've been absolutely fine not thinking about Harry, thanks.'

'Think again about what you do about it. About moving on. About us.'

Maria sounds like she's reading from a script. It's irritating. I take a deep breath.

'That's very easy for you to say. But whenever I think moving on might even be a vague possibility, I'm back there. With those feelings of shame, of fear. Of not knowing how to trust anyone I thought I knew. And I can't put myself through it again. Then to crown it all, out of nowhere, I meet someone who has actually seen that video. And I know, deep down inside, that one way or another, I will never, ever get away from it.'

I quickly fill them in on Andrew. Just saying it out loud to them has a weirdly therapeutic effect. Rosie still looks devastated but seems to find her voice. She speaks again, very quietly.

'We just want to find a way to go back to how things were. To all of us being friends again.'

I think about what Jon said, about talking to the people I love. These are two of the people I loved deeply. I realise how much I've missed them.

'I hear you,' I say. They're watching me, waiting to see what I'll say. There's too much to take in, I need time to think. 'Look. Maybe it would be a good idea to meet up. But you need to leave it with me to decide. I'll let you know, okay?'

I end the call, and for a split second the three of us are here together on the screen, frozen in our goodbyes.

34

I stare out at the fields, unmistakably northern with their dry-stone walls and flocks of hardy looking sheep. The sky is grey, that heavy kind of weather that Mum would call "set in" – a day that has no hope of sunshine, no chance of ever reaching full daylight. Absent-mindedly I click the earbuds I forgot to charge in my hand, until I notice the disapproving stare of the woman sitting opposite. Sorry, I mouth. Although this can't be as annoying as the packet of crisps she was crunching through earlier. A book. That would have been a good idea. Or a newspaper. I flick through a news app on my phone but nothing grabs my attention.

After I talked to Maria and Rosie, going home felt like the obvious thing to do. I called Jon to see if I could take Saturday off and he said yes straight away. He actually sounded delighted that I was following his advice. But this morning I woke up with a ball of nerves in my stomach that's getting bigger and bigger with every familiar station name we pass. The stations all look grubby, unchanged over years, the only updates the odd new sign or a rebranded café. It's ages since I've taken this train. Mum's been suggesting all term that I could go home for a weekend. But I didn't want to before now. I feel like a selfish cow when I think of how she tries to hide her disappointment every time I come up with an excuse not to see her. Hopefully she'll be pleased I'm making the effort. Maybe I should have called first.

I watch the little houses rushing past, compact and tidy, the setting for so many people's lives. How would it be to live so close to the railway, your life constantly interrupted by the sound of the trains roaring past? Maybe they like it, seeing other people on their way to somewhere, while they stay warm and cosy at home. I shift in my seat, pulling my jumper up to my chin, and check the time on my phone again. Halfway there. Time feels elastic when you're travelling. Part of me feels like I've been on this train my whole life.

Mum doesn't know I'm coming; I haven't really had the time to tell her. I'll walk to the house from the station and surprise her. It's been quite a rush, making the decision, calling Jon, updating my student railcard and booking a train... What am I on about, of course, there would have been time. I spent most of last night flicking through the channels showing rubbish Friday night TV and ended up turning it off. I could easily have called Mum, or even just sent a text. But part of me hadn't really believed I'd actually do it.

The carriage door swooshes open and a boy comes through carrying a paper bag that smells of coffee. I'm dying for a coffee. I look at my phone again, still at least an hour to go. Maybe I could just go and get one, it would kill a bit of time, maybe calm me down. I let the boy go past, root in my bag for my wallet and stand up. Through the glass doors I can see that the next carriage is rammed. The buffet car is at least two carriages away. I hesitate. That's a lot of people I'd have to walk past. And we're not that far from home. I sit back down. Mum will have coffee. I'll wait.

The train approaches my destination and the places I recognise start to come thick and fast. I spot the village where Mum's boss lived, where she used to drag me for drinks every Christmas and they always had flat lemonade. Over in the distance I get my first glimpse of the tower of the parish church, where I was christened and, years later, sang with the school choir. And somewhere to the left of that, not visible from the train but resonating even from this distance, school. I take a deep breath and start to pack up my things. The defunct earbuds, the empty bottle of water, my phone. The woman opposite looks relieved. I must've been fiddling with the earbuds the whole time.

I pull my coat on, turn up the collar and pull the hood over my head. I lift my rucksack onto my shoulder and head for the door.

'Next station stop is Oxenholme Lake District. Please make sure you have all your belongings on leaving the train.'

The station is much busier than I would have liked. I stand to the side of the platform as several other people get off. A man I recognise waits by the door to the buffet; I watch his face break into a smile as a girl in a navy-blue wool coat runs towards him. In front of me, an elderly couple struggle with their bags, trying to put up an umbrella to protect themselves from the Lake District rain. I go to help them, but out of the corner of my eye I notice a girl I knew from the year below at school. I pull my hood tighter around my face and shrink back against an advertising hoarding. My heart thumps. What made me think this was a good idea? I could bump into anyone, trying to walk through town on a Saturday afternoon. Stupid, stupid plan. Jon pops into my head, somehow juggling a lunchtime shift on his own. He'd be proud I've made it this far. I can't go back now. I take a deep breath to steady myself and do what I should have done hours or days or weeks before; I pull out my phone and call Mum.

35

The sound of the kettle, the squeak of the fridge door and Mum humming in the kitchen. I sit on the sofa, hugging a cushion, the sounds of the house so familiar I can almost believe my life at uni doesn't exist. I look round at the things in the lounge. A scented candle on the shelf between the photo frames. Coasters on the coffee table. A magazine rack next to the armchair, sparing the carpet from its usual clutter of papers and Sunday supplements. All new. But the photos are the same as ever; me as a kid on the beach; me with Gran, feeding the ducks; and Mum, in an orange dress, at someone's birthday party, years ago. Next to the TV, neatly tucked away but just visible with its patterned pastel cover, Mum's notebook and a pen. It still feels like home, but somehow it's less lived in.

Mum sounded so surprised and happy when I called from the station. She was there in less than ten minutes, racing down the platform, scooping me into her arms, shaking with emotion. But her hug felt too tight, too overwhelming. I stood still, letting it happen to me, my rucksack hanging off one shoulder, the rain sliding down my face. I pulled away, trying to pretend I didn't see Mum's tears, smiled and told her about the journey. As she steered me towards the car across the empty car park, I was so glad the other travellers had made faster getaways. Mum babbled happily about work and people I don't know as we drove through town, the rain making it difficult to see. I pulled my hood round my face. I didn't look out of the window and I wasn't really listening. Suddenly I didn't know why I'd come.

I can hear a teaspoon tinkling in one cup then the next, and Mum's clogs tapping on the tiles as she brings the tea into the lounge. She puts the mugs down on the two new coasters and fusses with the gas fire, wondering if I'm warm enough.

'So!' she says, brightly, settling down in the chair in the corner. 'You're here! What a lovely surprise.'

I sip my tea, knowing this is the moment I needed to start explaining why I turned up without warning. 'Urgh! Mum, I don't take sugar anymore.'

Mum looks crestfallen. I hate myself.

'Here, let me make you another...' Mum immediately stands up. I shake my head.

'No, no, it's fine, I can drink it. I should have said.' I try to smile and take another sip, fighting the urge to flinch at how sweet it is.

Mum nurses her own cup in her hands, the coaster redundant on the table. 'I suppose it's a while since I made you a cup of tea,' she says.

A silence hangs between us and we avoid each other's eyes and both take another mouthful of our drinks. Mum swallows and clears her throat.

'I wasn't expecting you home until Christmas. Do you not have any exams or...' She tails off.

God, Amy, say something! I think of Jon, and his insistence I needed to talk to Mum. Now I can't remember why I thought he was right.

'No, no exams. Just essays this term. I thought, maybe...' This is the moment: tell her why you're here.

'Maybe it would be quieter here for you to study?' Mum says quickly. Easily defeated, I nod agreement.

'Exactly.'

'You could maybe have called me,' Mum says, still cradling the tea, still avoiding my eye.

'Well, it's been a while since I've seen you. And I thought it would be a nice surprise!' I say, with a false brightness that Mum seems to want to fall for. Her face lights up. It would be so much easier not to talk about things. I watch Mum put her cup back on the table, and she comes over to give me another hug.

'It's a lovely surprise. I'm so happy to see you.'

She smells of washing powder and perfume and home, and I nearly break as she holds me. 'Why don't you go and settle yourself in upstairs? That will be the quietest place,' she says, pulling away. 'I'll have a think about lunch.'

The hand soap in the bathroom is new and different, something rose and geranium. I dry my hands and try to decide if I like it or not. Downstairs I can hear Mum in the kitchen, radio on, banging pans as she gets them out of the cupboard.

'We'll just have eggs for lunch, is that okay?' she says. 'Then I'll pop out this afternoon for something for later.' I decide not to mention my part-time veganism, after the awkwardness of the sugar in the tea.

I go into my bedroom. My bed is neat, pens and papers are stacked on one side of my desk and there's no sign of any dust anywhere. Looks as if I just went out. Or as if Mum was ready for me anytime I might come back. My rucksack looks untidy and out of place on the floor by my desk. I shove it into the bottom of the wardrobe where a few abandoned shirts and jackets are still hanging. Things I hadn't wanted to take with me. And my school blazer. I shut the door and go downstairs.

Mum's crashing around, cracking eggs, making the kind of mess only she can make. For the first time I realise why I've always felt so at home in Jon's disaster of a kitchen.

'Shall I help?' I say. Mum nods towards the bread bin.

'You can get some toast on?'

I've always found that talking and doing is easier than just talking. Especially when there's something that's hard to say. It was always in the car on the way home from school or helping Mum put the shopping away that I'd find the words to say that I'd fallen out with someone, or I hadn't done very well in a Maths test. Here in the kitchen with Mum there's something soothing about the sound of Radio 2 in the background, the regular scratching of the whisk in the pan, how we move around each other as we make lunch. I put four slices of the multi-seed bread Mum always buys into the toaster.

'Mum. Something happened. At work.'

Mum stops whisking. Without the bright smile, the worry creases in her forehead deepen. I realise she's been waiting for some kind of bad news from the moment she answered the phone.

'What, darling? You can tell me. Was it Jon?'

I shake my head. Girl meets man could only end badly in Mum's book. The curse of the single mum. For God's sake, why does she always need to jump to conclusions?

'No, Mum. How did you get that idea? Jon's great. The best boss you could ever wish for.'

Mum looks unconvinced.

'Honestly. We're friends. You'll meet him one day, then you'll get it.' The eggs are starting to solidify. 'Keep whisking, I'll tell you.'

Mum goes back to the eggs and I tell her what happened. How happy I'd been at work, until I met Andrew, how I'd always had an uneasy feeling around him. The toast pops up and I pause the story to butter it. Mum piles the eggs on top and we go to the table. Through mouthfuls, I carry on, about his constant questioning and realising that he came from round here. Mum finishes her eggs, puts her knife and fork down and listens, twisting a napkin in her hand.

'And then Maria came in,' I say, glancing up. 'But I think you know that bit.'

Mum looks a bit uncomfortable, but I carry on. How Andrew had put two and two together seeing me with Maria. How Jon had found me crying.

'And don't worry! He was just totally kind. Although I don't think he had a clue what was wrong with me.'

'Darling, I can't believe you were going through all this and you didn't tell me.'

I shrug, my mouth occupied with the last of the eggs. I swallow and put down my knife and fork.

'I thought I was okay. And I thought if I told you that, you'd be fine too.'

Mum shakes her head.

'That's so far from the truth. I've been…'

I cut her off.

'Mum, I haven't finished. So, Rosie. She'd sent me a message on Instagram so I knew something was going on. But I didn't really want to know what. Getting over what Rosie did has been one of the hardest things. So when she turned up at work…'

'But I think she wanted to apologise darling. She wants to help…'

So Rosie had obviously talked to Mum too. 'Yeah. She said. But it's not that easy. Then when I saw her with Maria… Well, it felt like the ultimate betrayal.'

'You shouldn't look at it like that. Those two girls. They were always good friends to you. Well, until… Everyone is just trying to do their best. Because they care.'

'Yeah, I guess so.' I frown, rearranging my knife and fork. 'So I suppose Rosie told you about Harry?'

Mum nods. 'She did. Actually I felt quite pleased. That boy finally got what was coming to him. I can't say I was at all sorry.'

Mum sounds angrier than I would have expected. But then I realise what's coming. She turns to me, hands clasped in front of her chest.

'You know, there are still things you could do. To put this all behind you. I think it might…'

I tap my fingers on the table.

'Mum, we've been over this a million times. It's way too late. And I don't want to go to the police.'

'But if you just listen! I've looked into it.' Mum leans forwards eagerly, like she's been waiting for this moment. She speaks quickly, her words tumbling out, talking with her hands, a deluge of information. It's the list-making, organised Mum from those very early days when the video was first shared. Back then, all I wanted was an adult to take charge and make it all go away, but now it feels like I'm being steamrollered.

'Stop, Mum!' I put my hands over my ears, like a child, the words coming out a bit louder than I meant.

Mum stops mid-sentence, hands in mid-air, startled. 'I was just trying to tell you what I've found out. There are options. You know, maybe it's time to deal with this.'

'No.' I soften a little as Mum looks hurt. But this isn't what I wanted. 'I know you're trying to help. But I'm not just a list of problems that you can solve by ticking things off. I didn't come home for you to fix everything. You can't. No one can. I just needed to talk.' I pause, then half-whisper. 'You only had to listen.'

Mum sags back into her chair, her hands falling into her lap.

'Darling...'

I push my plate away.

'So. You're up to speed now anyway, and thanks for lunch. I actually do have an essay to write so, if it's okay with you, I'm going upstairs for a bit.'

Mum just nods, deflated again, and I leave her with the dirty plates. Passing the open door to the lounge, I see the notebook and pen back out on the coffee table.

I flop down on my bed and look around my old room. There's still a gap where Banksy used to be. My pinboard looks like a shrine to my teenage years, with a thin layer of dust across the top. If Mum's been keeping my room clean in my absence, she missed that bit. There's a collection of old photos still stuck there and a couple of cards with quotes I'd thought, at seventeen, were inspirational.

If you're tired of starting over, stop giving up.

It's never too late to be what you might have been.

I reach up and pull them off the board, dropping them into the bin. Downstairs, I can hear Mum stacking the dishwasher – I'm feeling a bit guilty at having left her with the clearing up, but on balance it was better for me to get away from any more conversation, before I said anything I'd regret.

My phone pings. Jon

Just to let you know, I'm surviving Saturday. Hope you're having a good time with your mum. But don't stay away too long.

I put the phone down. Having a good time? I don't think that's why I'm here. I'm here for... well, what? To let Mum know how I really am? To tell her about Andrew? I honestly don't know now. Our conversation didn't go well by anyone's standards, and now I'm hiding up here in my childhood bedroom again. Like nothing has changed.

I can't get comfy on this bed. Adverts for posh mattresses always say you spend a third of your life in bed. If that's true, I must've spent at least six years in this little bed, which is starting to feel a bit narrow. Well, more than that if you take into account the hideous summer of exams, when Mum would probably have liked to go on holiday. I swing my legs off the bed and sit up. I'm supposed to be writing an essay, I should do something. What's the point spending even more time staring at this ceiling?

'Amy! I'm popping out to get something for dinner. Any requests?' Mum calls upstairs.

'Whatever, Mum, you choose,' I shout back. At least she hasn't asked me to go with her. I'm just thinking about whether I should offer, but the jangle of keys and the sound of the front door opening and closing tell me it's too late.

On my desk are various bits and pieces I left behind. None of the pens seem to work so I chuck them in the bin. There's a tin of cartridges for an ink pen I don't have any more, and a couple of rubbers that have seen better days, so I bin them too.

A bottle at the back catches my eye. My signature scent. I remember picking it out with my friends, spraying hundreds of different smells on little strips of paper until I couldn't tell one from another. It was a man's fragrance – I smile at my younger self for wanting to be different. I look at the bottle, chunky, solid, monochrome, something I'd got so used to seeing I didn't notice it. Suddenly I realise – I haven't worn it since the night of the party. It's just been sitting there, untouched, all this time. I don't know if I remember how it smells. Cautiously, I undo the lid, daring the citrus and spice to send me back to those days and nights that now feel like a different lifetime. I sniff hard. The smell is still familiar, but not in the way I expected. A scent I recognise, but I don't know why, as if I've smelt it on a stranger walking past. I drop that into the bin too. I'll never wear it again.

I pull my rucksack out of the wardrobe, looking for my laptop and some mints I stuffed in the pocket. No mints. Just a creased piece of paper. The flyer for the Half Moon, with Jamie's number on the back. It gives me a jolt, a piece of my other life here in my little room. I'm about to put that in the bin too, but something stops me. Maybe one day, I think, unconvinced, as I put it down on the desk.

As usual, my laptop isn't charged, and I'm not bothered enough about the essay to plug it in. I'm just wondering whether to start sorting through the wardrobe, while I'm in a throwing away mood, when I hear Mum's car in the drive. I look out the window as Mum gets out, waving enthusiastically, holding a Co-op bag. The rain's stopped, there's a watery sunset, a vague promise that tomorrow might be a better day. I close the laptop and put it back into the rucksack with the carefully refolded flyer. Well. As I'm here, I should have another go at talking to Mum.

'I got stuff for lasagne and some ice cream, that okay?' Mum's trying to rearrange the freezer to find space for a tub of Ben and Jerry's. She shoves the drawer closed with a huff.

'Mum. I'm really sorry. I was snappy before, and…'

Mum carries on putting the shopping away but there's a very slight hesitation before she says, 'It's okay, darling, you've had a lot on. I realise that now.'

I put my hand on her arm and turn her to face me. 'Don't give me any more excuses. Lashing out at you isn't going to help anything.'

Mum's eyes shine with fondness and she pushes a strand of hair off my face.

'If you only knew how I've missed you,' she says.

'You too,' I say, though my throat seems to have closed up with the effort of not showing any emotion. 'Mum, could we talk?'

Mum looks at the shopping, still on the side.

'This can wait, I've put the ice cream away. Come on, let's go and sit down.'

The lounge is still warm from earlier. Mum draws the curtains and I sit in my usual place on the sofa.

'Before you start, I have a few things I'd like to say too. Move up a bit,' Mum says, squeezing in next to me. 'You said earlier that you think I want to turn your problems into a list of things I can tick off.'

I cringe. 'I'm sorry, that was a horrible thing to say.'

Mum gives a half-smile. 'Well, it was a bit. But I do like my lists. And more than that. If someone has a problem, I want to help. Especially when that someone is you.'

I hug a cushion in front of me to stop myself tensing up again. 'I know you do, Mum, but...'

Mum puts her hand on my arm. 'Please. I know you want to talk. But it's your turn to listen.'

I sink back into the sofa and let her speak.

'You and me, we were always so close. Like our own little unit against the world. Some people thought we were too close, that you need some distance between mother and daughter. But it isn't easy being a single mum, and I thought I was doing okay.'

'Mum! You were. None of it was your fault. I just...'

Mum pats my arm gently, like I'm still five years old.

'Shhh, I haven't finished. So when all that stuff with the video happened, you pushed me away. I didn't understand. Rather than turn to me when you needed someone more than ever, you just seemed to get more and more distant. I didn't know how to reach you. And I tried so hard. But I just kept getting it wrong.'

I try to protest again, but Mum gently stops me with a wave of her hand.

'Let me carry on, please. I've wanted to have this conversation for a long time.' She clears her throat. She's holding it together but I can tell I'm not the only one choking back the tears.

'The only thing you seemed to want was to get away from here. And from me. I guess that's the sad truth of being a parent. If you're successful, every milestone and every step take your child further away from you. Maybe that's what they all meant, the ones who said you should have some distance. Maybe that makes it easier.'

Mum looks wistful, staring at the wall. I take a deep, shuddery breath and wait for her to carry on.

'I told myself this was what you needed. A new start. There wasn't any way I could repair what happened to you. The video. Harry. God knows, I would have done anything. I'd tried so hard, all your life, to limit how much not having a dad would affect you. I haven't been able to give you a good role model for a relationship, I know that, but I did what I could. Then that happened. And I was so scared it would damage your feelings about men, about sex, about everything. I wanted to wrap you up and never let you out of my sight. But you didn't seem to want me to. You just wanted to get away, so all I could do was support you in that.'

I think back to those early days. The pain, the depression, the shame. It was all about me. I've never thought about how Mum felt. In all that time, all the conversations about going to the police, Harry, school, what we could do. When we said goodbye at university, I didn't give a second thought to Mum coming back here on her own. To Mum's own confusing feelings about uni. I've been so wrapped up in my own head, I haven't considered Mum at all.

She's still talking. 'I missed you so much. I tried to be cheerful whenever we talked. But everything felt so empty without you. Although you seemed to be having a good time.' She pauses, looking straight at me. 'Or that's what you told me.'

I curl myself more tightly into the cushions and think of our slightly awkward FaceTimes, the made-up nights out and social events. Of course Mum was never going to buy all that.

'I know I wasn't honest with you, Mum. But I was trying to protect you from it all. The shit I was living with.' Mum has her chin in her hands and seems to be okay with me talking now.

'The thing was, it just wasn't the escape that I'd hoped for. I thought I'd be there, anonymous, among a load of other students where no one knew me.'

'Hiding in plain sight?'

'Yeah, something like that. But that wasn't how it felt. Not at all. It's such a small world, you're always coming across people who know each other, or they know someone's cousin or best friend or something. When anyone talks to you, it's like they're obsessed with finding a connection with you. Question after question. But I didn't want to be connected. I didn't want someone to go, "Oh my god! You're that girl from the video!" So I tried my best to stay away.'

Mum shakes her head, looking tearful.

'I knew it. I wish I'd been able to do something.'

I carry on.

'You couldn't. Because I didn't let you. I wanted you to think I was okay. I tried to tell myself I was okay, and to find ways to live. I thought I could just do it differently. I kept people at arm's length, didn't try to make friends. I didn't trust anyone and it seemed easier not to try. In my head, I was managing.'

Mum strokes my leg as I keep talking. 'But I was so lonely. Getting the job in the café was the best thing I could have done.'

Mum frowns slightly, the line between her brows deepening.

'So why did you do that? If you wanted to hide? Surely lots of people saw you there?'

'It was different. People were normal. Not students. Not all my age. I felt comfortable with older people, working people, families. No one asking me about my school or looking for connections. Until Andrew.' His name still makes me shudder. 'And then, suddenly, my nightmare came true. And I realised I was right all along. That I can't ever escape.'

'And he had the video?' Mum looks nervous. I shake my head.

'He said he did. But Jon checked his phone and he swore it wasn't there.'

Mum breathes a huge sigh of relief.

'That's good. Really good. Look, darling. Please don't go mad at me and please just listen. This is what I was trying to tell you at lunch.'

Mum picks the notebook up off the coffee table and waves it in the air. 'Just to prove my lists have their uses.'

She settles back down and opens it a few pages in. 'I needed to feel I was doing something. I felt so useless and I felt I'd failed you.' She waves away my protestations. 'So I decided all I could do was to keep an eye on things.'

I can see the trademark scrawl of her writing, lots of notes all over the page.

'Do you remember the Revenge Porn Helpline? I told you about them.'

I nod, it sounds vaguely familiar; I remember hating the name and the very idea of it.

'Well, they've been lots of help. Supporting me. And making sure the video wasn't still appearing anywhere. And they have basically closed the case.'

What case? I don't understand what she just said.

'What does that mean?'

'Well, to the best of their knowledge and ability to check, the video isn't anywhere on the internet. Never really has been, after that first day.'

This sounds like an outrageous claim. I raise an eyebrow.

'Really? They have searched the whole internet?'

'No, of course not. And they can't guarantee it. There's always the possibility someone might still have it, as an individual. They can't check that.'

'Like Harry you mean?'

'Yes. Or Andrew. Or anyone.' Mum flicks a few pages and looks at her notes, nervously. 'I mean, anyone who had it could share it. That's what I've been worried about. To be honest, when Rosie told me what Harry had done at Durham, I had a bit of a panic. I got them to check again. Just in case. But I just heard back from them – yesterday, in fact. Nothing.'

I try to take it all in. Mum on some kind of cybersecurity mission on my behalf. It seems so unlikely I almost laugh, but Mum's earnest expression stops me.

'So why didn't you tell me?' I ask. 'Before, I mean. That you were doing this?'

Mum gives her head a little shake. 'I didn't think you needed to know. I thought you were trying to move on and forget about it. I hoped you were, anyway. And I wanted to be able to tell you that was possible. To give you some good news.' She gives me a very steady look. 'But now I think I can.'

I pull at the trim of the sofa cushion. Mum seems to be saying the video has gone away. I ought to feel relieved. Or something at least. The notebook is face down, back on the table and Mum's waiting for me to say something. And she's getting a complete lack of reaction.

'Amy? Aren't you pleased?'

I nod. 'I am. I think. It's just…' I look down at my hands, twisting a ring around my index finger. 'I know should feel happy. But I don't. Like when Rosie told me about Harry. I didn't feel anything.'

Mum nods, knowingly.

'You're numb. I think that's probably quite a common reaction. Maybe it's time you talked to someone?'

I laugh, out loud this time.

'Oh for God's sake! You sound like Jon,' I realise. 'And isn't that what we're doing?'

Mum laughs too.

'It is what we're doing. At long last! But I mean talk to a professional. Get some help. You're not the only person this kind of thing has happened to, sadly.

'You never wanted to go to the police. Back then I thought that was a mistake, but now I think maybe you were right. Without Rosie's evidence it would have been really hard for you to prove what happened. But whether it still exists or not, that video is still affecting your life. Every day. You need to deal with it, one way or another.'

I feel the familiar prickles of resistance starting at the suggestion I should have gone to the police, but they're not as strong as they used to be. I'm about to speak when the landline starts ringing. Mum jumps up at the first ring, as she always has. It cracks me up, this urgency to get to the phone. It can wait! I want to say. But I let her go, pick up her notebook and start to flick through the pages. There's such a lot to take in. I could use a minute's thinking time.

The call goes on a while. I can't really hear any words, but her voice is all giggly and soft. I put the notebook down and crane towards the door to try and catch what she's saying. I hear the handset click back into its holder and hurriedly rearrange myself on the sofa before Mum walks back in.

'Sorry about that, shall I put the kettle on?' She looks a bit flushed.

'Who was it?' I ask casually.

'Oh, it was just… a friend. He, umm… we were going to go to the cinema maybe, but I told him we can go another day.'

I note the "he/him" pronouns but keep quiet. I've got enough to think about without trying to compute the idea of Mum on a date.

'Cup of tea would be great!' I smile. 'Don't know about you, but I think maybe I've done as much talking as I can for one day.'

'Oh… okay.' Mum nods, but I detect a slight trace of resignation, as if she's thinking we've been here before. I make light of it, tapping my head.

'Lots to mull over. And what time's dinner? I'm starving.'

36

I wake from a completely dreamless sleep feeling like I haven't moved all night. The old alarm clock on the bedside table tells me it's 9.24 a.m. No! I was going to get up early and make breakfast. I jump out of bed and pull back the rather too effective blackout curtains. I blink in the winter sun and remember how pretty the view of the fells is.

I grab the dressing gown from the back of the door – it's too pink and way too short, but it will have to do. I head downstairs, feeling the stillness of the house. Mum must have gone for some bread or something. The kettle's still warm and there's already washing on the line. I smile at the mug and tea bag she's left out for me. While I'm waiting for the kettle to boil, I watch Mum's jeans and tights blowing in the breeze.

Yesterday took it out of me. I didn't realise how tired I was until my head hit the pillow. We had a lovely evening, though. Mum took the hint and we didn't talk any more about anything heavy. We made lasagne together; Mum did the bolognese and I took the béchamel sauce, which I thought was pretty ambitious of me. We cooked, ate, shared a bottle of rosé and chatted. It felt like old times – we had a good laugh about things we hadn't talked about for years. Old family stories and shared memories of holidays, trips to the beach. How much we both miss Gran and how we lost her way too young. I stopped myself from telling Mum that she looks more like her every day. She might have thought I was saying she looks old. She doesn't, she just reminds me such a lot of how I remember Gran, with wise eyes, lines from smiling, beautiful.

'I wanted to tell you something, Mum,' I said, as she poured the last drops of rosé into our glasses.

Mum sipped her wine.

'Thought we were done talking for today?'

'Yeah. Not about that, really. I just wanted to you know that it's always been enough. Just you and me. I mean, not knowing my dad. It hasn't mattered. You've been enough.'

Mum nodded, tears in her eyes.

'And you have been more than enough for me, my darling. The most precious gift I could ever have wished for.'

It was late when we went to bed. I don't think either of us really wanted the day to end. When we said goodnight, I felt like I needed to say something profound, something to mark the moment, and how I felt about it. But I couldn't find the words.

So Mum said, 'I'm so glad you came home.'

And I said, 'Me too.'

And we stood and hugged on the stairs for a long time.

I'm sitting on the stool at the breakfast bar, drinking my tea and flicking through the news on my phone, when I hear footsteps on the drive and Mum throws the back door open. Well, it looks like Mum. But this person is red in the face and wearing Lycra and running shoes.

'Morning, darling,' she says. 'Bet you never thought you'd see me like this!'

'Mum!' I put my phone down in surprise. 'When did you start running?'

'Oh, couple of months ago. I decided it was time I got fit.'

She pushes off some smart looking running shoes and pads through the kitchen leaving sweaty footprints on the shiny tiles.

'Quick shower then I'll need breakfast. I did 5k!'

I sit down again and stare blankly at the shelf of familiar-looking cookbooks in front of me. Mum's running? How weird. That, and the mystery caller from last night. Plus the fact that, when she's not frowning, Mum looks really great. I get up, pull some porridge oats from the cupboard and measure them into a pan. Good on Mum, I think, stirring the porridge. She seems to have got herself a life. How have I missed this?

I leave the porridge to stand and take bowls, glasses and fruit juice into the dining room. It's a lovely morning – yesterday's rain has completely gone and the winter sun is almost warm as it streams into the room. I set the table as nicely as I can; I should've got Mum some flowers or something. Breakfast will have to do.

'Ooh, porridge, lovely.' Mum's fresh-faced and damp-haired, her curls springing up from her shoulders. Now her face isn't red and sweaty, she's glowing.

'You look really great, Mum,' I say. 'I didn't really notice yesterday, think there was too much going on. But you do. Must be the running! What's all that about then?'

Mum pours herself some juice and tries to hide the fact she's really pleased with the compliment. 'Oh, you know. Just looking after myself in my old age.'

I laugh. 'Forty-one is hardly old!'

Mum shrugs. 'I know. I'm joking.' She shakes her head and smooths a damp curl away from her eyes. She stops smiling and looks suddenly serious. 'Without wishing to go back to our conversation from yesterday, it's been hard at times. For me, I mean. I needed to do something to make myself feel better. Being obsessed with tracking your video down on social media wasn't quite enough.'

She laughs awkwardly. I stir my spoon through the porridge, suddenly not at all hungry. Eyes bigger than your belly, Gran would have said. I look up at Mum from under my eyelashes.

'Mum. I'm really sorry. I...'

Mum waves her hand. 'Darling, it's okay. I know you said you were trying to protect me, but I felt myself getting quite down. And I didn't want to load that on you. So, I talked to a few people, read some stuff online. And much to my amazement, running seems to help.'

There's a silence broken by the sound of Mum's spoon in her bowl as she scrapes it clean. She looks up at me when she's finished.

'Porridge too hot, little bear?' she says. I try to smile, but it doesn't work and the tears I've been holding back spill out.

'Hey! What's this for?' Mum comes round to my side of the table and puts her arms around me.

'I don't know. Just... just we've wasted so much time. Me not telling you stuff. You not telling me stuff. It just seems... so pointless now.'

Mum rubs my shoulder gently and presses her damp hair against my cheek.

'It's alright, you know. It's not too late. We're talking. We're getting our shit together. We're going to be okay.'

I nod slowly. 'We talked a lot yesterday. Both of us. And I was really listening. And now I've thought about it all. Well, I think you're right.'

Mum draws away and tries to look serious, but she's smiling.

'Oh my goodness! Let me get my phone! I need to record that.'

I sniff through the tears, a half-laugh and a cry rolled into one, and nudge her.

'Okay, point taken. But the helpline you mentioned. I've been thinking about it and... well do they have any victim support? I hate that word, and I hate that I'm a victim. But I think that's what it would be called.'

'You were a victim, darling. A victim of a crime. There's no shame in that at all. And yes, they can definitely help. Let me get you the number, although I don't think they'll be open on a Sunday.'

Mum's instantly out of her seat, heading for the door. I grab her arm before she can go and start another list.

'Mum, it's okay! There's no rush. I... I just want the number. And maybe a name, if you've talked to someone in particular. But then you can leave it with me. I've got it from here.'

Mum looks slightly worried.

'Are you sure? You're not just saying that to get me off your case? Because...'

'No. I promise. No more lying or pretending. '

She sits back down, the worry lines relaxing again and the post-run glow coming back. 'I'll get it after breakfast then.'

Scraping the remains of my porridge into the bin, I almost wish I'd been on a run too. That was definitely more carbs than I needed. Mum wipes down the surfaces and sticks her bowl and a couple of mugs into the dishwasher.

'What time is your train?' she asks.

'Four thirty-five.' I reach round and put my bowl into the dishwasher too. 'Mum, do you remember that garden centre we used to go to sometimes?'

Mum pauses, her hand reaching for the dishwasher tablets.

'Garden centre? Webbs maybe?'

'You remember, the one where one time you let me paddle in the fountain and the guy went mad at you.'

Mum laughs out loud. 'How could I forget? We were in so much trouble. It was a such a hot day though. Yeah, Webbs. Why?'

'Do they still have a nice café? I thought... I'd like to take you out for lunch.'

Mum freezes, the dishwasher door half-way open, her eyebrows up somewhere near her hairline.

'Out for lunch?'

She shuts the door and turns to look at me. She speaks really gently, as if she doesn't really want either of us to hear. As if saying it too loud might break the new understanding between us.

'You know, sweetheart, you don't have to do that. Don't rush into things, I mean, are you sure?'

I put a hand up to stop her.

'Don't react. Yes, it's surprising. Yes, we haven't been out for lunch for a very long time. Or out, anywhere. But don't question me on it. I might change my mind. I told you, you were right. You said maybe it's time. And I think it is.'

She turns back to the dishwasher and opens it again, very deliberately. I look away so she doesn't realise I've noticed that she's crying.

'Well, that would be very nice. Webbs it is then. Although it might be a bit cold for paddling today.'

Back upstairs, I get my stuff together. I shove the few clothes I brought with me into the rucksack, make sure the flyer's still safely in the pocket, and do a quick scan for phone leads and other things I might have forgotten. This room really does need a bit of an update. And something to fill the space where the poster used to be. Maybe I could ask for some new prints or something for Christmas. And a new dressing gown. I pull the bed cover up, straighten the pillow and close the wardrobe door. Just before I go, I take my phone out of my pocket and write a quick text.

Had a weekend at home, it's been great. Done some thinking. Let's talk again soon. X

Maria gets straight back to me with a grinning emoji.

I stick the phone away and hoist the rucksack onto my back.

'Mum, I'm ready!' I say, coming down the stairs.

Mum's by the door, car keys in hand. She gives me a piece of paper.

'Here's that number you wanted.'

I look at it and put it carefully into my jeans pocket. Another number. Another number I should definitely ring.

'Thank you.' I take a deep breath and exhale fully. 'Now let's go. Maybe we can go for a walk along the river on the way?'

37

I sit rocking the table; it seems to have one leg shorter than the others. I've tried it in three different positions and only succeeded in making it worse. This wouldn't happen in *Common Grounds*. Jon would have appeared with some kind of levelling device made from a wedge of kitchen paper before now.

'If there's anything you can't use kitchen paper for, I haven't discovered it yet,' he'd say.

Mum's at the counter, nattering with the lady who's taking our order. Doesn't look like the mushroom medley vegan special is going to be arriving any time soon at this rate. Between the two of them, they seem to have discovered a load of people they both know. I've heard names I vaguely recognise flying around, along with noises of incredulity, laughter and sympathy. It's nice. And I'm not in a rush. I'm sure at some point they'll exhaust their discussion of everyone they have in common and I'll get some lunch.

I chose the table carefully, in the corner of the glass-fronted dining area, where I can see but not really be seen. Just in case. It does feel weird to be out, in my hometown. I meant what I said to Mum, but you can't just switch it all off. The paranoia. It's going to take me a while, I think. There's a nice view from here anyway – I'm looking out at the grounds where we had a wander before lunch. The garden centre hasn't aged that well. The only plants we saw were just sticks in pots, as far as I could tell, with ridiculous price tags and a promise of somewhat unlikely blossom and autumn fruits. The famous fountain I paddled in, aged five, is now empty and cordoned off with red and white tape. I can clearly remember the irate manager pulling me out of it though. He looked totally horrified that there was a bare-foot child playing in the centrepiece of his "Outdoor ornamentation" department.

As I flick through the memories, I find my eyes drawn to a man loading sacks of something heavy onto a flatbed trolley. He's tall, well-built, with floppy blonde hair sticking out from under a cap. He drops a bag onto the pile and pushes his hat back, wiping his forehead, and suddenly the sunny memories of childhood happiness evaporate and a shiver goes through me. It looks like Harry. Rosie said he was leaving the country, what the hell is he doing here? I can't really see that clearly, so I lean closer to the window. The person who can't be Harry is a couple of steps down from the café terrace, leaning against the trolley, swigging from a large bottle of water. If I crane my neck, I can see over the edge of the patio to watch him. He's maybe ten metres away, with only a patio and a thin pane of glass separating us. He nods to a couple of customers and exchanges a few words with them and, as he turns his head, he smiles. Harry. It's definitely him. I'm so close to this person who's had so much impact on my life. And he's oblivious. I glance quickly back at Mum, who's still talking, then, propelled by something unconscious that might be a death wish, I stand up, push back the French doors and walk out into the winter sunshine.

The doors clearly haven't been opened for some time, and by the time I've shoved them shut again, the squeaks of rusty metal have caused him to look up. I stride towards him, pretty sure that until this moment he hadn't seen me. He puts down the sack with a thump, letting sand spill out of the top, and stares up at me, his face uncertain, as if deciding what on earth to say after all this time.

'Amy! Wow, is that really you?' So, we've gone with casual familiarity. I want to punch him.

'Yes, it's me.'

If I didn't know him, I'd still have found him attractive. He looks a bit older, chin dark with stubble, and his rugby physique looks a bit soft round the middle, but his smile still glows with boyish charm. I'm soaked by a wave of anger. Everything he's put us through – me,

Rosie, the girl in Durham – it's had no visible effect. Maybe that was too much to hope.

Quickly I check over my shoulder – through the window I can see Mum on her way to the table with a tray. Her quizzical look suggests she's noticed I'm not there but hasn't quite clocked what's going on outside.

'So what are you doing here?' I ask, glad that from my vantage point on the patio, I am looking down on him. 'Rosie said you were leaving the country.'

His smile falters slightly.

'Oh, yeah, I'm just here until Christmas, saving up. Got the chance to do a bit of travelling, work abroad. You know...' He looks a bit flushed. I, on the other hand, am feeling steady and amazingly calm. Thank God I saw him before he saw me. I clear my throat.

'Yeah right. She also told me what you've done. Nice one.' I want a reaction. Frustratingly he's not even looking up at me. Twat. 'Maybe I should have gone to the police, back then. Stopped you in your tracks. I hadn't realised you were heading for a life as a serial sex pest.'

He looks up. Finally. I've needled him. The sun's behind me, low in the sky, making him squint, his hands shading his eyes.

'Amy, I'm sorry. If I could take it all back...'

As if he thinks now's his chance to apologise. I stop him with a wagging finger.

'Uh-uh. No. You don't get to speak. It's my turn.'

Behind me I can hear Mum tapping on the glass. I throw her a quick glance – she's simultaneously trying to slide the doors open and miming 'What the hell are you doing?' without trying to look too alarmed. I give her a little nod and turn back to Harry. He's fixed to the spot, as if awaiting my next instruction.

'You've made me scared to live in my own town. And I never wanted to see you again. But as you're here, I have something to say.' I move slightly so my shadow blocks out the sun and I can see his expression. My voice surprises me, so steady and firm. So grounded. As if talking to Harry was what I needed to do, and now is the time.

'I've hated you, really hated you. I've wished over and over again that I'd never even gone to that party, not fallen for your shit. I've wasted so much time and energy because of what you did to me. So many opportunities. But enough already. I'm done.' He looks away again, and takes a breath as if he might be about to start speaking, but I don't leave any gaps for him to cut in.

'I wanted to see you suffer for what you did to me. But I wasn't strong enough. And now you've gone and committed crimes against other girls. And for that, I am really sorry. For them. But at least it gives me some pleasure to see that you are finally getting some pay back for what you've done.'

He's looking at the floor now, at his dirty workman's boots. The dead leaves around his feet. 'Amy...'

I don't let him carry on. 'I'm still talking. So what I know now is this. There are shitty, awful people like you in the world. And all this time, you're the ones I've been trying to hide away from. It's taken until now to see that I got it wrong. There are many, many more good people. Kind people. People you can trust and rely on. People who love you for yourself and don't judge you because something awful happened to you, once. Something you couldn't control. People who show you that you have nothing to be ashamed of by being yourself. If you're lucky, maybe one day you'll find that out for yourself.' I pause, ever so slightly. 'But I really hope your luck's run out.'

A rusty squeak breaks into the end of my speech as Mum succeeds in pushing the French windows open and bursts onto the patio.

'Amy! Your lunch is here,' she says for something to say, although I have the distinct impression that what she really means is, 'What the fuck is going on?'

'Okay, Mum,' I call, with a little smile of encouragement as I realise Mum is still hovering in full rescue mode, just in case. 'Just coming. Close the doors, it's cold.' Reluctantly, she retreats and I turn back to Harry. I take a last look at him, standing there uselessly in the pile of sand.

'Goodbye, Harry,' I say, turning away. I feel strong, confident, satisfied. It's over.

The French doors squeak loudly as they open and close for the third time, and I squeeze myself back indoors. Mum's sitting back down, her hands balled into tight fists on the table. I slide into my seat. Our lunch sits on the table, cooling on the plates. I remove a basil leaf garnish off my delicate-looking mushroom concoction, look enviously at Mum's bacon bap, and then up at her face. The worry lines are back.

'Is everything okay, darling?' she asks.

I nod, smiling broadly, and reach out for her clenched fists.

'I am absolutely fine, Mum. Honestly. I really, really am fine.' I feel her relax under my hands. 'Now let's eat.' I point towards the disappointingly small plate of mushrooms. 'Did you notice if they do cakes too? I think I'm maybe a bit hungrier than I thought.'

38

I haven't used this big case for ages, and I'd forgotten that one of the wheels is jammed. On most days, it would have annoyed the hell out of me – I'm half-dragging and half-carrying it from the bus stop. But today I'm not bothered at all. I'm almost smiling as I walk through the little arcade, all lit up for the Christmas shoppers. It really could do with lightly falling snow or a sparkly frost to complete the scene, rather than today's grey sky and light drizzle. But these now very familiar streets actually feel like home. Well, not home. But somewhere I belong. Somewhere I can be happy.

I push open the door to the café with my shoulder, half-fall in backwards and almost laugh out loud. Jon has gone to town. There are garlands of fairy lights across the front windows, a spectacular tree in the corner made up of candy canes and red and white striped lollipops, Mariah Carey is blasting out over the sound system and the whole place smells of cloves and cinnamon.

'Happy Christmas!' he calls, from the top of a step ladder behind the counter. 'What do you think?'

'Wow. Just wow. And I don't even like Mariah Carey.'

'What? How can you not like this song? Pure Christmas cheese. If Christmas cheese was a thing.' He's dangling a string of raffia hearts woven with tiny lights. 'Does this look okay here?'

'Yeah, lovely. It's all lovely. Apart from the music, it's actually really tasteful. I love it!'

I give him a smile and he notices the case.

'Oh! It's today?'

'Yeah, I'm leaving straight from work in the end. Maria reckons we might make it in time for a few drinks in the Brewery. Old haunt,' I add, by way of explanation.

'That sounds fun.' He stops trying to hang the string of hearts and turns to look at me properly. 'You good with that?'

I chew my lip but nod, slowly.

'I think I am... I'm going to try anyway. I can always ask Mum to come and get me.'

'Ah, the joys of parenthood. Abandoning your own social life for the sake of a possible taxi request.'

Good point. I still haven't asked Mum about that overheard phone call. Wow, maybe Mum has a social life. There's so much more we need to talk about, hopefully over some long evenings with mulled wine in front of the fire. I can't wait.

'Stick your case in the staff room and come and give me a hand with this, will you? It's a two-person job, I've been up here an hour and I can't get it straight. Oh, and check out the toilets on your way back. I've gone for a snowfall effect.'

I laugh, dragging the problematic case out of the way. Trust Jon to be the kind of guy who goes nuts over Christmas. It does all look really festive though, I must admit. Not tacky at all. Not even the sparkly toilet.

The good mood seems to be rubbing off on the customers. Could be the decorations. Or the Christmas music, jingling away in the background all day. Or maybe the fabulous smells of cinnamon and ginger and the vast array of stollen and mince pies. I've got so many photos and videos; it's as if it was all designed to give me lots of good Instagram content.

'Jon, who's doing the social media while I'm away?' I ask when there's a bit of a lull.

'Ummm... Hadn't thought, really. Is it a problem if we just leave it for a few weeks?'

'Yes! Blimey, all this work I've put in. I'll tell you what. I'll take a load today and then I'll post every couple of days as if I'm here.

Then after Christmas you'll have to send me new photos and I'll post them. Can you manage that?'

'Yes, I can probably manage the odd photo.' He looks a bit sad. 'I'll miss you.'

I'm a bit unnerved by his honesty, but I'll miss him too. 'Don't worry, I'm coming back.' I hesitate, suddenly aware of how little I know about Jon compared to the width and depth of what he knows about me.

'Do you have Christmas plans?' I ask. He looks a bit brighter but I'm not totally convinced.

'I do. Fun and games all the way. Don't you worry about me. I have my Christmas traditions. Not quite the same as other people's, but all good.'

And he thinks I'm a conundrum. Maybe my New Year's resolution should be to get to know Jon better.

Lunchtime is a blur of soup and savoury orders. Things calm down around three, and I restock the mince pies for the afternoon tea slot. The door goes and I look up from my display.

'Hey.'

Oh no.

'Oh, hi.' It's weeks since I've seen him. He's wearing a really nice winter coat and a beanie hat. I was kind of hoping if he ever came in again that either I wouldn't be here, or I wouldn't think he was at all attractive anymore. Neither of those things happen. Here he is, here I am. Last time he was here I disappointed him big time. Which had really nothing at all to do with how I feel about him. Not in the slightest. But I'll have to do an awful lot of explaining for him to understand that.

'Look, Jamie. I… I owe you an apology.'

He's looking at the string of hearts, the fairy lights, anywhere but at me.

'You don't owe me anything. I misread the signs. It's okay. I'm fine about it now.'

He's fine about it now? What does that mean? I don't want him to be fine about it. God, I've really messed up.

'No, I mean...' He is looking at me now at least. And he doesn't look annoyed. Kind of hopeful.

'Look. Without going into too much detail. I was having quite a bad time then. Well, it's been a long bad time really. And you coming in was... Well, I always liked to see you here, and everything, but I couldn't, I wasn't ready...' I'm making such a mess of this. What does "and everything" mean? I can see Jon hovering at the kitchen door, probably not wanting to interrupt.

Jamie shakes his head and drops his eyes again.

'You don't have to explain. It's okay. I stayed away, to give you space. Well, and because it was hard to come in. If you didn't want to see me. But... well I thought...' He shoots Jon a look. 'I thought maybe it was time to come back.'

I look at Jon too. He's doing a very bad impression of someone who isn't listening. I smile at him and turn back to Jamie.

'Well, the little bird that told you that was probably right. It's good to see you. I'm glad you came back. Can I make you a coffee?'

Jamie looks relieved. He pulls off his hat and ruffles his hair.

'I'm going to try one of those gingerbread lattes I've seen so many photos of.'

What? 'You follow our Instagram?'

He points at himself. 'Guitarboy.' Of course.

Jon comes over as I'm making the coffee.

'Hey, Jon. How you getting on with the new strings?'

Jon starts chatting animatedly about the ease of bar chords and the fresh sound. Jon plays guitar? How did I not know that?

'Gingerbread latte.' I smile and place it down in front of him.

'On the house,' says Jon, looking at me. 'Least we can do to welcome back one of our regulars.'

The door goes suddenly, the jingle and the sound of girls' laughter cutting through the Christmas music. In burst Maria and Rosie.

'Hey!' I rush out from the counter. I throw my arms around Maria, enthusiastically, then hesitate. Rosie hangs back, looking at the floor.

'Come here,' I say, pulling her into a hug. As we move apart, I look over at Maria, whose eyes are wet.

'Big softie,' I say. 'Get a grip.' I wink at her. 'Nothing to see here. So, who wants a coffee? I'm going to be another half hour or so.'

Rosie and Maria settle down in the corner, not too far from where Jamie sits at his usual table. I serve a couple more coffees and then glance at the clock. Jon catches me looking.

'You can go a bit early if you like. Call it a Christmas present.'

'You sure?' Without meaning to, I shoot a glance over at table four. Jon nods.

'Yes. But I think there is something you need to sort out before you leave.' He gives me a direct look. 'There's only so much match-making a boss can do without looking like a bit of a dick.'

I tip my head on one side.

'I haven't played my guitar for eighteen years.' He holds out his left hand and the pads of his fingers are all red. 'Had to play it when I'd had it all restrung, didn't I? The lengths I go to for my staff.'

'Thank you.' I give him a quick hug, and he looks embarrassed.

'You're welcome. Try not to mess it up this time.'

I hesitate, only for a couple of seconds.

'Off you go then!' he says, and I step out from behind the counter. Jamie looks up as I walk over.

'Is it okay if I sit down for a minute?' I ask. For a split second, he looks taken aback. Then he gives me his full, one-hundred-watt smile and moves his coat to one side to free up a chair.

'Sure. Take a seat.'

I sit and shift in the chair, suddenly tongue-tied. He looks at me, expectantly.

'Can I ask you something? Does anyone call you anything other than Jamie?' I blurt. What a weird question. Oh well, it's been on my mind since the first time he told me his name. I don't think that's what he was expecting, but he covers his surprise well.

'Umm. Not really. Most people call me Jamie. My mum calls me James when she's cross with me about something. My surname's Harrison so my old school friends sometimes call me Harry. Why do you ask?'

I widen my eyes and almost laugh out loud. He looks a bit confused. 'What?'

'Oh... well for reasons that will one day become clear, I don't think Harry will work. It's just...' Slight hesitation. Just say it. 'It's just, Jamie and Amy sounds a bit ridiculous.'

He starts to laugh. 'Oh my god, I'm so glad you said that. I've been thinking the same. Maybe I'll have to come up with a cute nickname for you or something instead...' He stops laughing and blushes. 'I mean. If... well, you know.'

I've never seen him blush before.

'I'm going to be at home for a couple of weeks,' I say. 'For Christmas and a bit longer. There's stuff I need to do. But when I come back... when I come back, I'd really like to go to another gig with you. Or maybe a quiet drink. Or, well, anything really. If you still want to, that is.'

It was almost worth all of it to see how his face lights up. That and the blush. He really does like me.

'Oh wow. Yeah. That would be really great.' He drops his chin and looks up at me with one eyebrow raised. It's so cute I nearly stop breathing. But then he comes out with, 'So... you're giving me another shot?'

'Another shot? Was that a dad joke? Is that a thing of yours?'

'Might be... would that be a problem?'

I shake my head, laughing. 'I think I could get round it. As long as there aren't too many of them.'

We sit here, grinning at each other, not sure what else to say, but I'm pretty sure the real conversation has only just started.

Maria and Rosie get up from their table and clear their throats loudly, Maria looking very unsubtly at her watch. I glance over at them and turn back to Jamie.

'I have to go now. But I'll be back. And we can take it from there.'

I smile a goodbye, stand up and drag myself away. If I could trust myself not to trip over anything, I'd walk backwards so I could keep looking at him for as long as possible. Jon's there in the staff room before me, holding my coat and my case.

'Here you go. And happy Christmas.' He hands me an envelope with my name on the front. 'Christmas bonus. Make sure you get yourself something nice.'

'Thank you! Thank you so much. I'll see you in January. And don't forget to send me photos!'

In a split second I decide it's not weird to give him a kiss on the cheek, then as he smiles and brushes it off, I pull my parka round my shoulders, grab the case and head for the door.

'Amy!' I turn back as Jamie calls my name. 'Can I have your number? So I can stay in touch. Wish you happy Christmas?'

I pull the Half Moon flyer, only slightly crumpled, out of my pocket and wave it at him. 'I've still got yours. I'll message you. This time it's a promise.'

His face lights up even more. I can't resist.

'Everyone deserves another shot,' I say, laughing. He meets my eyes for just a second before putting his head in his hands.

'Amy? You ready?'

Rosie and Maria are standing by the door, Maria jangling her car keys. I take a quick last glance round the café. Jon is throwing beans into the grinder and simultaneously knocking coffee grounds out of the machine. Jamie is looking at his phone, pretending not to watch me leave. I turn away.

'I'm ready. Bagsy me in the back. I'd rather not watch too closely if Maria's driving.'

Maria knocks me with her elbow, laughing. Rosie picks up my case, and we stride off, just three old friends hooking up for a trip back home.

AUTHOR'S NOTE

I hope you enjoyed Amy's story, which is purely fictional. But sadly, many people, mainly women, are affected by similar issues in the UK today. If you have found any of the incidents depicted in the novel triggering, or if you have been affected by intimate image abuse in any form, you can get help.

Everyone deals with trauma in different ways. In the novel, Amy's mum is the character who tries to get help, where Amy herself can't face talking to the police or trying to press charges, even though what happened to her was against the law.

While writing this book, I had help and advice from Hayley Laskey at the *Revenge Porn Helpline*. They are an organization set up in 2015 to offer support to victims of crimes relating to intimate image abuse, and the organization Amy's mum contacted to help her in the book. Here is their statement.

> *Intimate image abuse is a cruel and invasive crime. It's important that victims are aware that they are not to be blamed, that support is out there, and that they deserve access to it. We see the rise in cases of intimate image abuse as both positive and negative. Positive because victims are increasingly aware that a crime has been committed against them and feel empowered to take action. Negative because these crimes continue to be committed.*
>
> *Victims of intimate image abuse need to know that there is support available to them and that they can take some immediate steps to regain control of the situation.*
>
> - Don't panic – remember you have done nothing wrong and are the victim of a crime

- Screenshot all evidence – whether it is of the content itself or messages from the perpetrator

- Report the crime to the police – using 101

- *After you have contacted the police, or if you are unsure on how to do so, call the Revenge Porn Helpline on 0345 6000 459 or email help@revengepornhelpline.org.uk. We can advise on reporting to the police and on the law as it applies to each case, signpost to other relevant services and help with content removal – 90% of content reported to us is removed. Calling us can and will help.*

The *Revenge Porn Helpline* is for victims over eighteen years of age, but unfortunately this issue affects people much younger as well. If you are under eighteen and need help, a good place to start is *Report Remove. Childline* and the *Internet Watch Foundation (IWF)* work together to run *Report Remove,* enabling young people under eighteen in the UK to confidentially report sexual images and videos of themselves and remove them from the internet. Their website is https://www.childline.org.uk/info-advice/bullying-abuse-safety/online-mobile-safety/report-remove/ or you can call 0800 1111

If you are a victim of intimate image abuse, know that you are not alone, that you can find help, and with the support of your friends and family and organizations like the Revenge Porn Helpline, you will get through it.

ACKNOWLEDGEMENTS

A few years ago, I found a box of old letters and notebooks in the loft. One of the notebooks was from when I was seventeen, and it confirmed what I'd been telling myself all my adult life – I had always wanted to write a book. That's all very well as an ambition when you're seventeen; when you have kids who are nearly that age, you have less time to think about it.

My new year's resolution in 2020 was to start writing. I started with a short story, shared it with a few people, and was encouraged to keep going. And then, of course, the pandemic hit us. Lockdown was kind to me and gave me lots of time to write and explore characters and ideas. I wrote more short stories, and thought a lot about the freedom of my own adolescence whilst seeing my teenage daughter forced to stay at home at the very moment she should have been finding her wings. Lockdown also made me miss cafés, and somewhere in this journey of nostalgia, lack of freedom and imagination, Jon's café appeared, and Amy's story started to take shape.

I have been humbled by all the support I have had from my family and friends. Many people read the manuscript as it developed, I am worried I will forget someone if I try to list them all, but everyone's comments and words of encouragement have made a huge difference, thank you all. A special thank you to my husband, Vaughan, your ongoing support and encouragement has allowed me the time and space to follow my dream. Thank you to my kids, Annie Rose and Ben, and my step-children, Tony, Carla and Luisa for any ideas you unknowingly provided for the story and characters, and to all of my family for being interested enough to read and ask questions while I have been working on this book.

I was lucky enough to do the Ultimate Novel Writing Course with Jericho Writers, where I met a great group of people, and we supported each other as we wrote and edited our novels. Thanks to Helen Francis, our mentor, and to my group, especially Nicky Downes, Alan Fraser, and Harriet Martin who were kind enough to read and report on my full manuscript.

Special thanks to Kate McDermott and Mark Camilleri who went the extra mile as beta readers and have continued to read, support and encourage me throughout the whole, long journey. Thanks to Cheryl Palin who was my lockdown writing buddy and who got me on the right track with creative writing. Thank you, Paul Taylor, for throwing down the original challenge to pick up a pen, and for encouraging me to keep going when it seemed too difficult - I will always be grateful, even if you did get into print before I did.

This book is for my children Annie Rose and Ben, for every teenager navigating adolescent life and the internet, and for every parent trying valiantly to do and say the right thing.

CONTINUING WITH THE STORY

Follow the author on
Instagram @books_by_becky_jones
www.booksbybeckyjones.uk

Sign up for newsletter, free content and book recommendations
www.ELMbooks.uk

Published by ELM Books 2025

ELM BOOKS

Paperback ISBN 978-1-0684810-0-0
eBook ISBN 978-1-0684810-1-7

Cover and Interior Design by Andy Magee
Elm Books logo designed by Lucy Covell